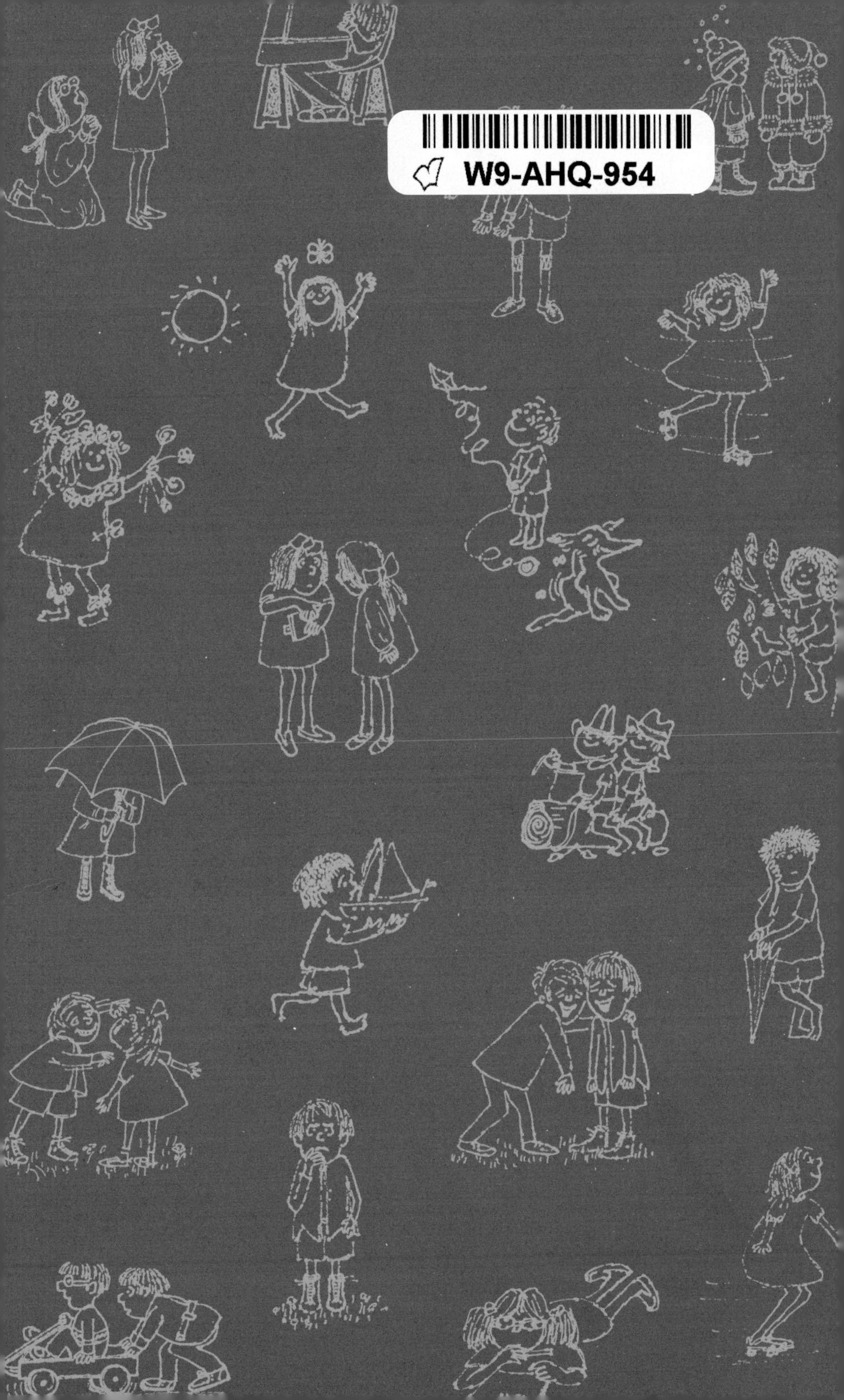

NOBODY IS PERFICK

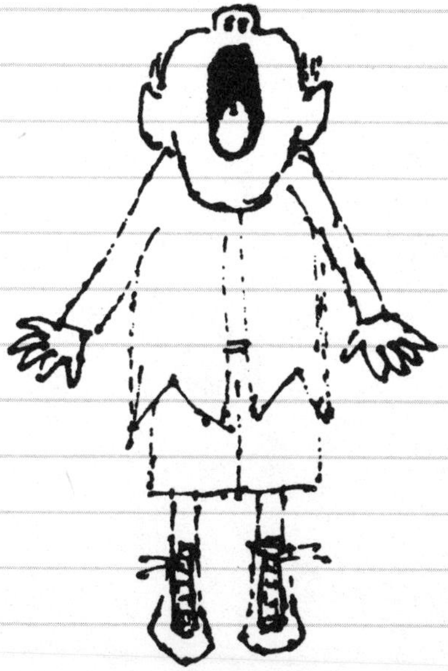

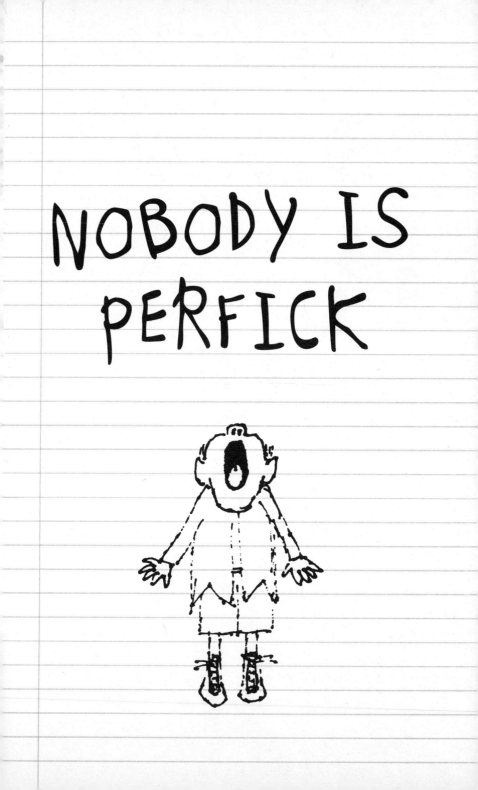

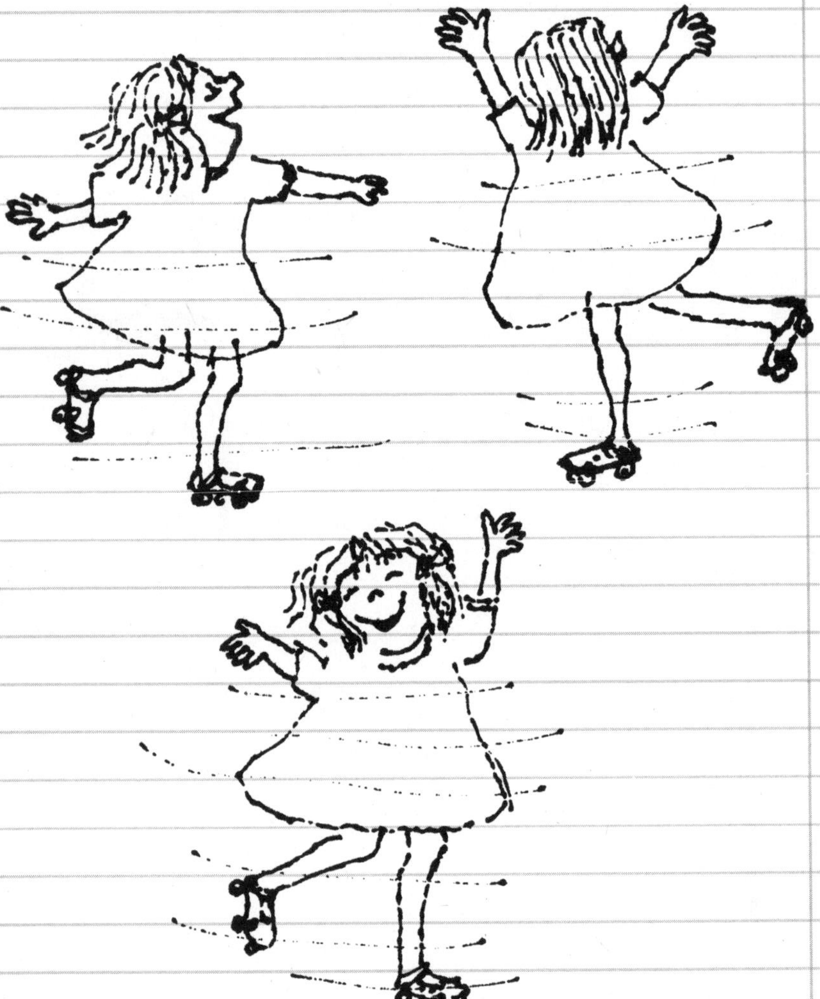

NOBODY IS PERFICK

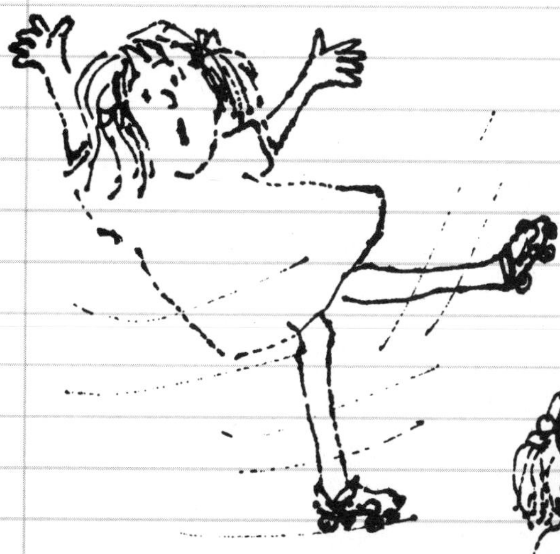

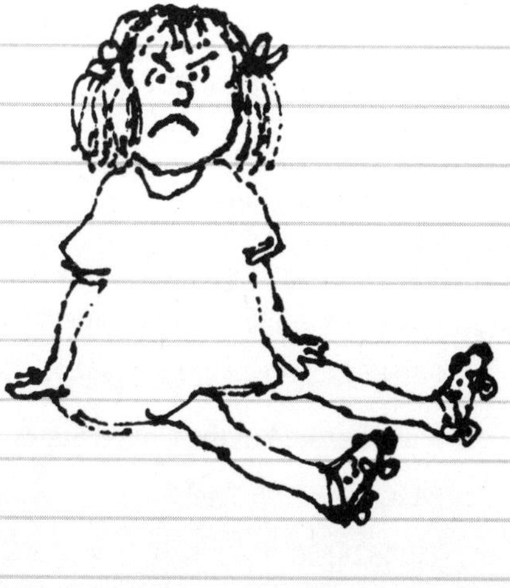

By Bernard Waber

Houghton Mifflin Harcourt
Boston New York

Speech bubble illustrations by Elliot Kreloff

www.hmhco.com

ISBN 978-0-395-31669-6 paperback

ISBN 978-0-544-84214-4 paper-over-board

Manufactured in the United States

DOC 10 9 8 7 6 5 4 3 2 1

4500628520

Nobody Is Perfick

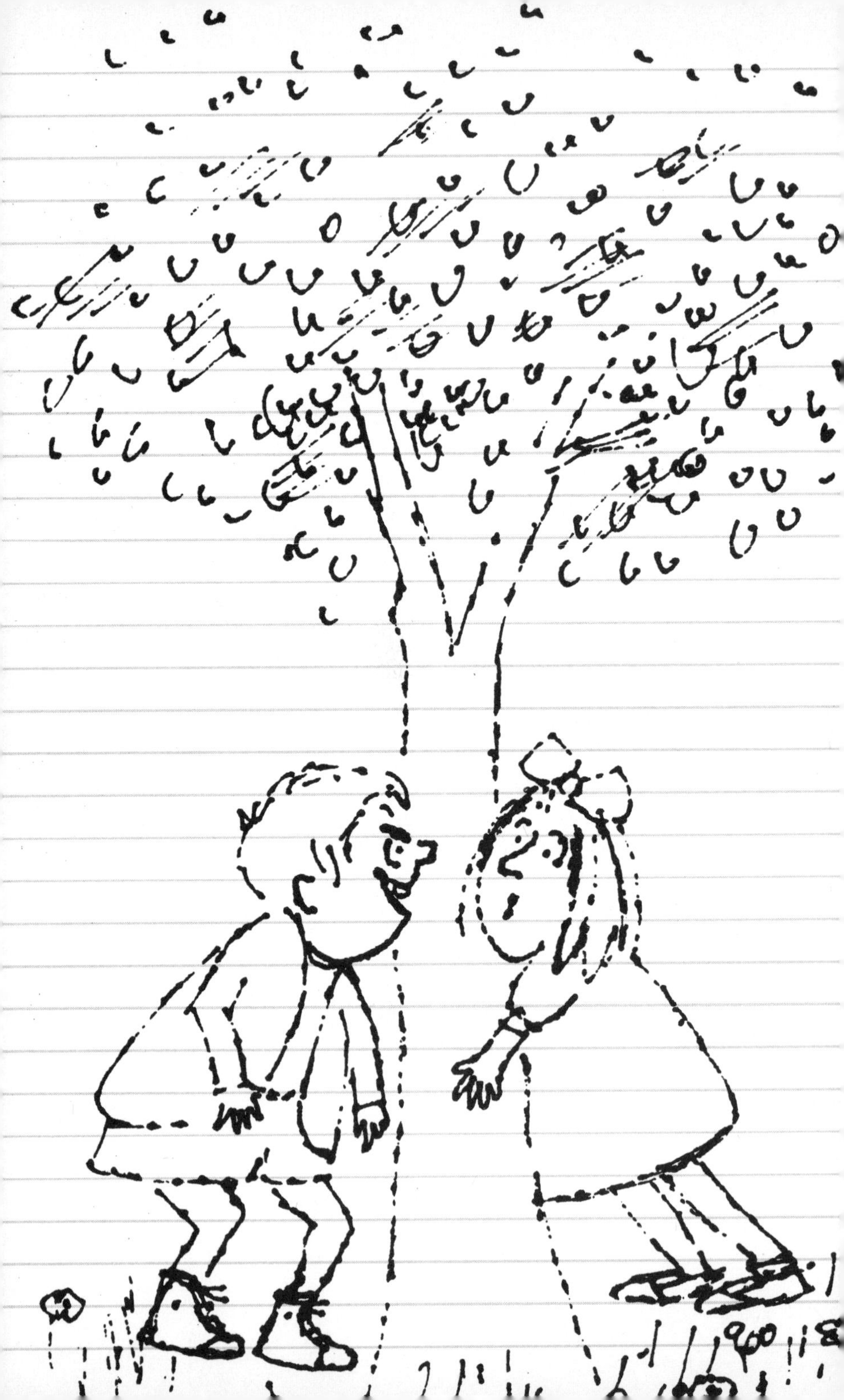

SAY SOMETHING NICE

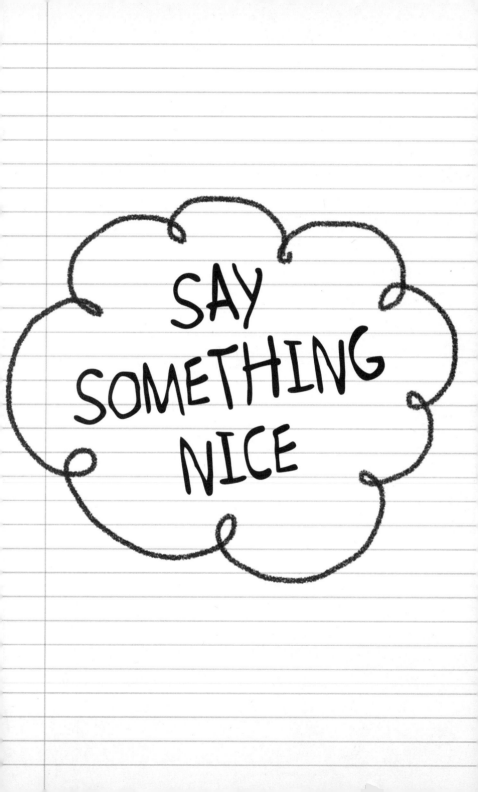

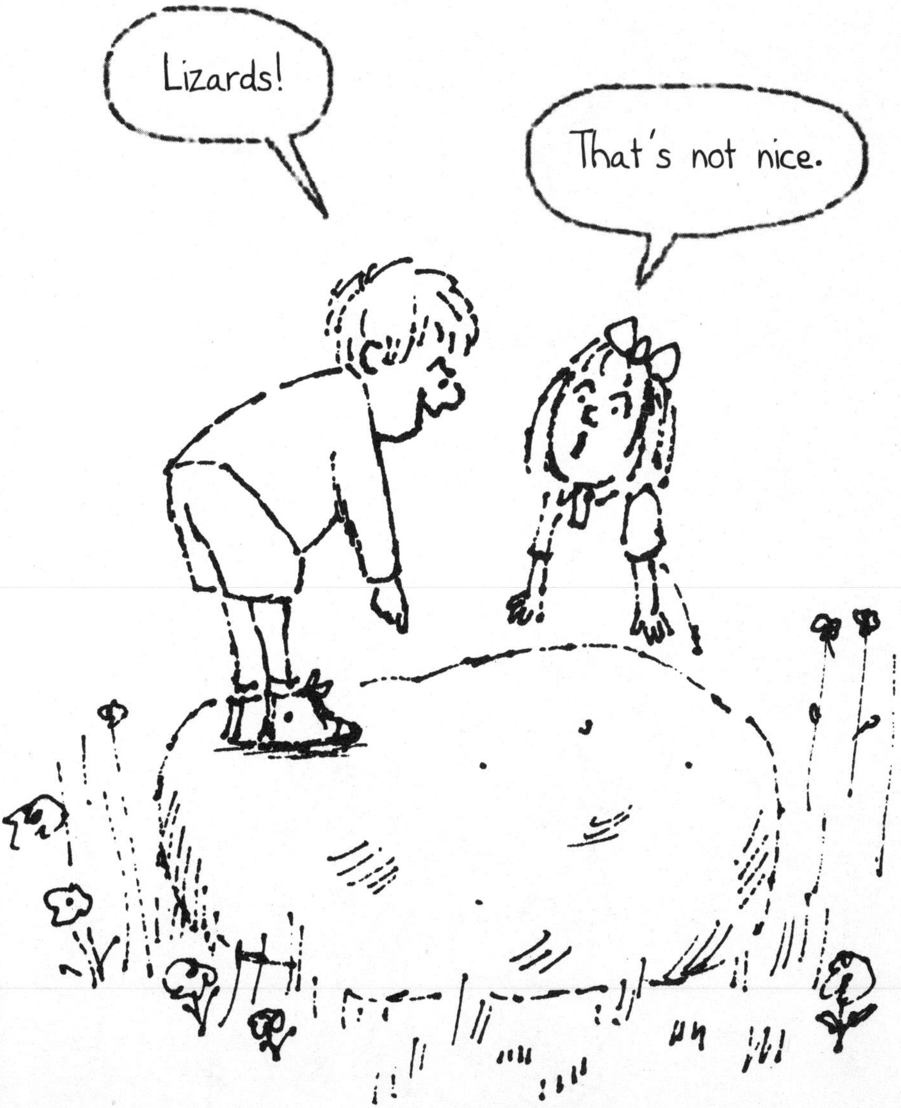
Lizards!
That's not nice.

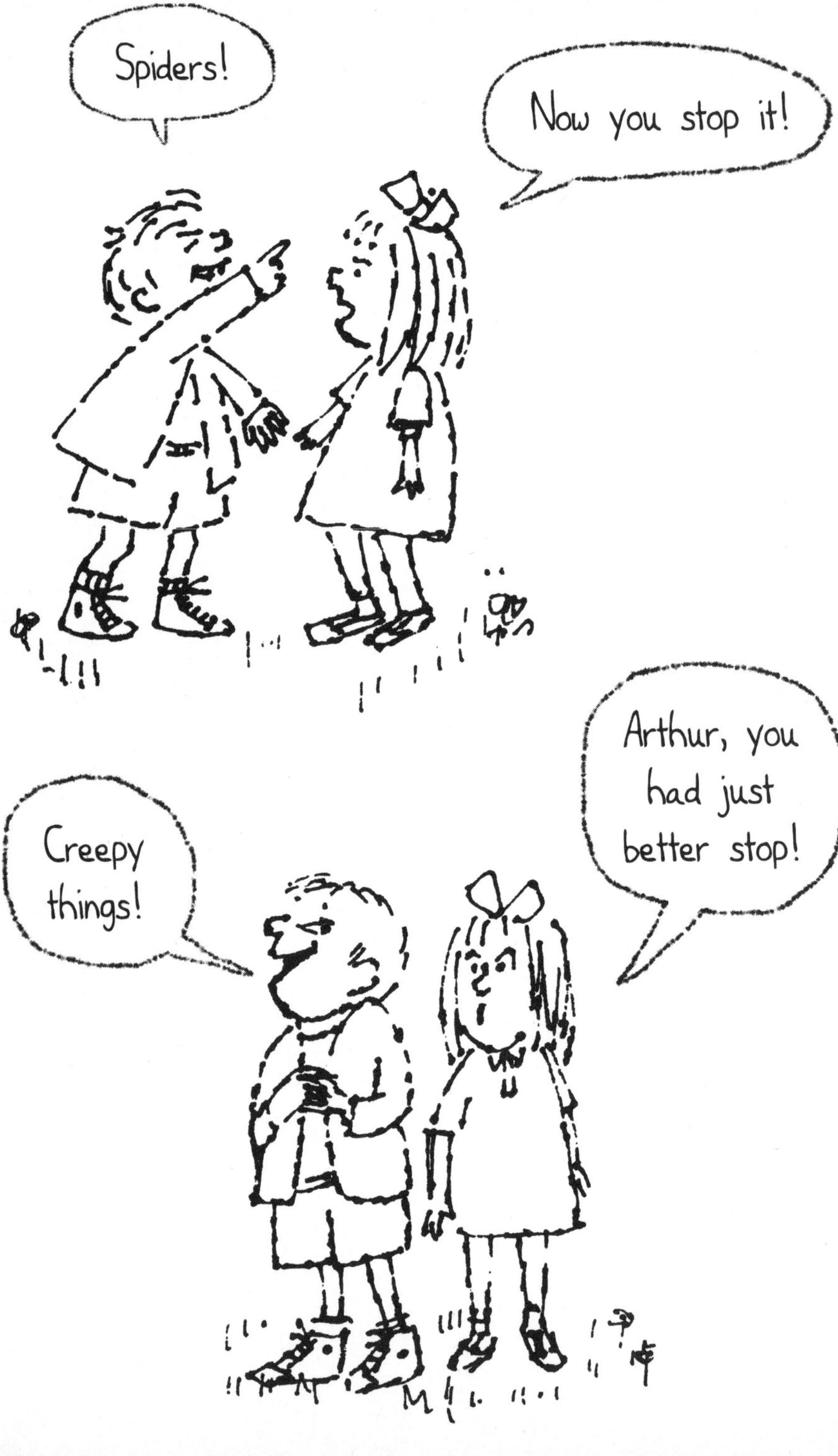
Spiders!
Now you stop it!
Creepy things!
Arthur, you had just better stop!

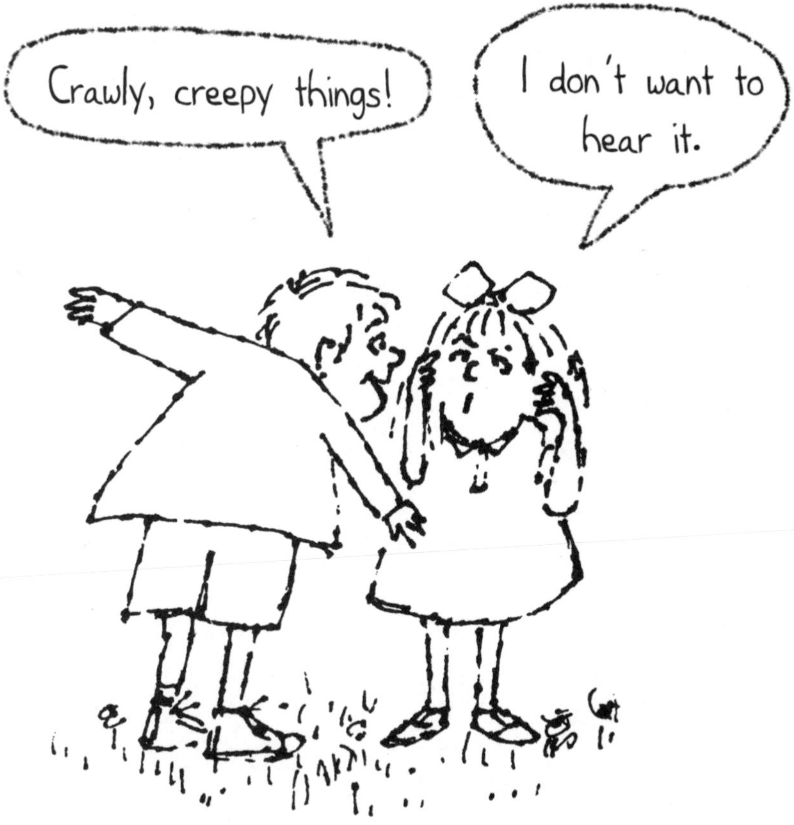
Crawly, creepy things!
I don't want to hear it.

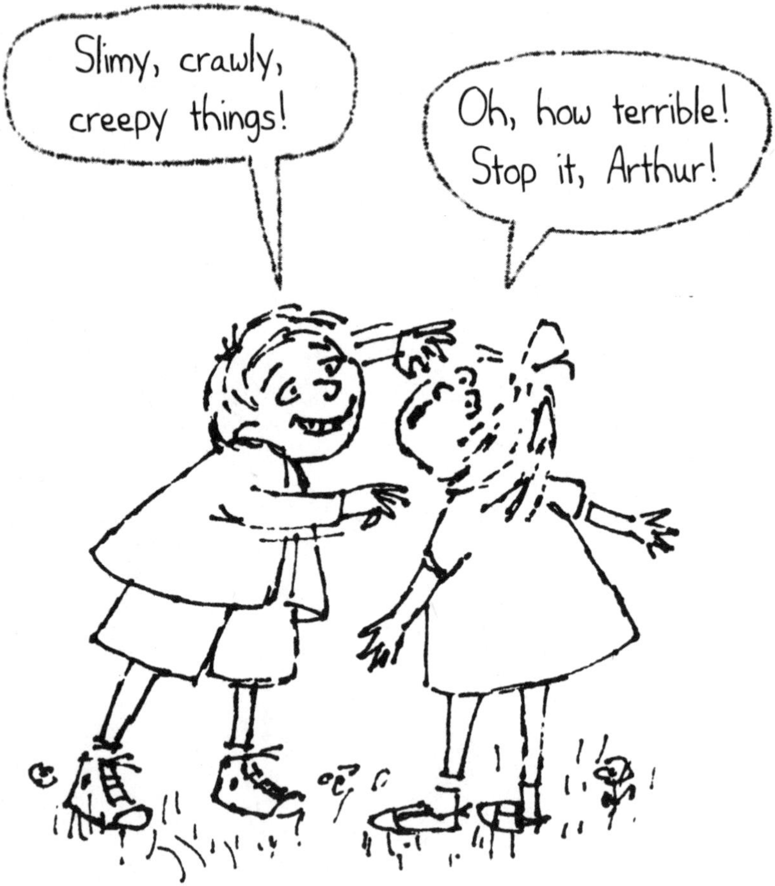
Slimy, crawly, creepy things!
Oh, how terrible! Stop it, Arthur!

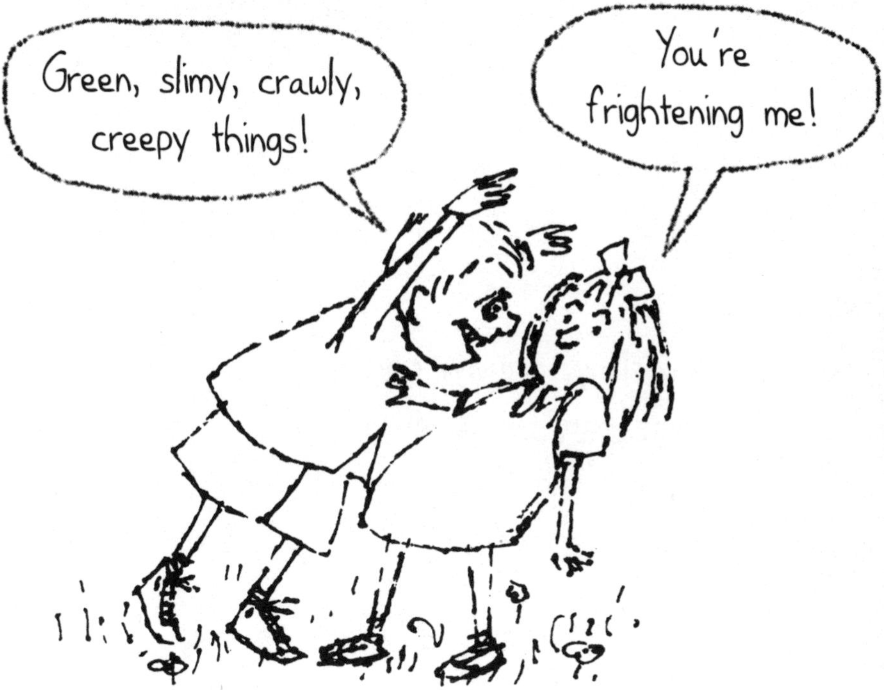
Green, slimy, crawly, creepy things!
You're frightening me!

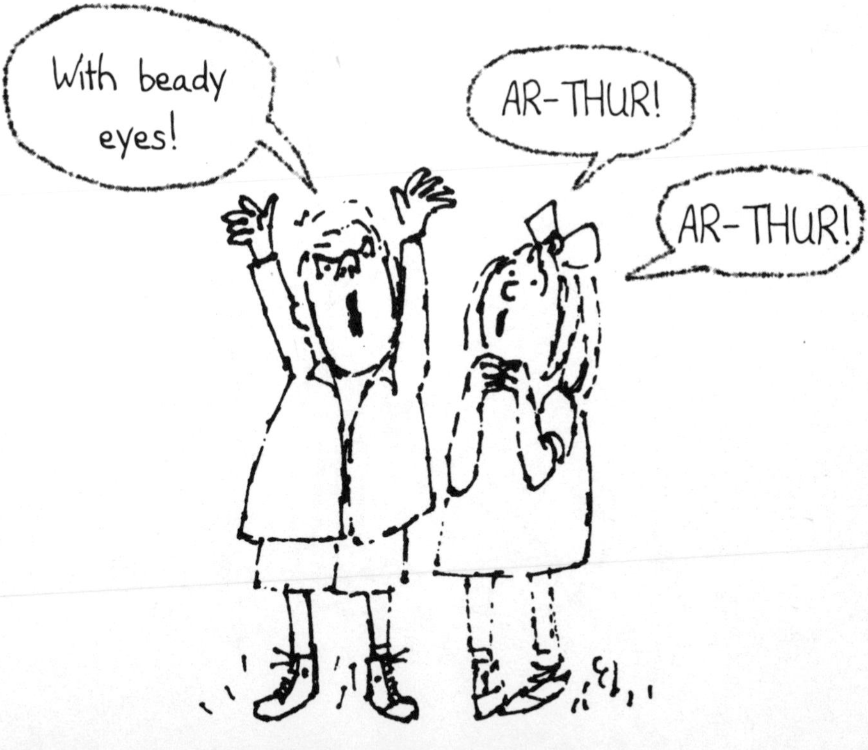
With beady eyes!
AR-THUR!
AR-THUR!

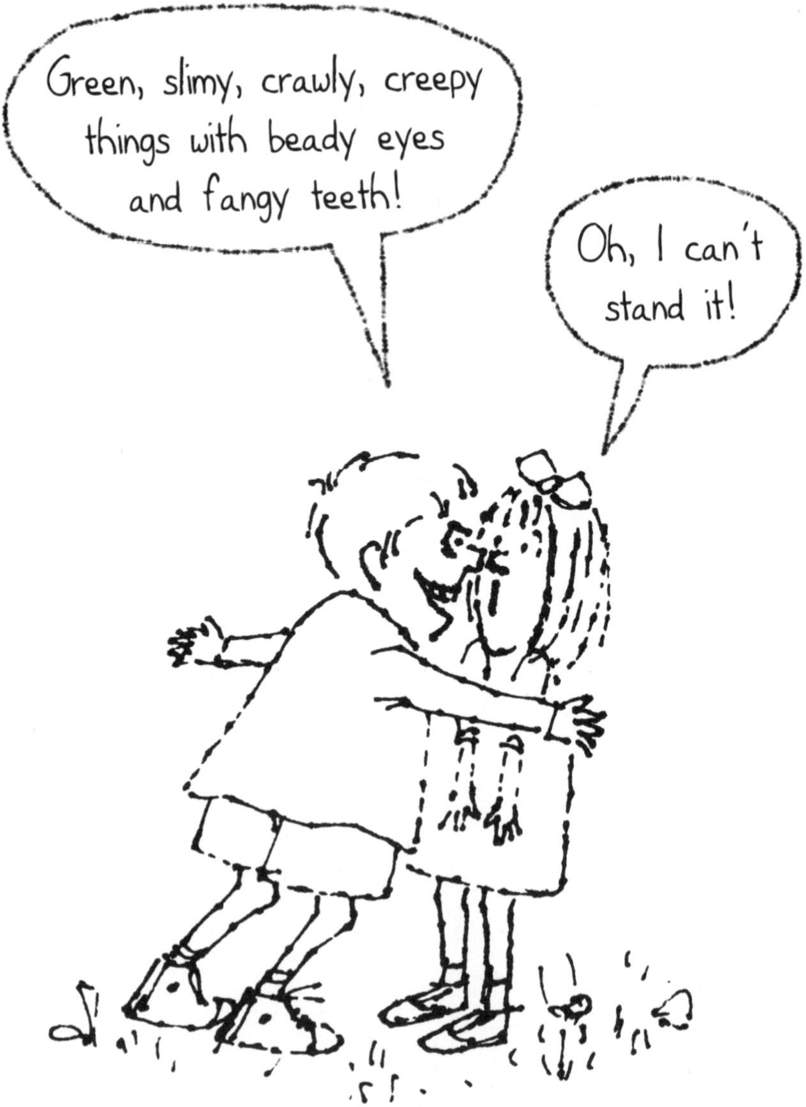
Green, slimy, crawly, creepy things with beady eyes and fangy teeth!
Oh, I can't stand it!

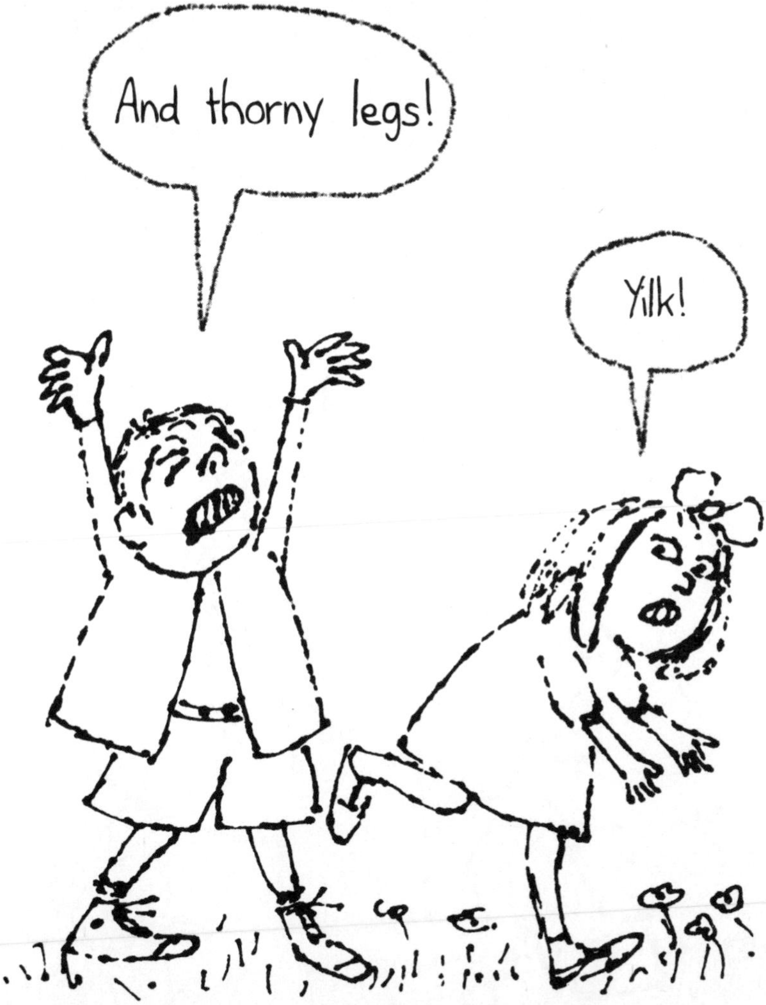
And thorny legs!
Yilk!

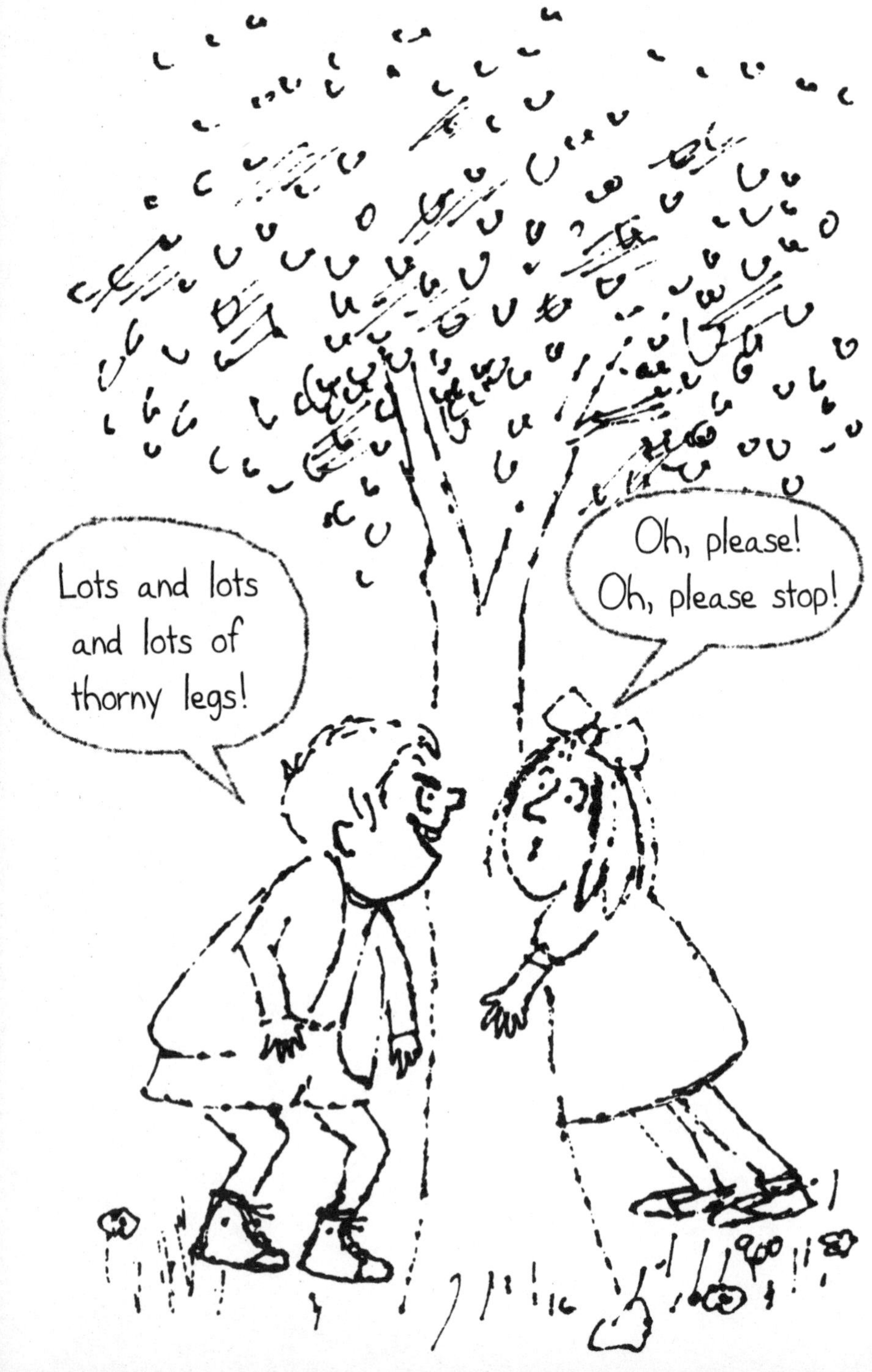

Lots and lots and lots of thorny legs!
Oh, please! Oh, please stop!

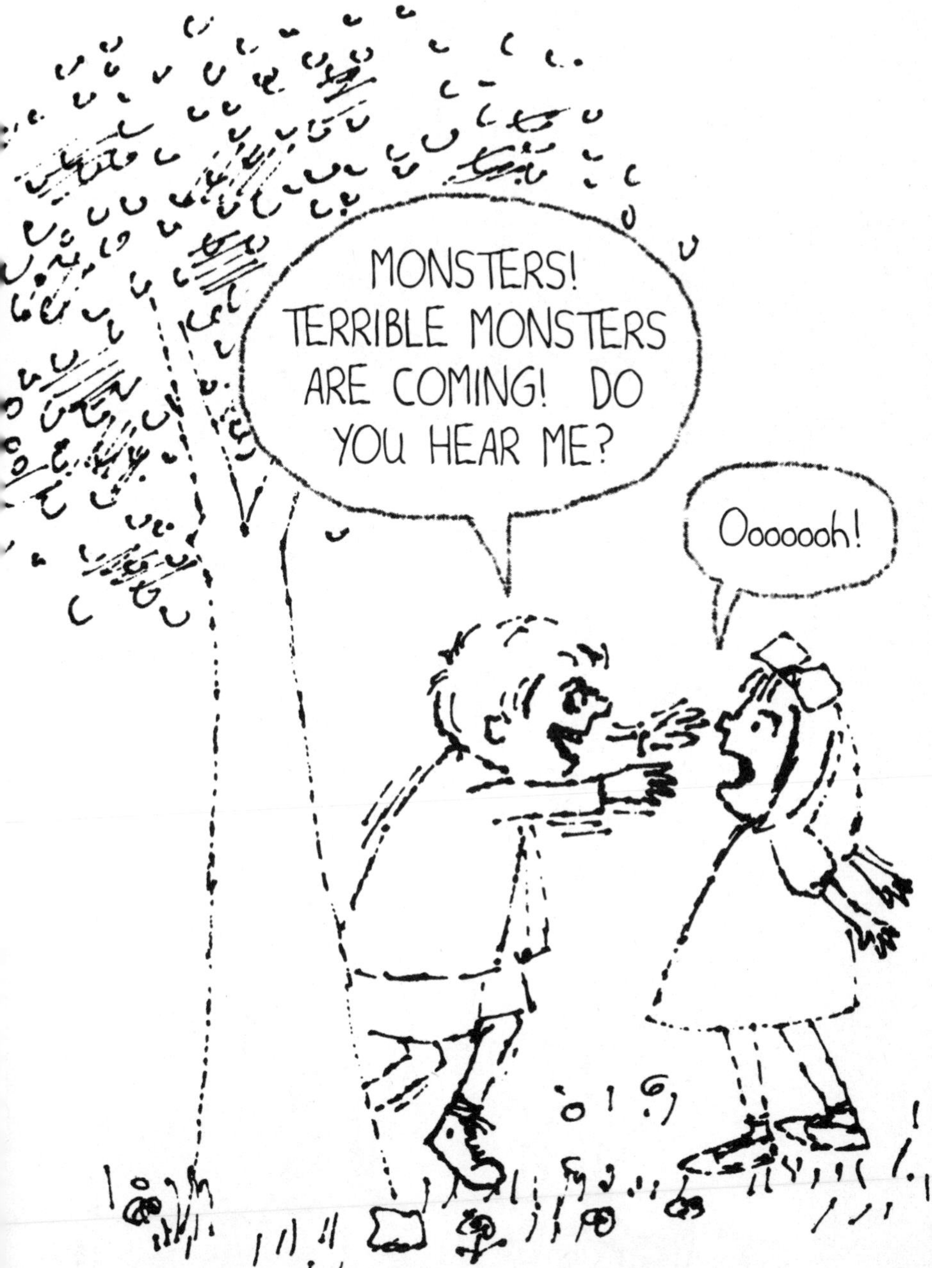
MONSTERS! TERRIBLE MONSTERS ARE COMING! DO YOU HEAR ME?
Ooooooh!

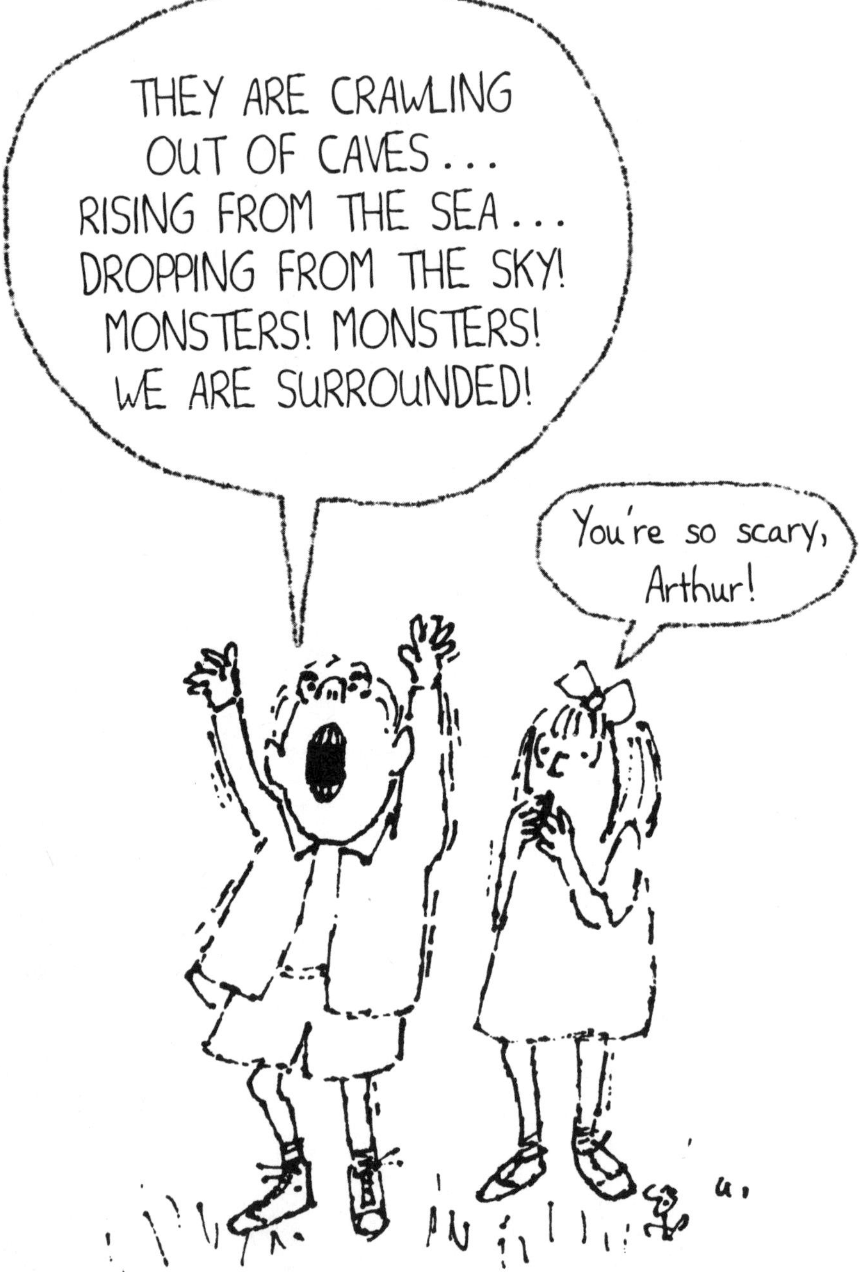
THEY ARE CRAWLING OUT OF CAVES . . . RISING FROM THE SEA . . . DROPPING FROM THE SKY! MONSTERS! MONSTERS! WE ARE SURROUNDED!
You're so scary, Arthur!

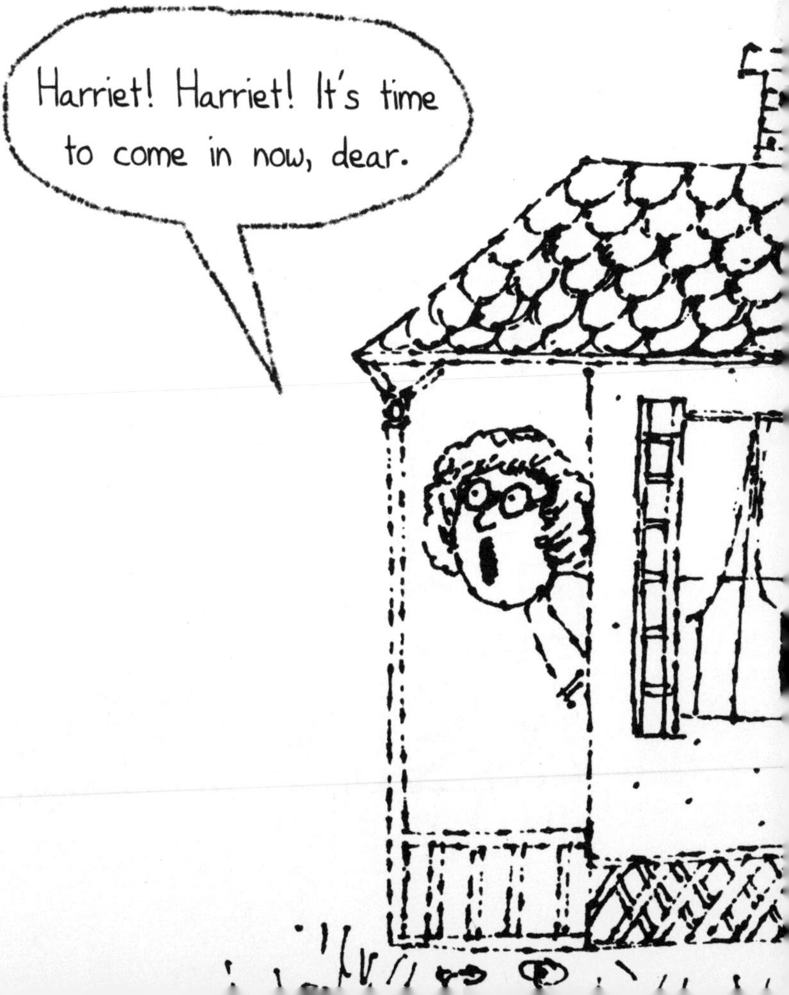
Harriet! Harriet! It's time to come in now, dear.

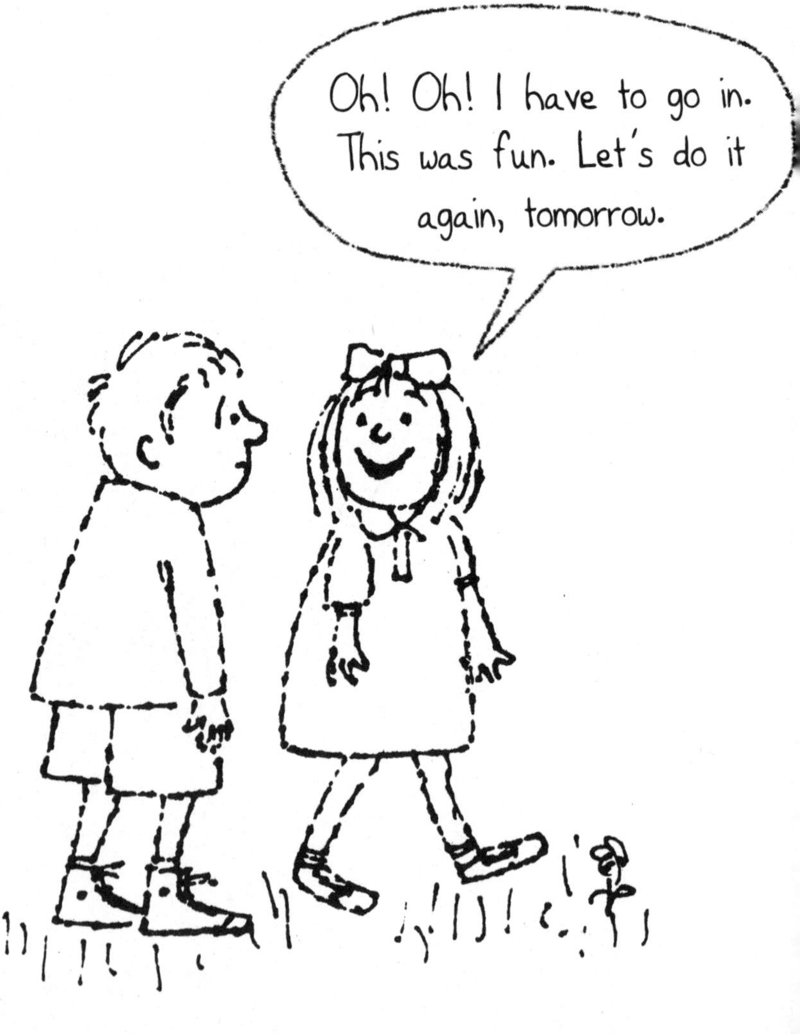
Oh! Oh! I have to go in. This was fun. Let's do it again, tomorrow.

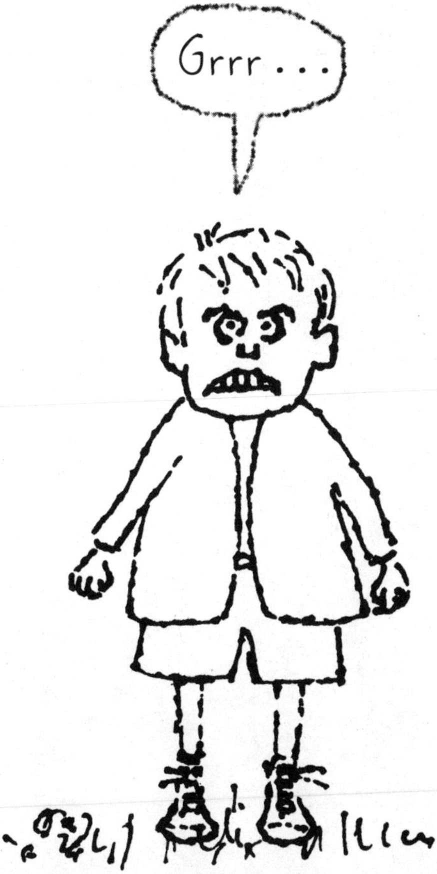
Grrr . . .

THAT WAS SOME DREAM

HA! HA! HA!

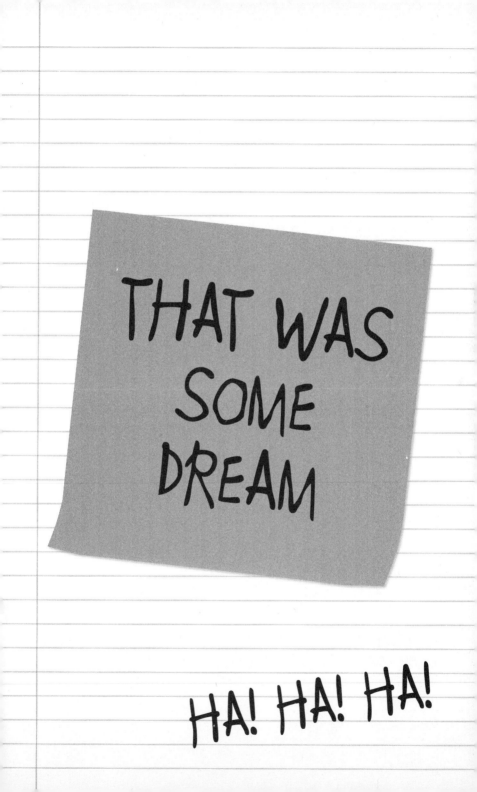

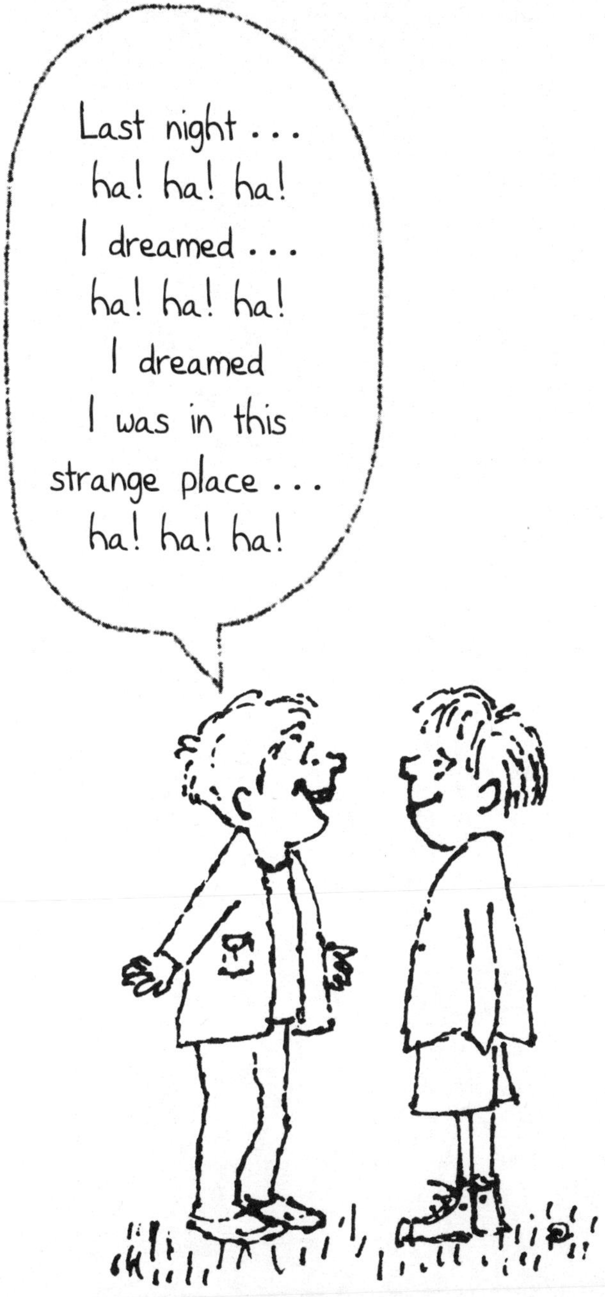
Last night . . . ha! ha! ha! I dreamed . . . ha! ha! ha! I dreamed I was in this strange place . . . ha! ha! ha!

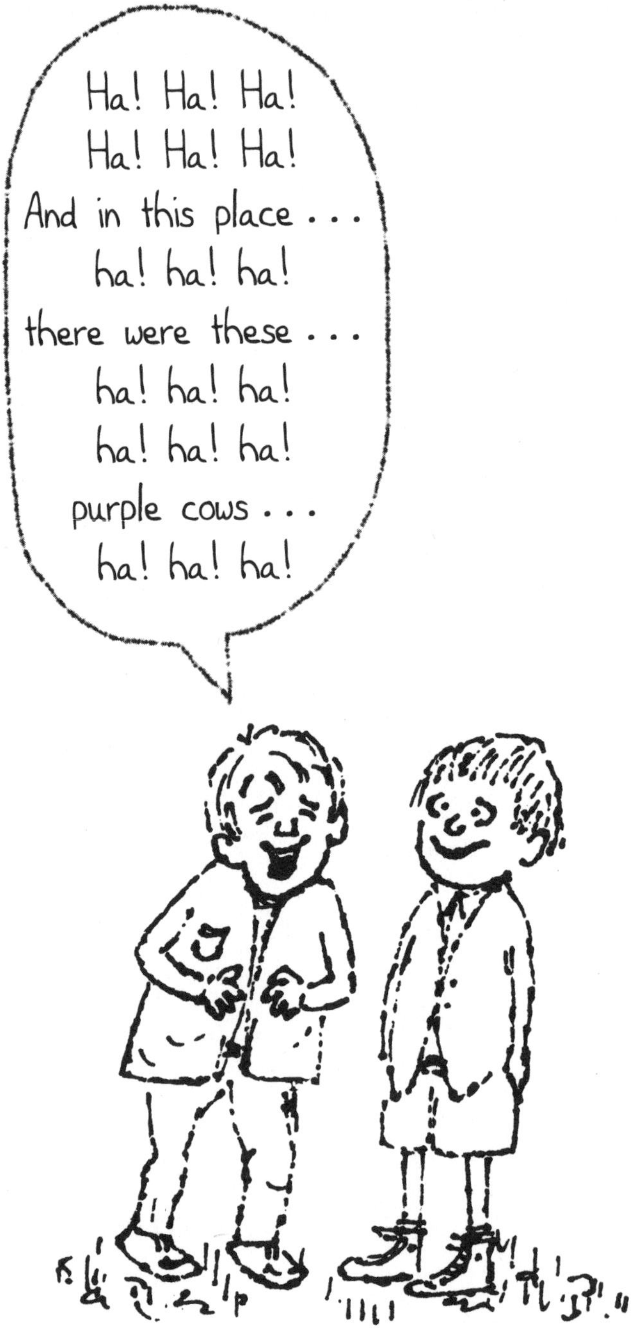
Ha! Ha! Ha!
Ha! Ha! Ha!
And in this place . . .
ha! ha! ha!
there were these . . .
ha! ha! ha!
ha! ha! ha!
purple cows . . .
ha! ha! ha!

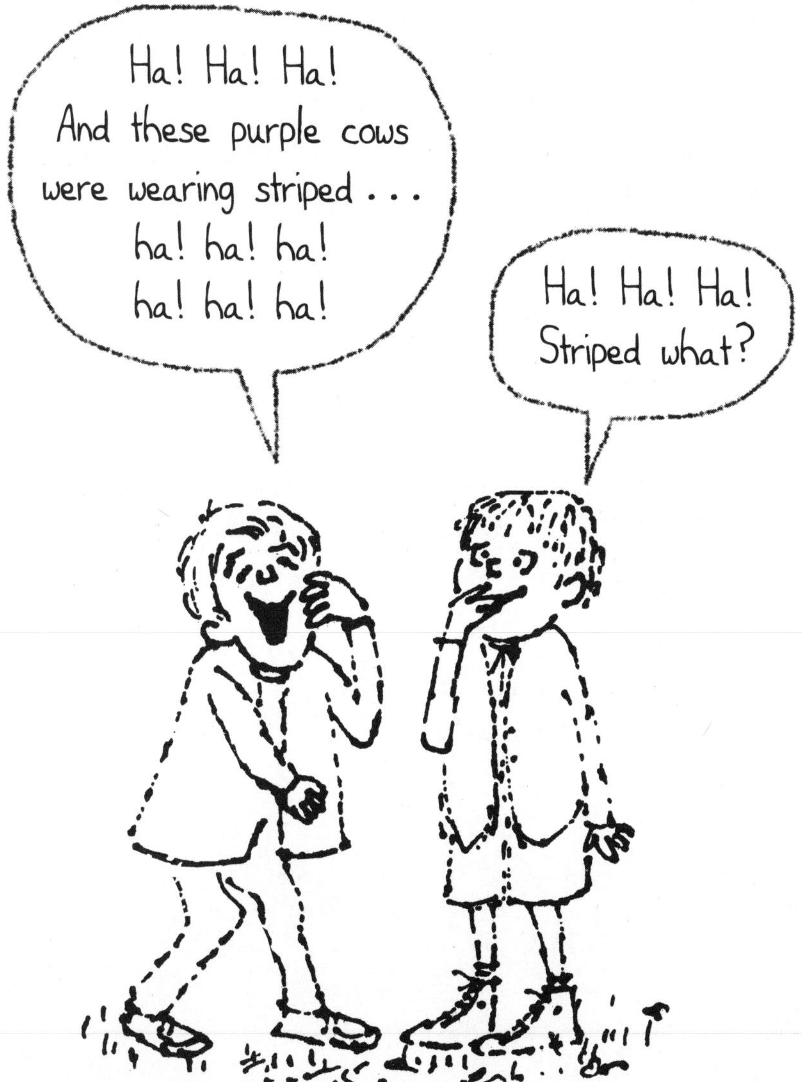
Ha! Ha! Ha! And these purple cows were wearing striped . . . ha! ha! ha! ha! ha! ha!
Ha! Ha! Ha! Striped what?

Ha! Ha! Ha! Ha! Ha! Ha! Striped . . . ha! ha! ha! ha! ha! ha! ha! ha! ha!
Ha! Ha! Ha! Ha! Ha! Ha! Striped what? Ha! Ha! Ha! Ha! Ha! Ha! Ha! Ha! Ha!

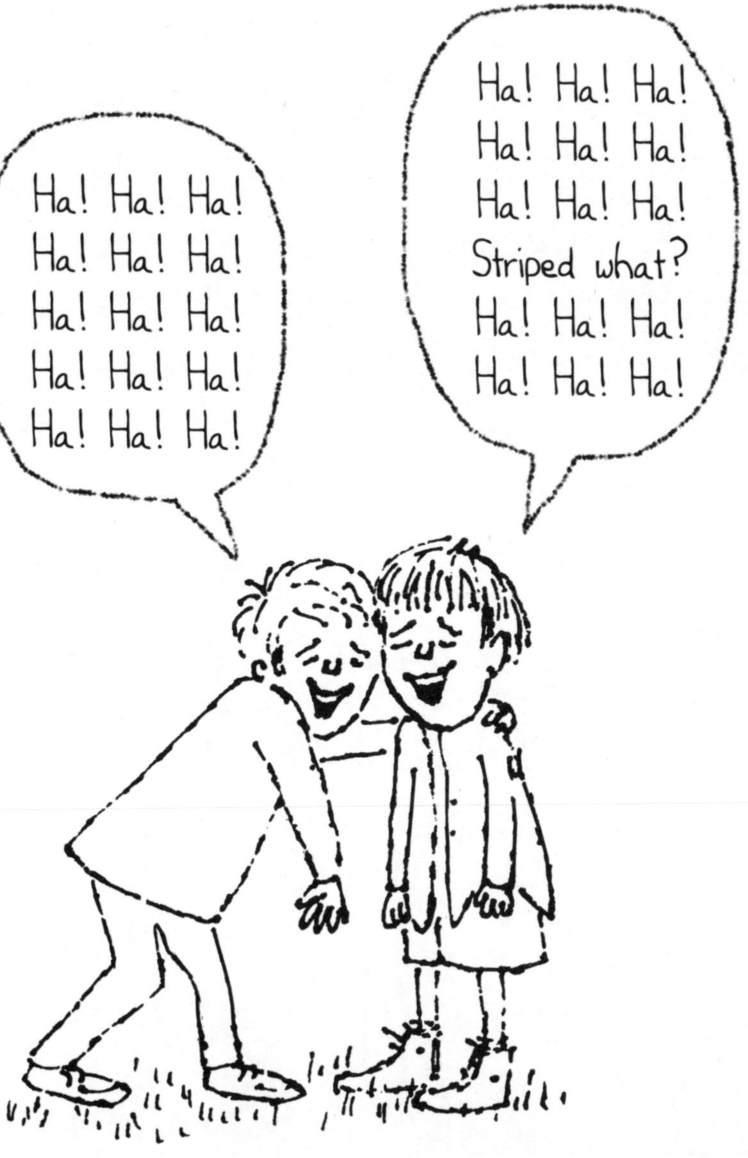
Ha! Ha! Ha! Ha! Ha! Ha! Ha! Ha! Ha! Ha! Ha! Ha! Ha! Ha! Ha!
Ha! Ha! Ha! Ha! Ha! Ha! Ha! Ha! Ha! Striped what? Ha! Ha! Ha! Ha! Ha! Ha!

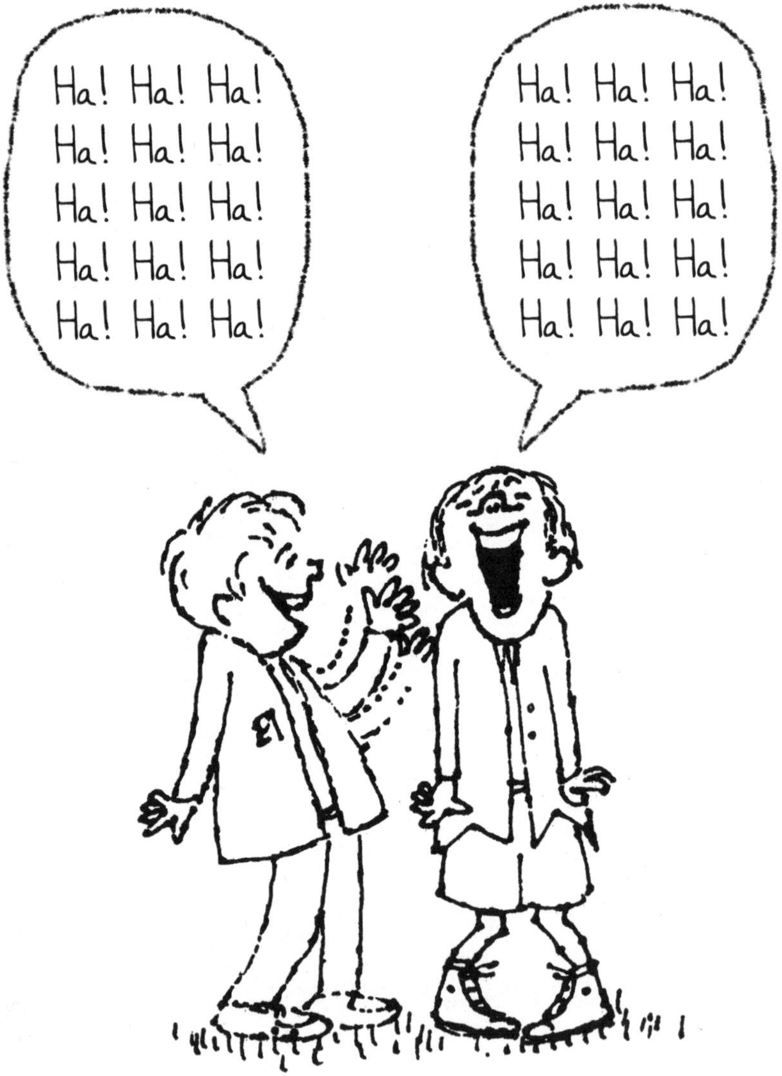
Ha! Ha! Ha! Ha! Ha! Ha! Ha! Ha! Ha! Ha! Ha! Ha! Ha! Ha! Ha!
Ha! Ha! Ha! Ha! Ha! Ha! Ha! Ha! Ha! Ha! Ha! Ha! Ha! Ha! Ha!

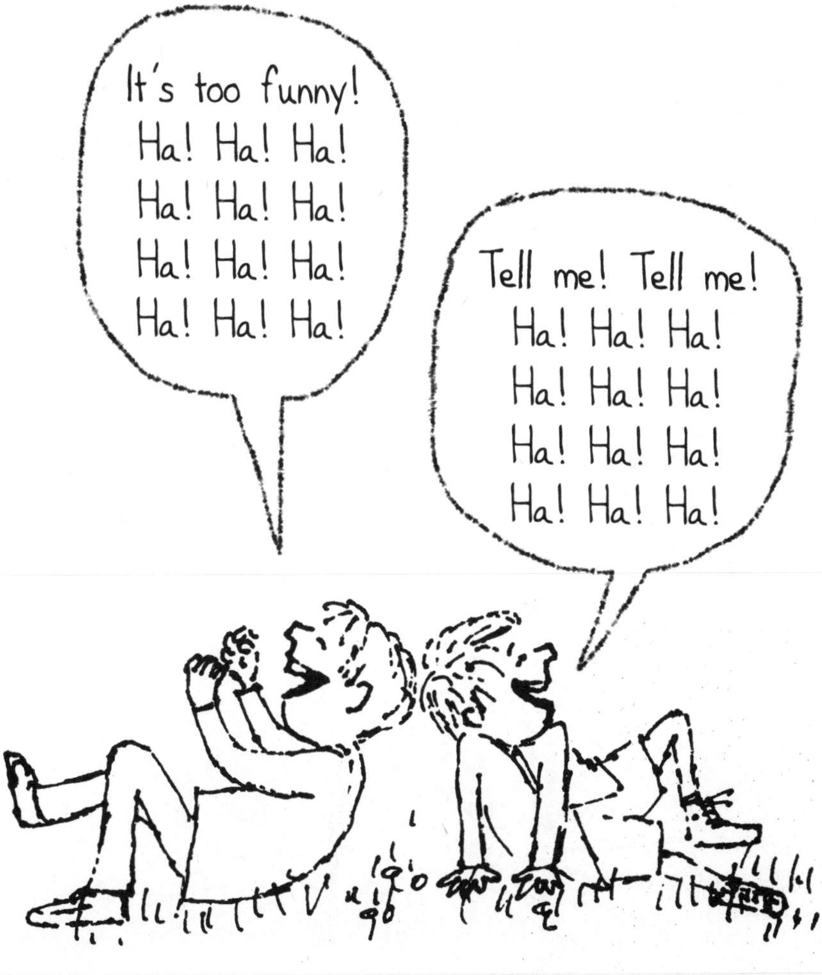
It's too funny! Ha! Ha! Ha! Ha! Ha! Ha! Ha! Ha! Ha! Ha! Ha! Ha!
Tell me! Tell me! Ha! Ha! Ha! Ha! Ha! Ha! Ha! Ha! Ha! Ha! Ha! Ha!

I'll have to . . . ha! ha! ha! ha! ha! ha! tell you . . . ha! ha! ha! ha! ha! ha! later . . . ha! ha! ha! ha! ha! ha!
Ha! Ha! Ha! Ha! Ha! Ha! Ha! Ha! Ha! Ha! Ha! Ha! Ha! Ha! Ha!

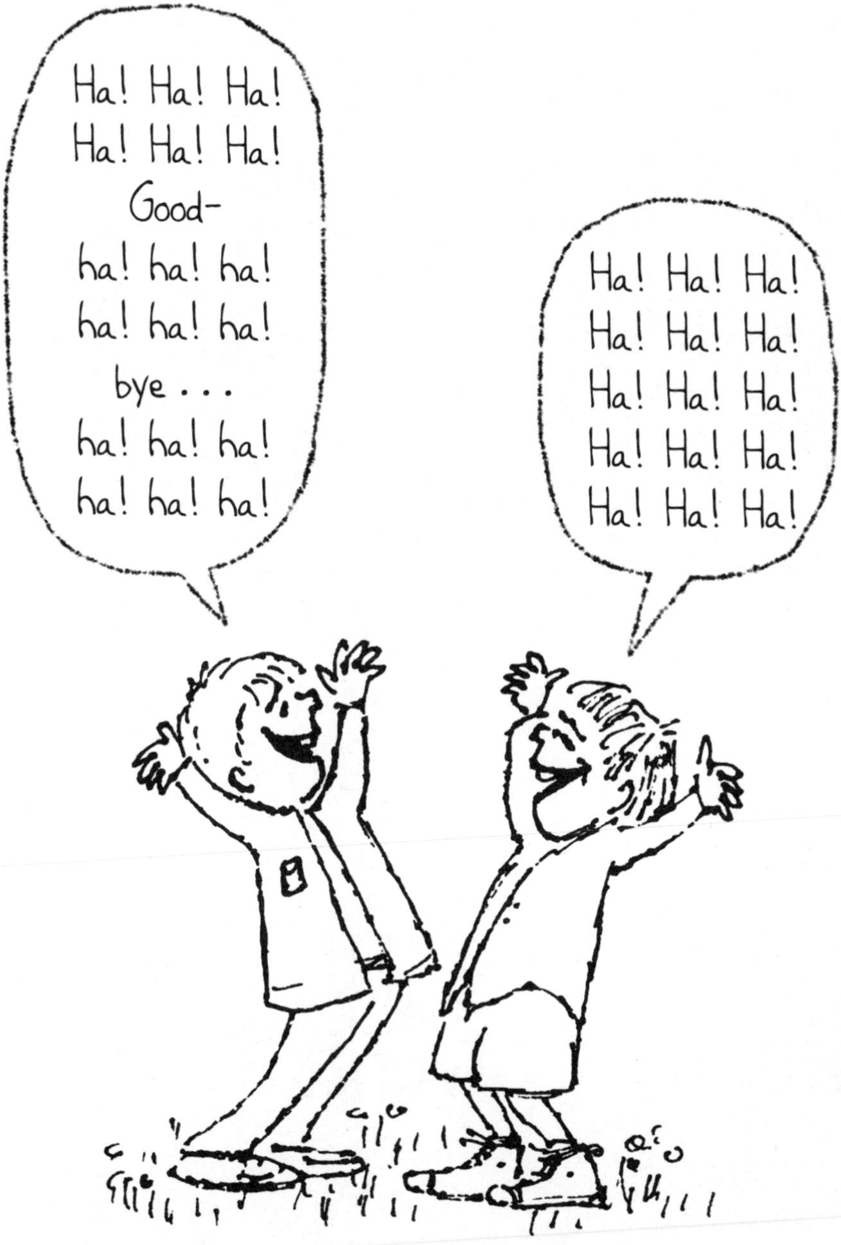
Ha! Ha! Ha! Ha! Ha! Ha! Good- ha! ha! ha! ha! ha! ha! bye . . . ha! ha! ha! ha! ha! ha!
Ha! Ha! Ha! Ha! Ha! Ha! Ha! Ha! Ha! Ha! Ha! Ha! Ha! Ha! Ha!

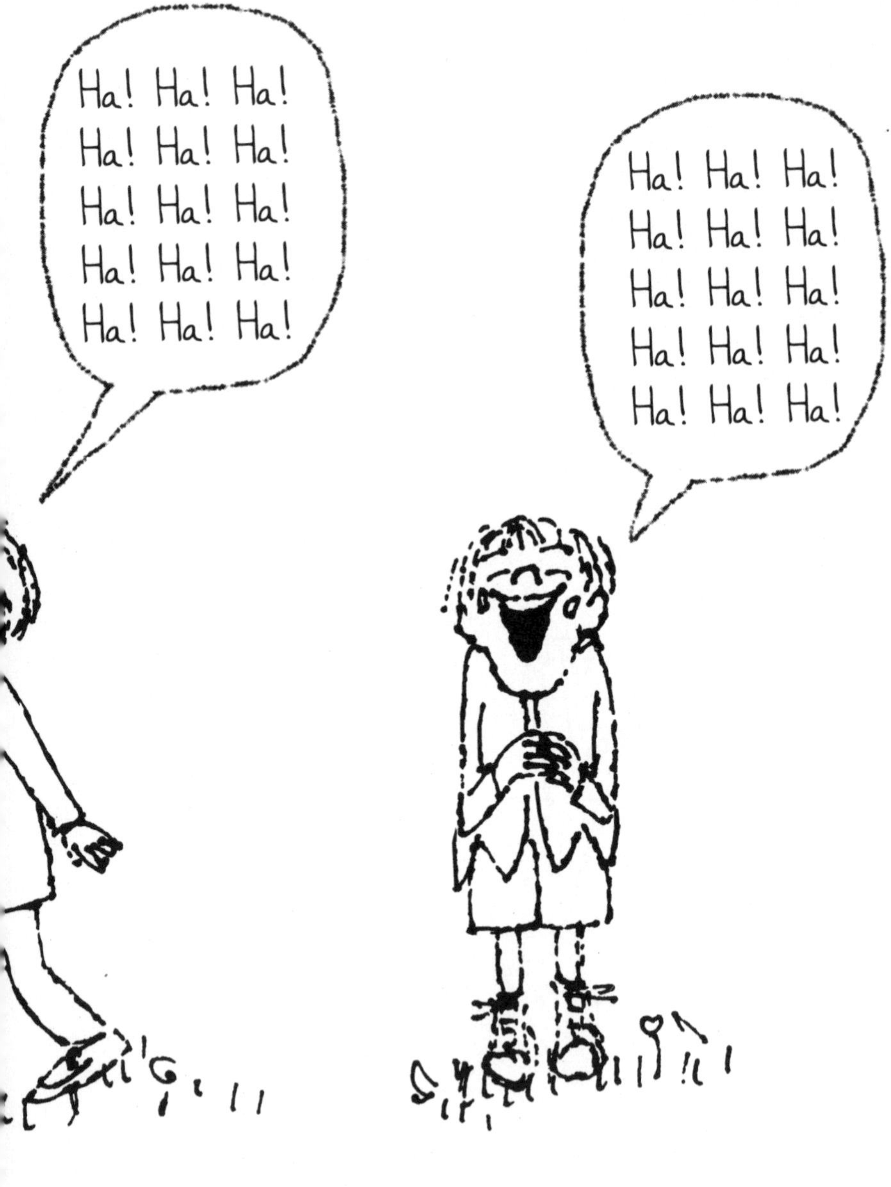
Ha! Ha! Ha! Ha! Ha! Ha! Ha! Ha! Ha! Ha! Ha! Ha! Ha! Ha! Ha!
Ha! Ha! Ha! Ha! Ha! Ha! Ha! Ha! Ha! Ha! Ha! Ha! Ha! Ha! Ha!

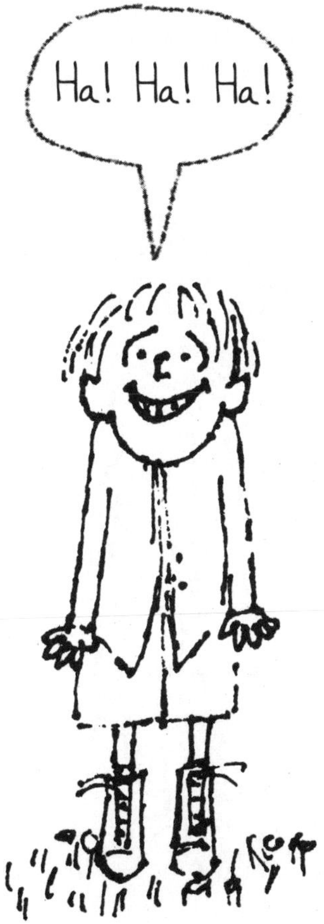
Ha! Ha! Ha!

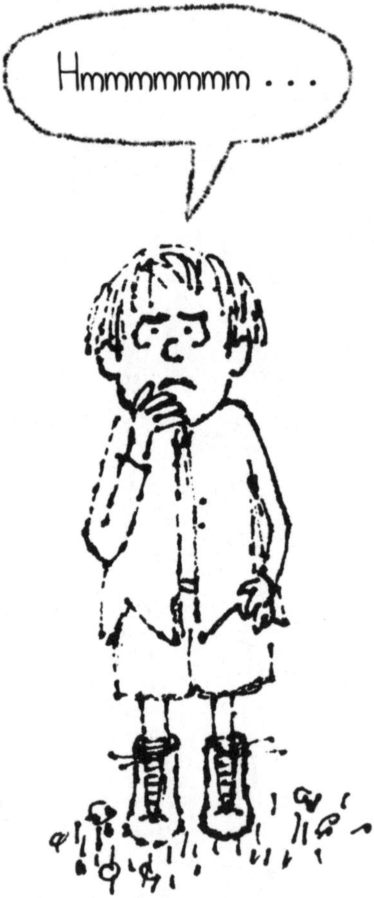
Hmmmmmmm . . .

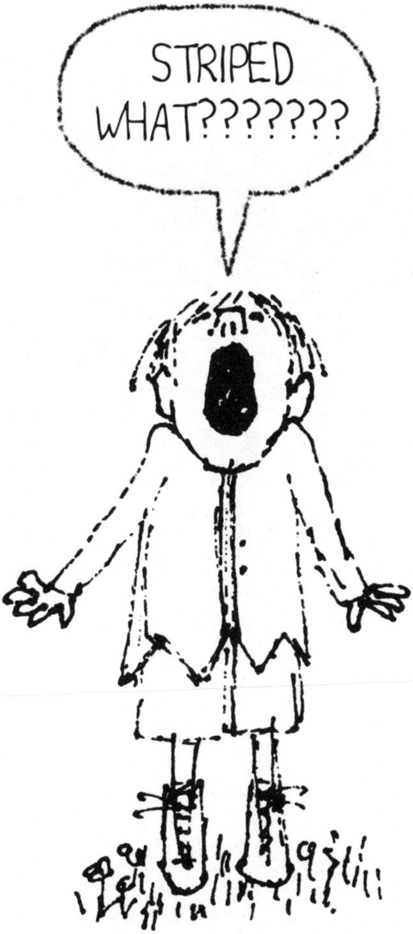
STRIPED WHAT????????

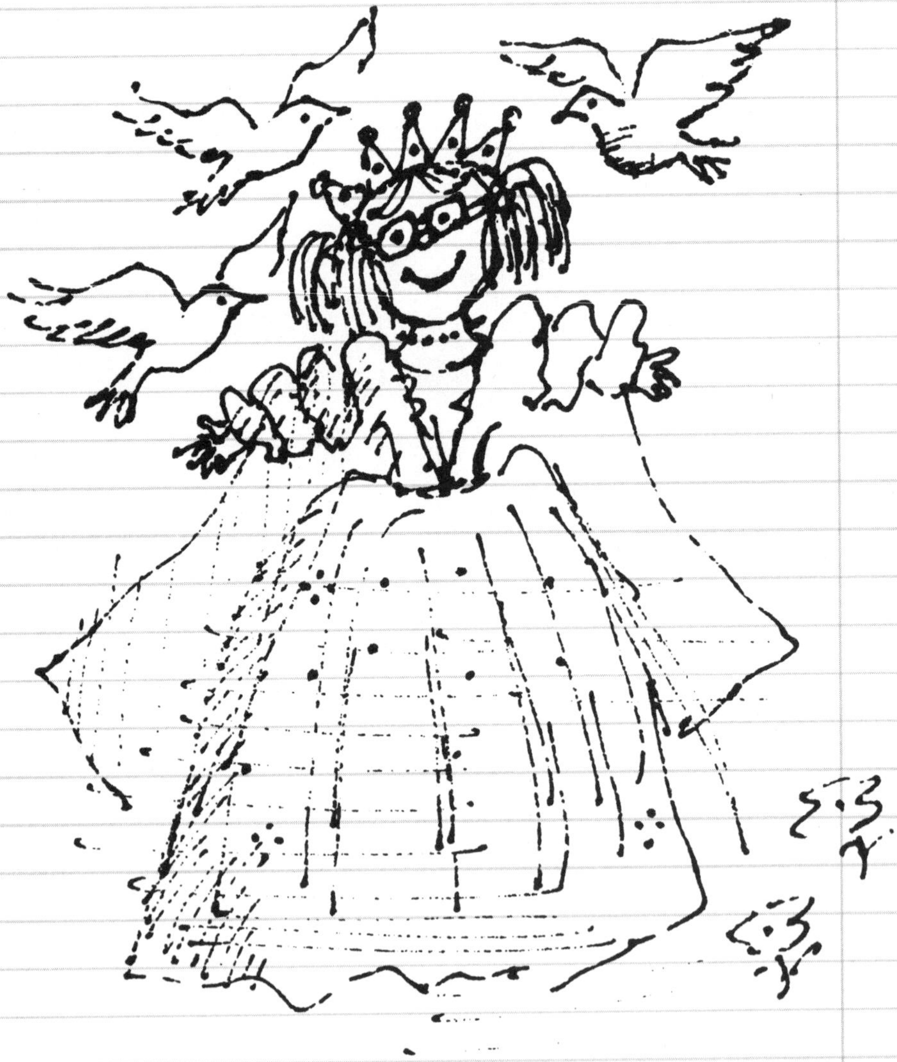

THAT WAS
SOME
DAYDREAM

Mmmmmmmmmmmm!

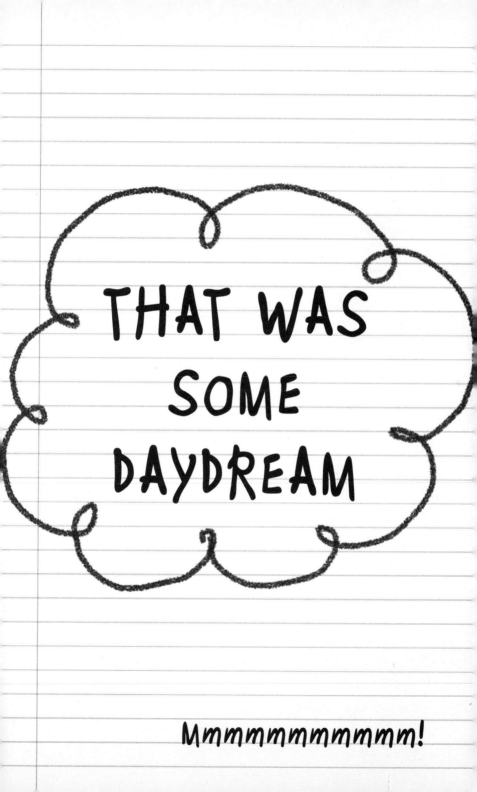

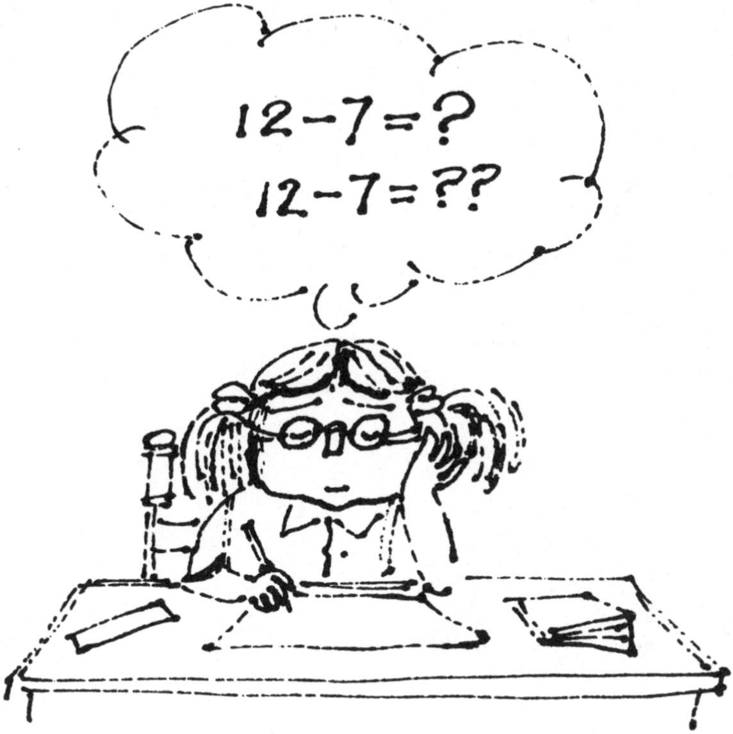
12−7=?
12−7=??

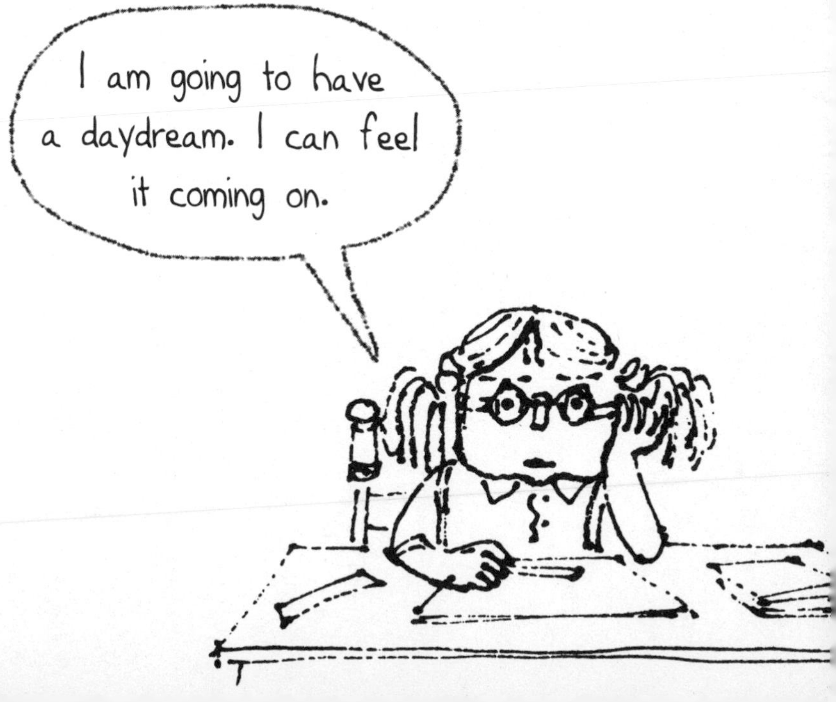
I am going to have a daydream. I can feel it coming on.

But I don't want to have a daydream. I really don't want to have a daydream.

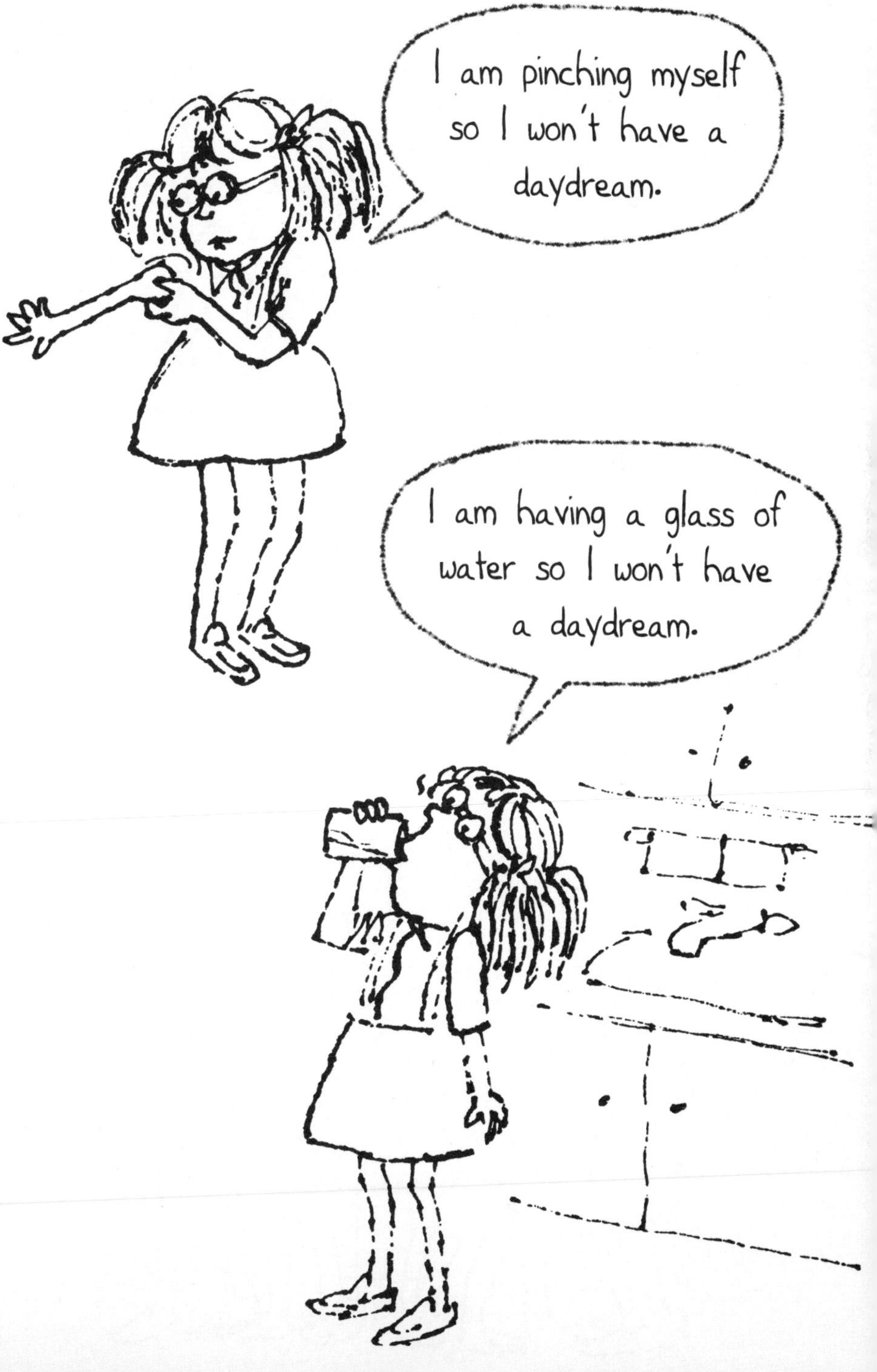
I am pinching myself so I won't have a daydream.
I am having a glass of water so I won't have a daydream.

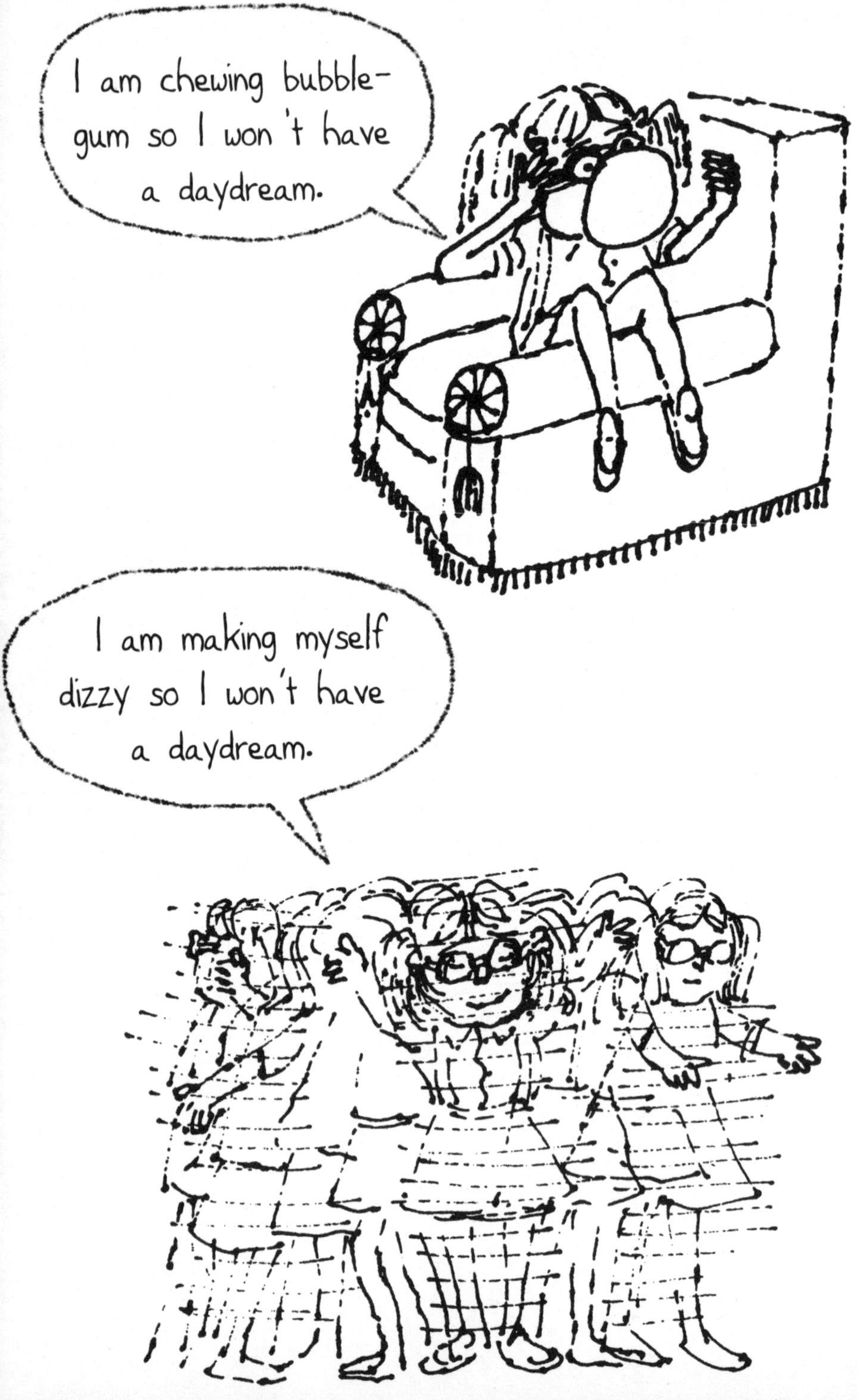
I am chewing bubble-gum so I won't have a daydream.
I am making myself dizzy so I won't have a daydream.

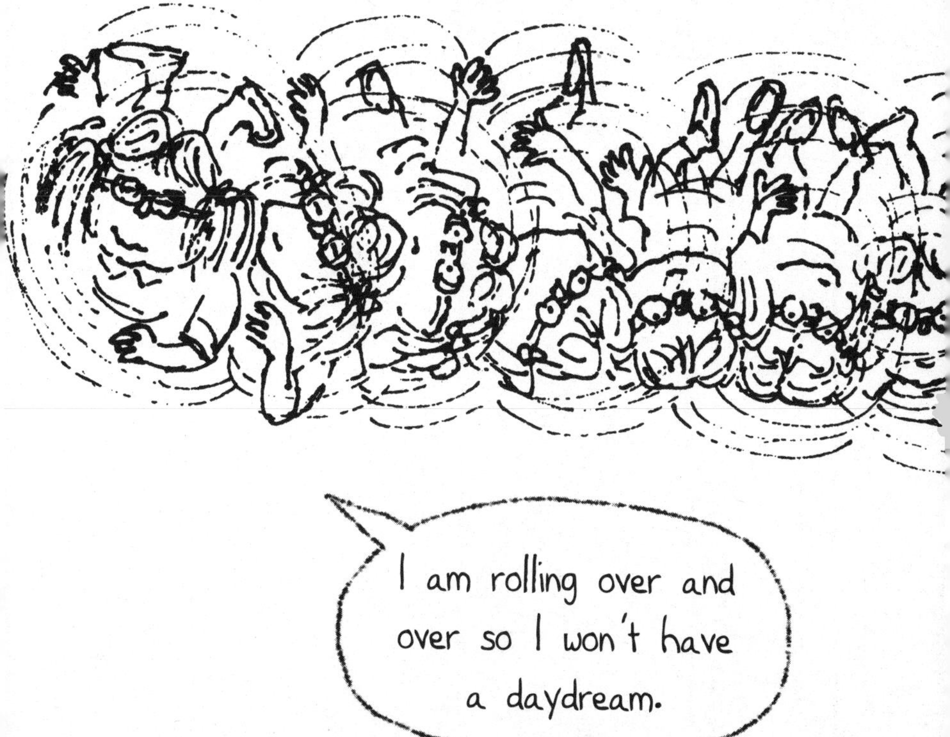
I am rolling over and over so I won't have a daydream.

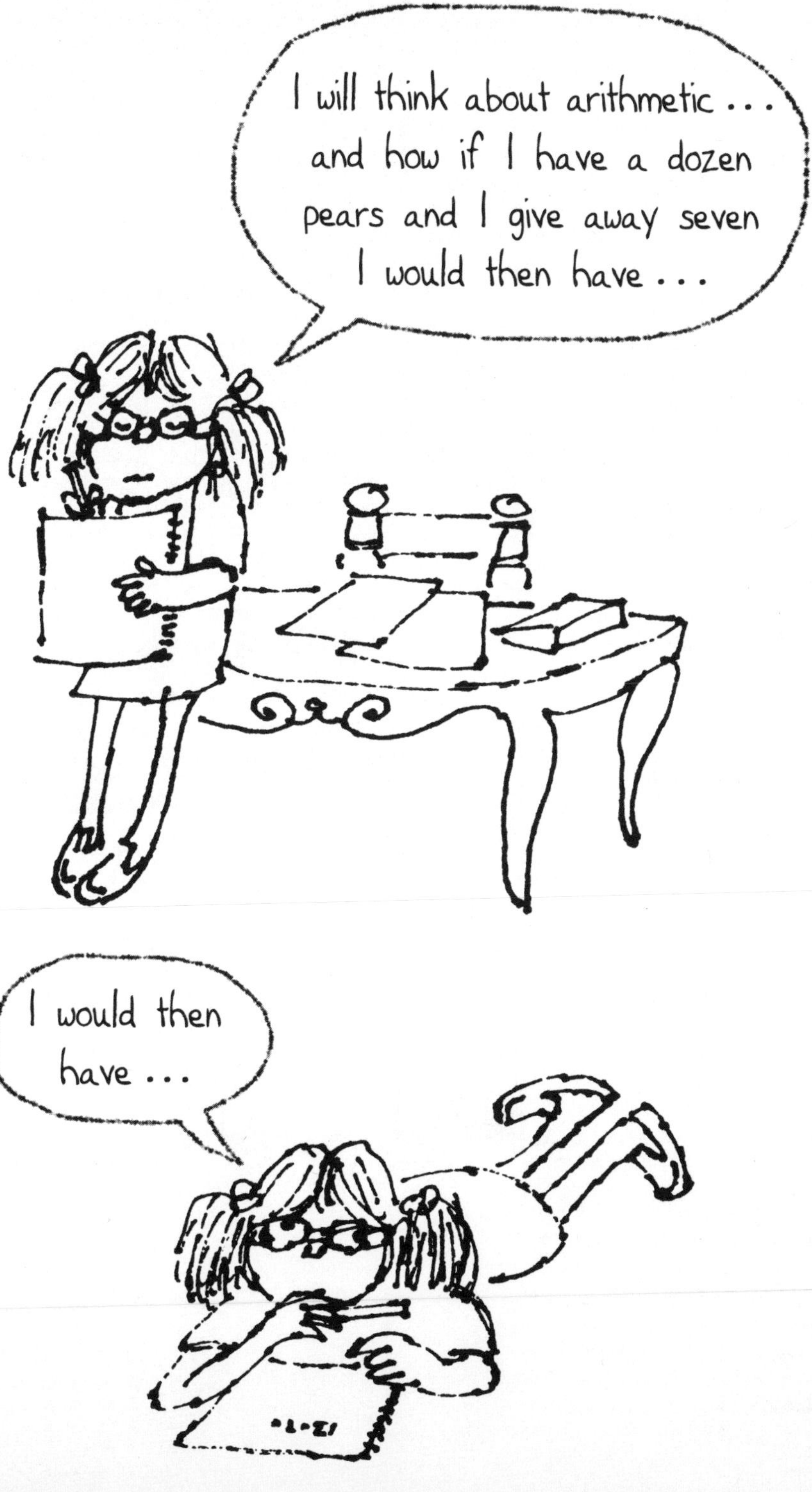
I will think about arithmetic . . . and how if I have a dozen pears and I give away seven I would then have . . .
I would then have . . .

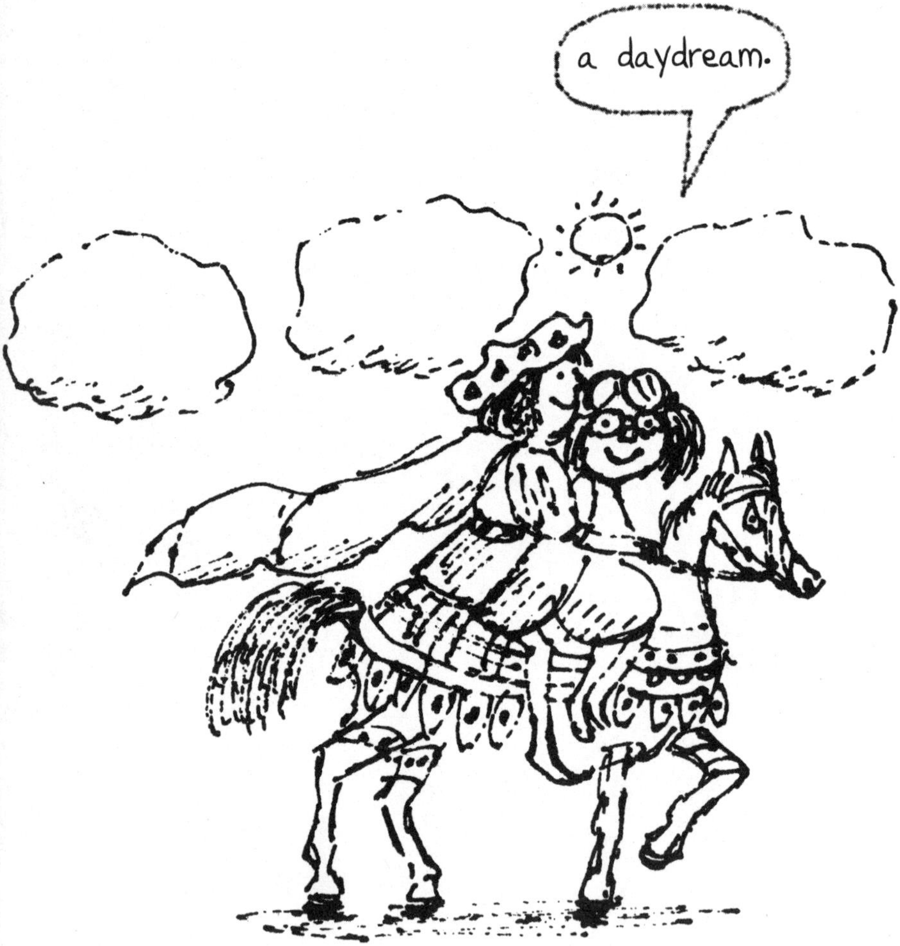
a daydream.

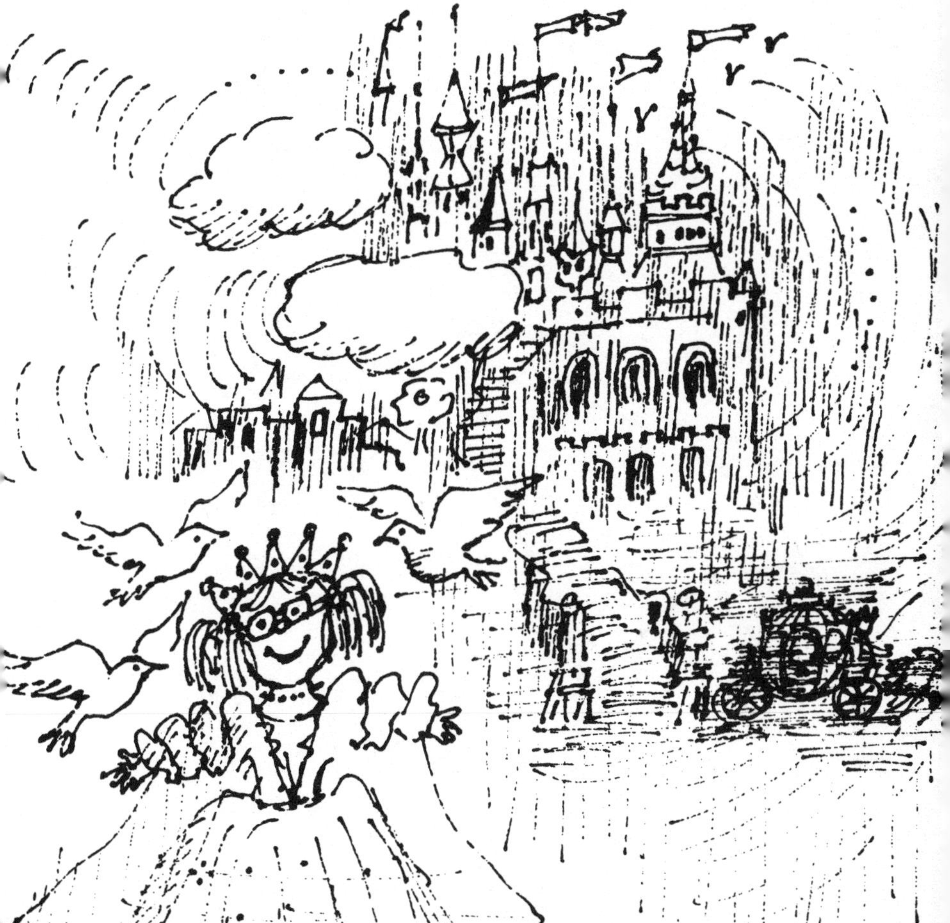

NO RAIN AGAIN TODAY

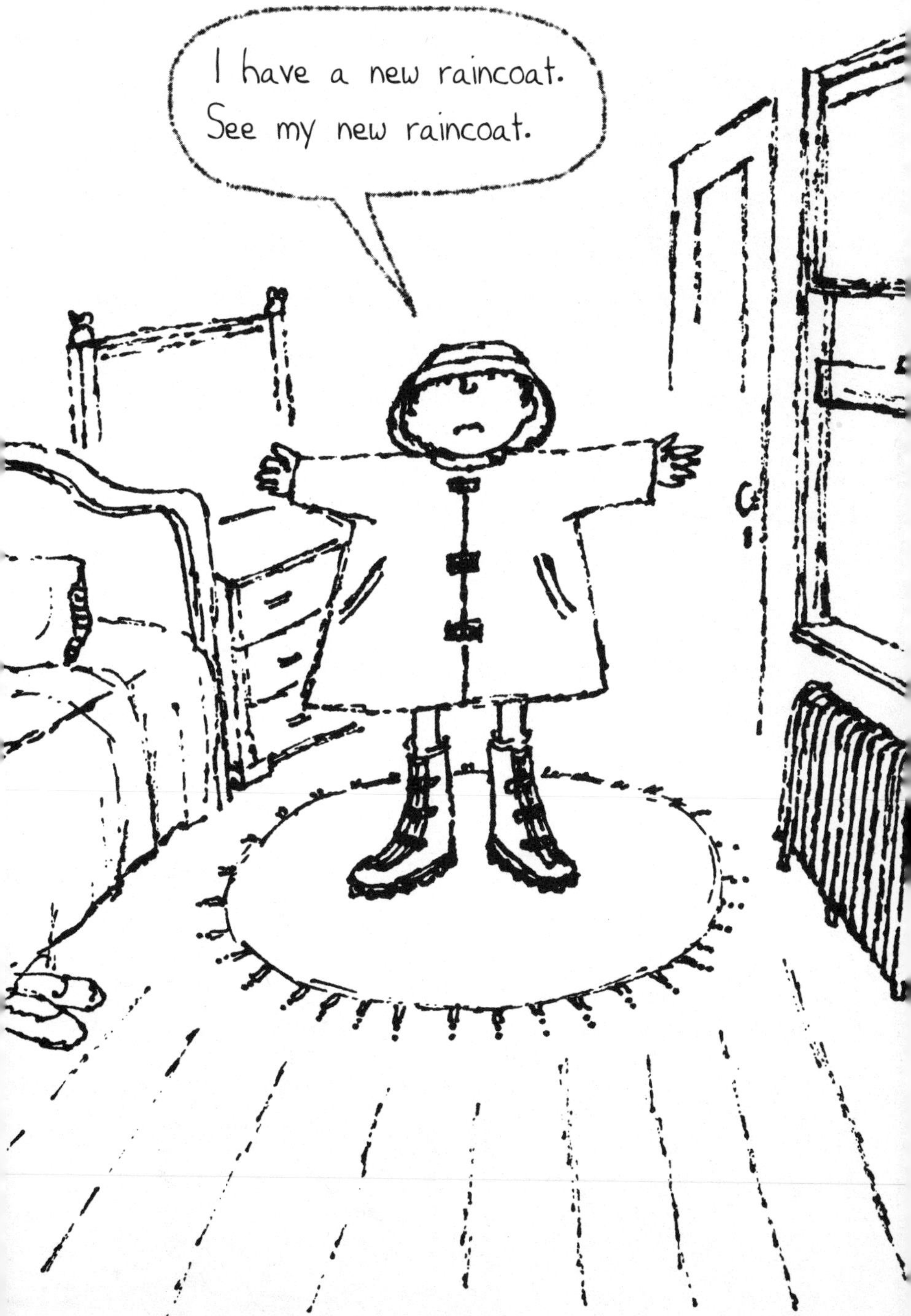
I have a new raincoat.
See my new raincoat.

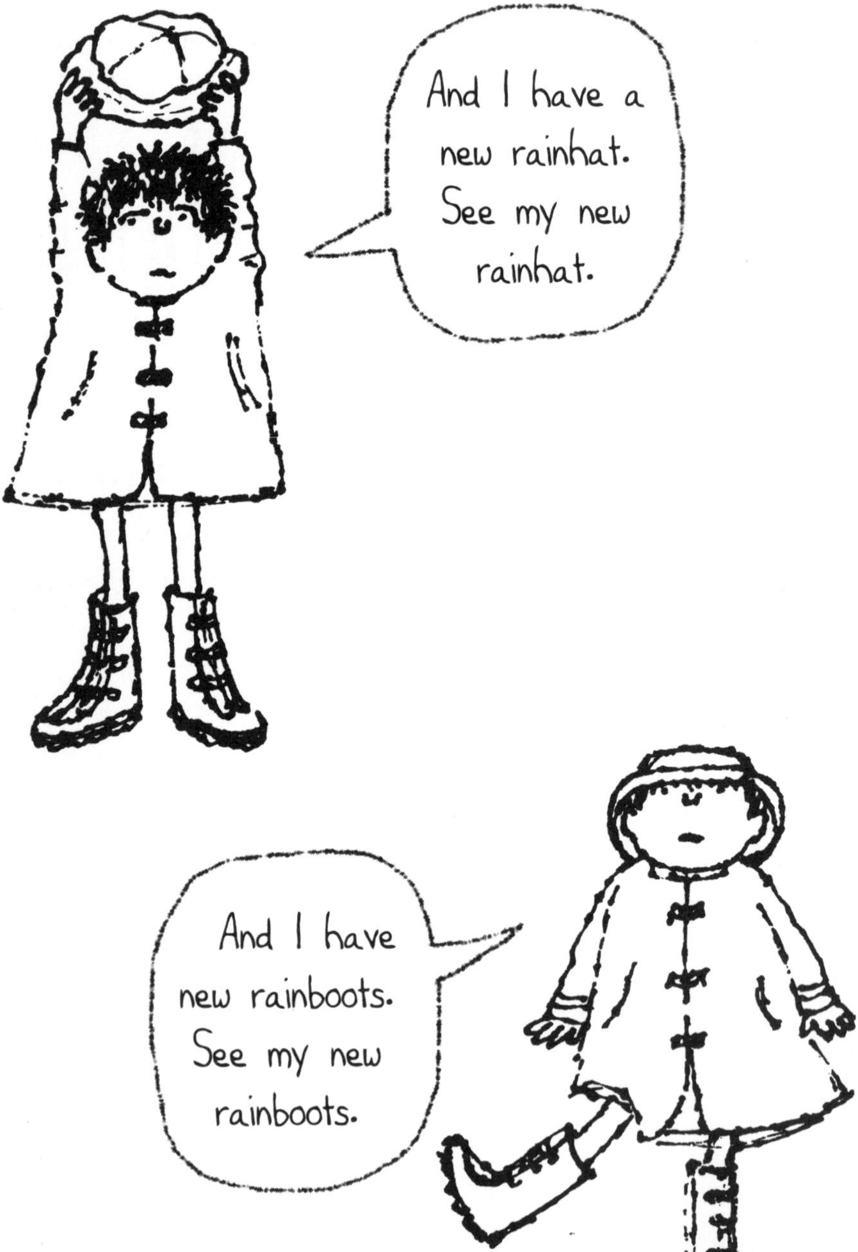
And I have a new rainhat. See my new rainhat.
And I have new rainboots. See my new rainboots.

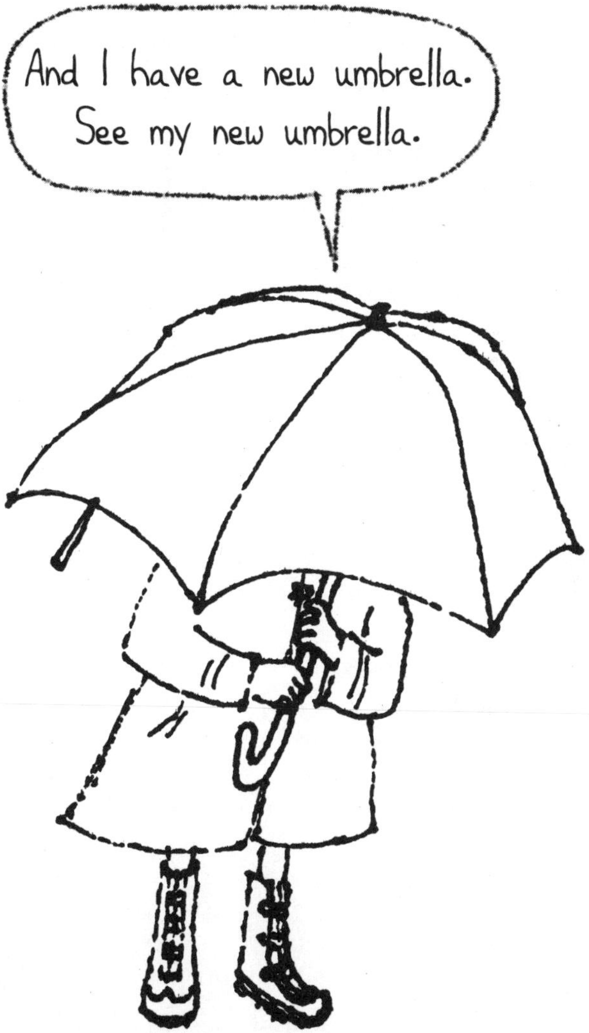
And I have a new umbrella.
See my new umbrella.

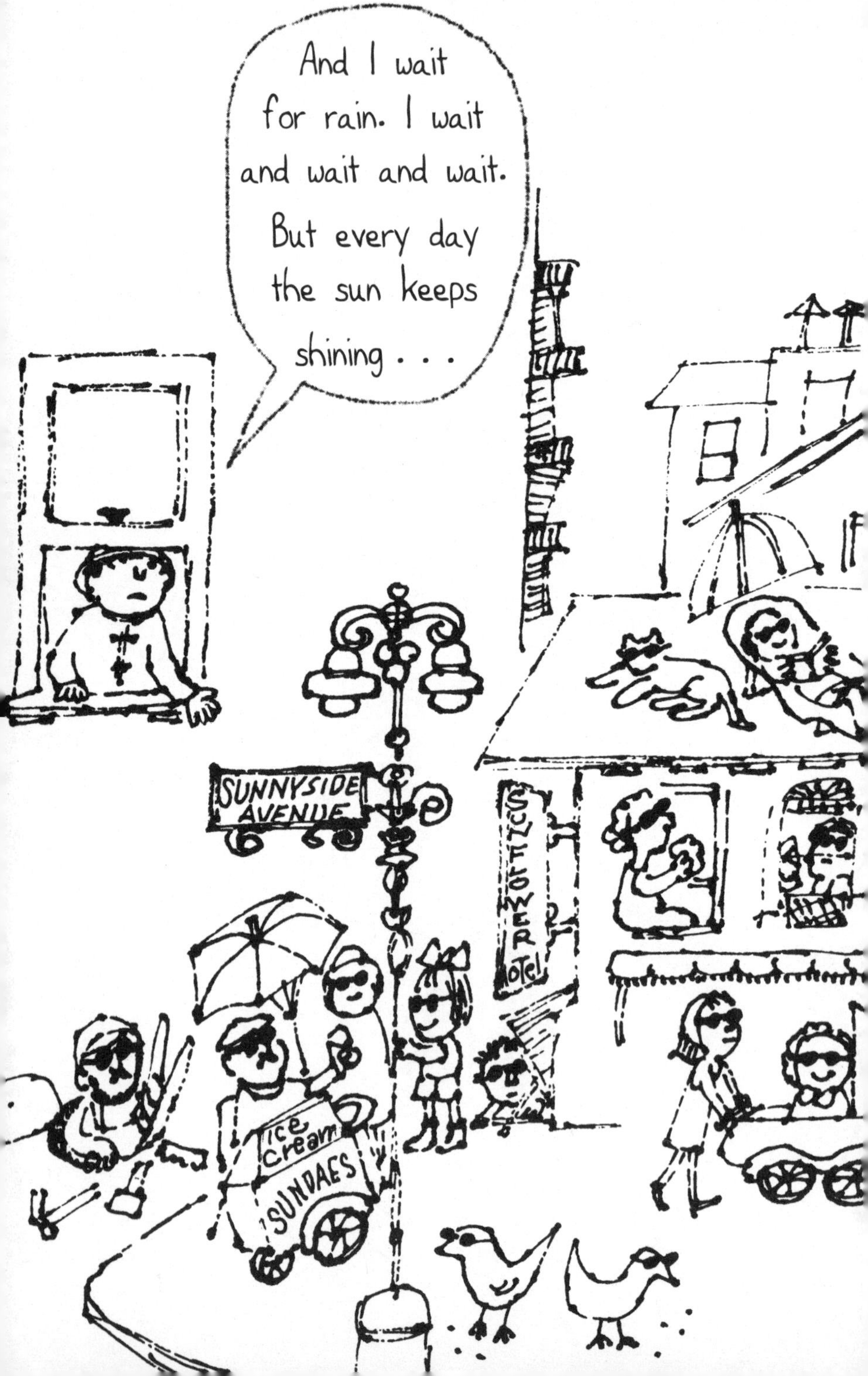

And I wait for rain. I wait and wait and wait. But every day the sun keeps shining . . .
SUNNYSIDE AVENUE
SUNFLOWER HOTEL
ice cream
SUNDAES

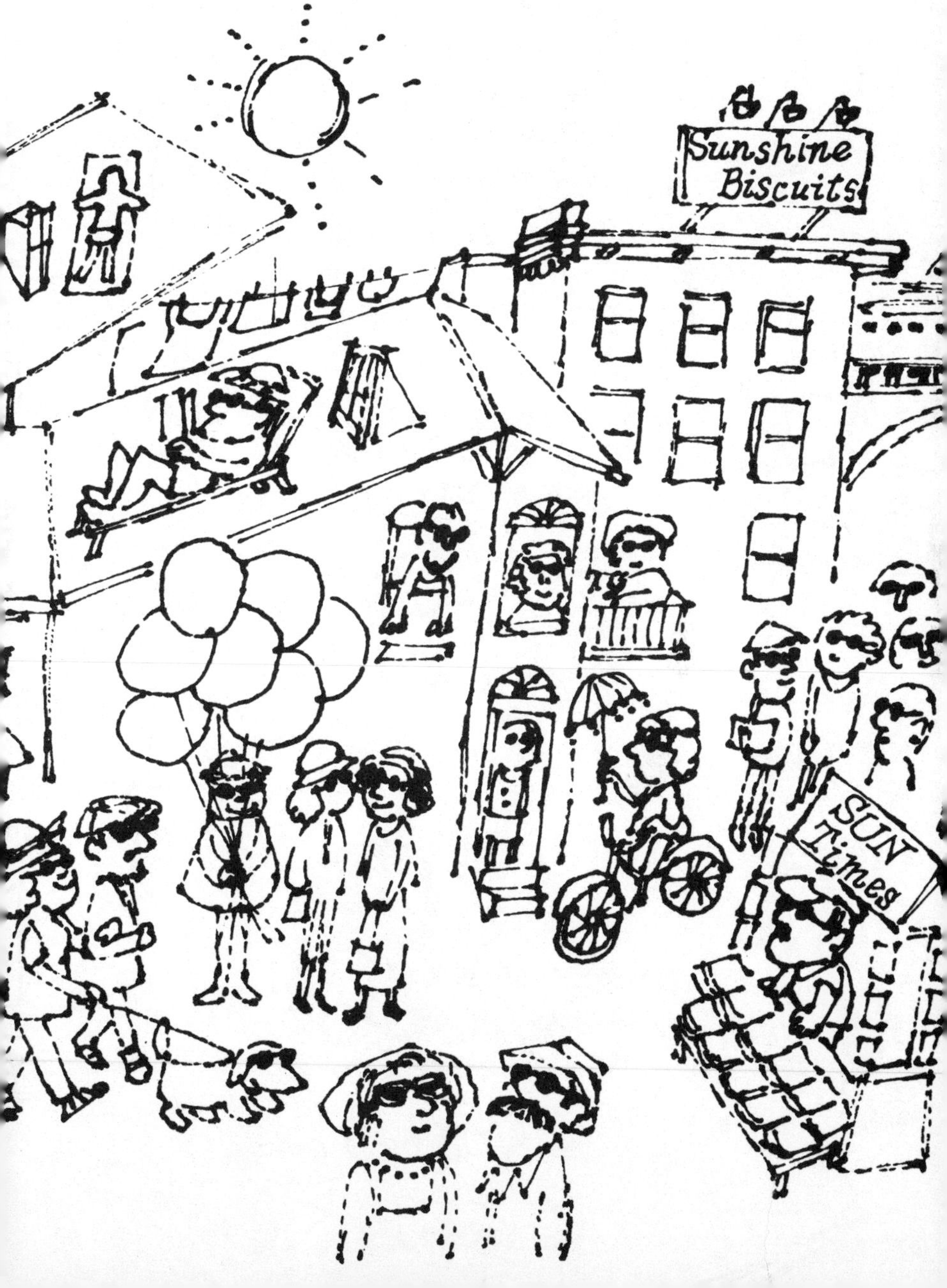
Sunshine Biscuits
SUN Times

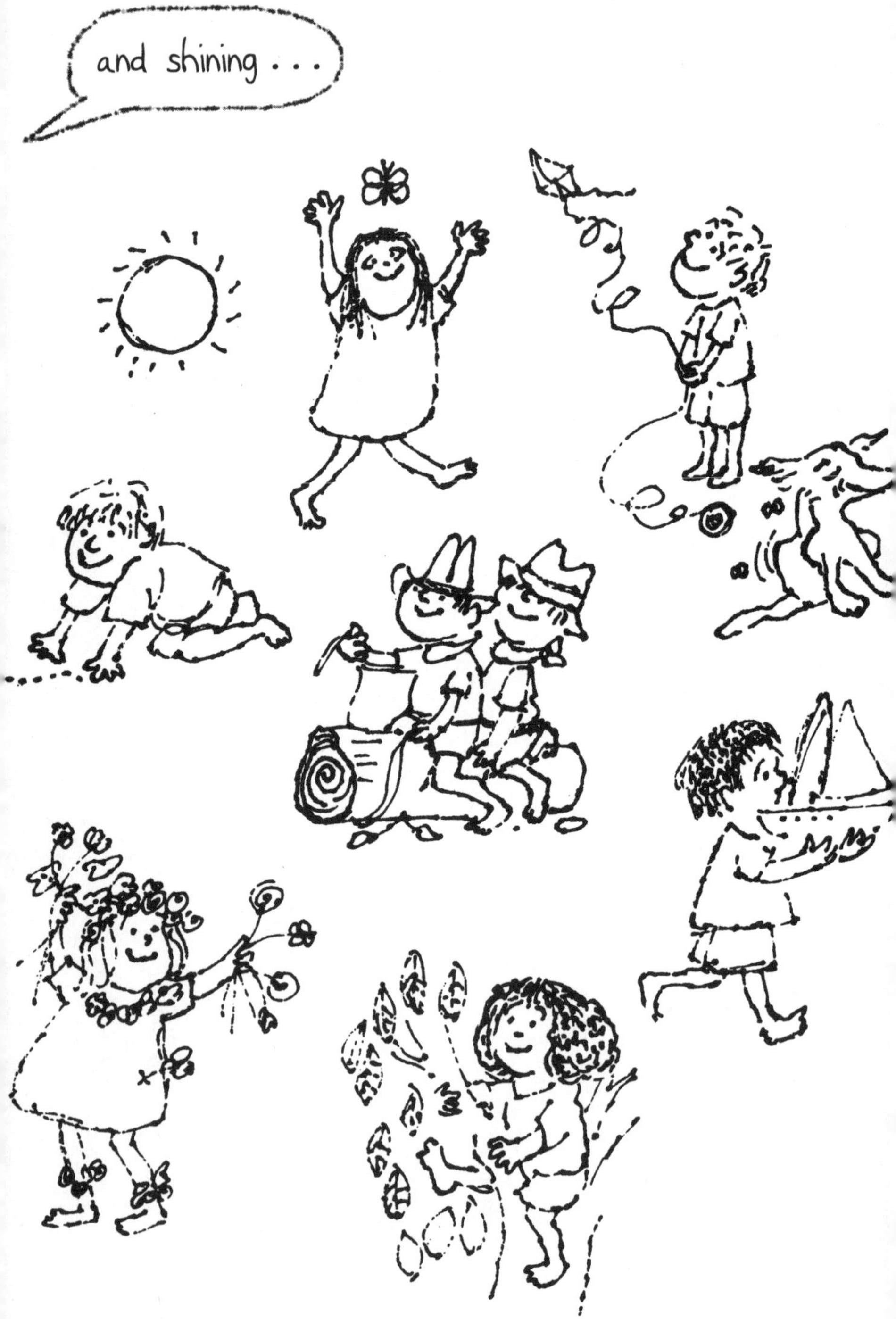
and shining . . .

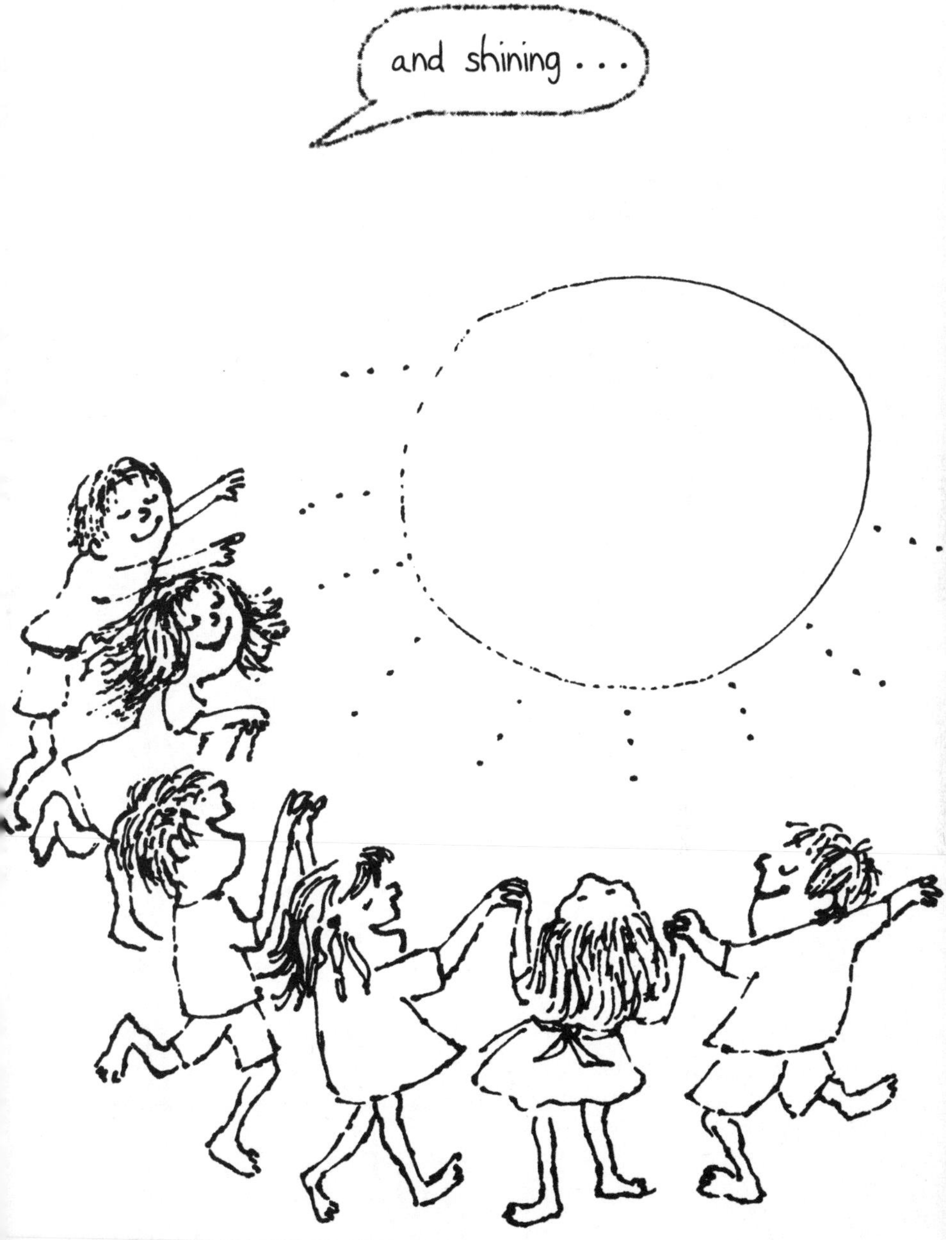
and shining . . .

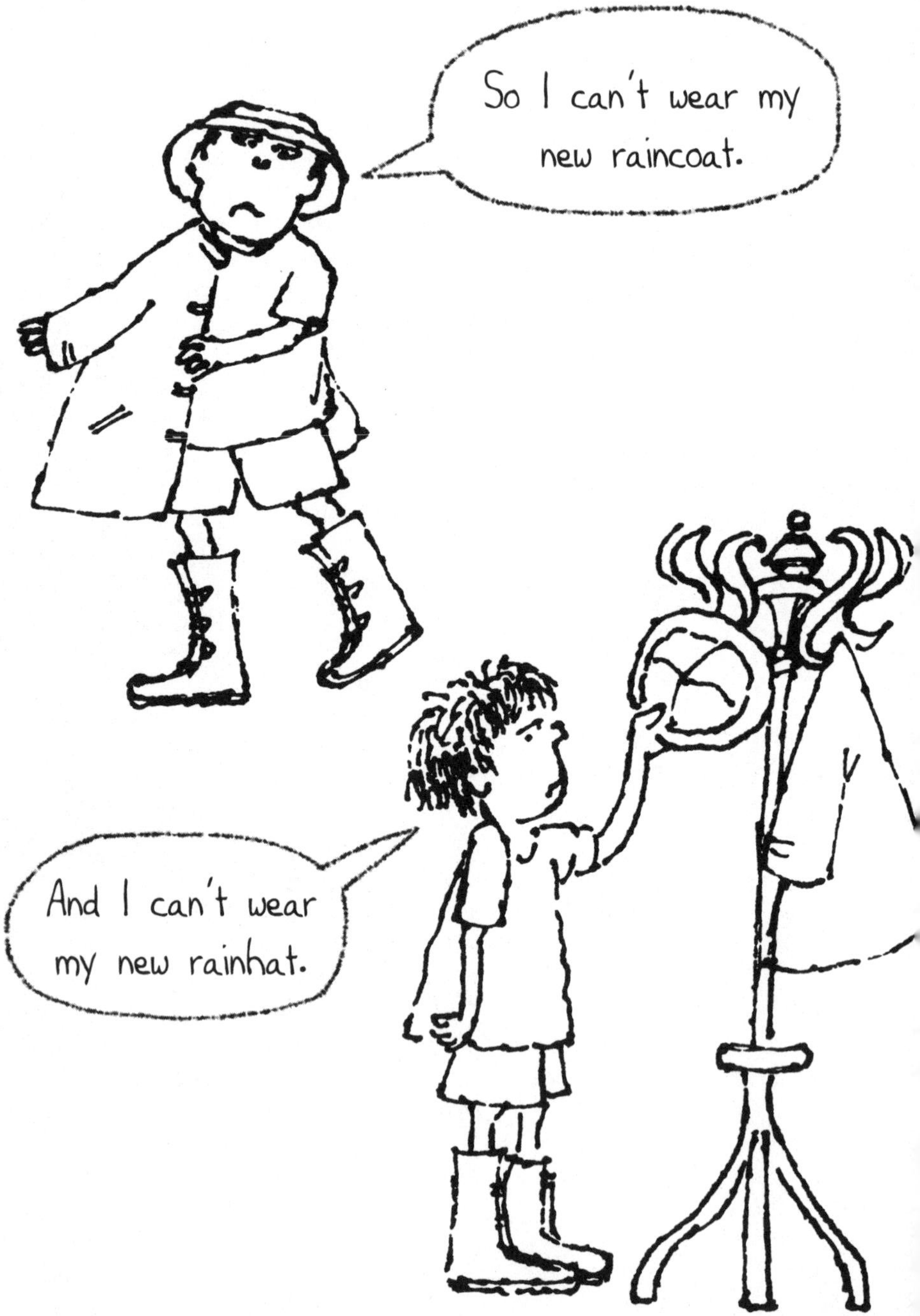
So I can't wear my new raincoat.
And I can't wear my new rainhat.

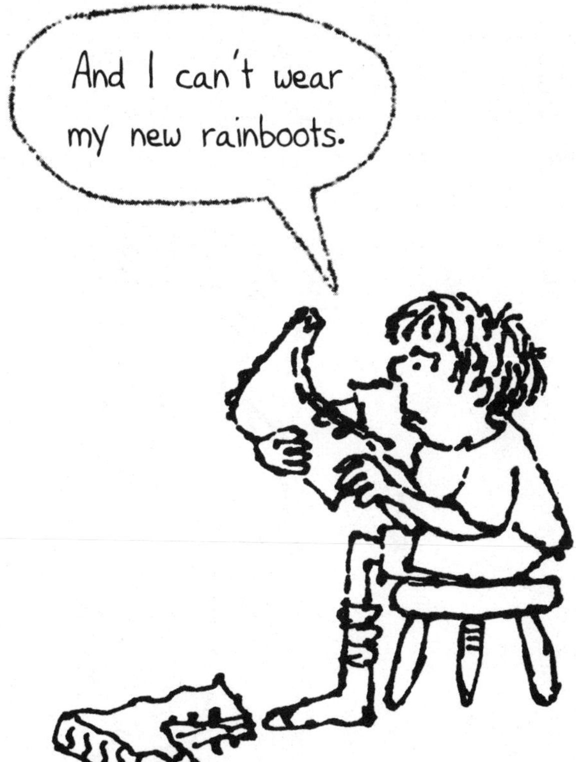
And I can't wear my new rainboots.

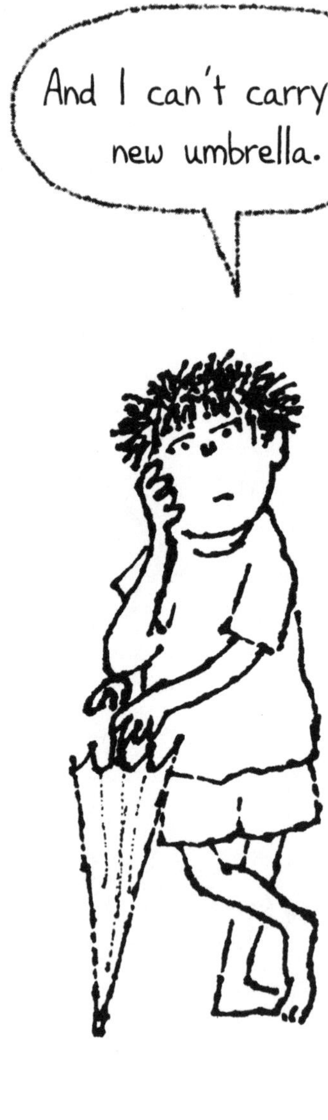
And I can't carry my new umbrella.

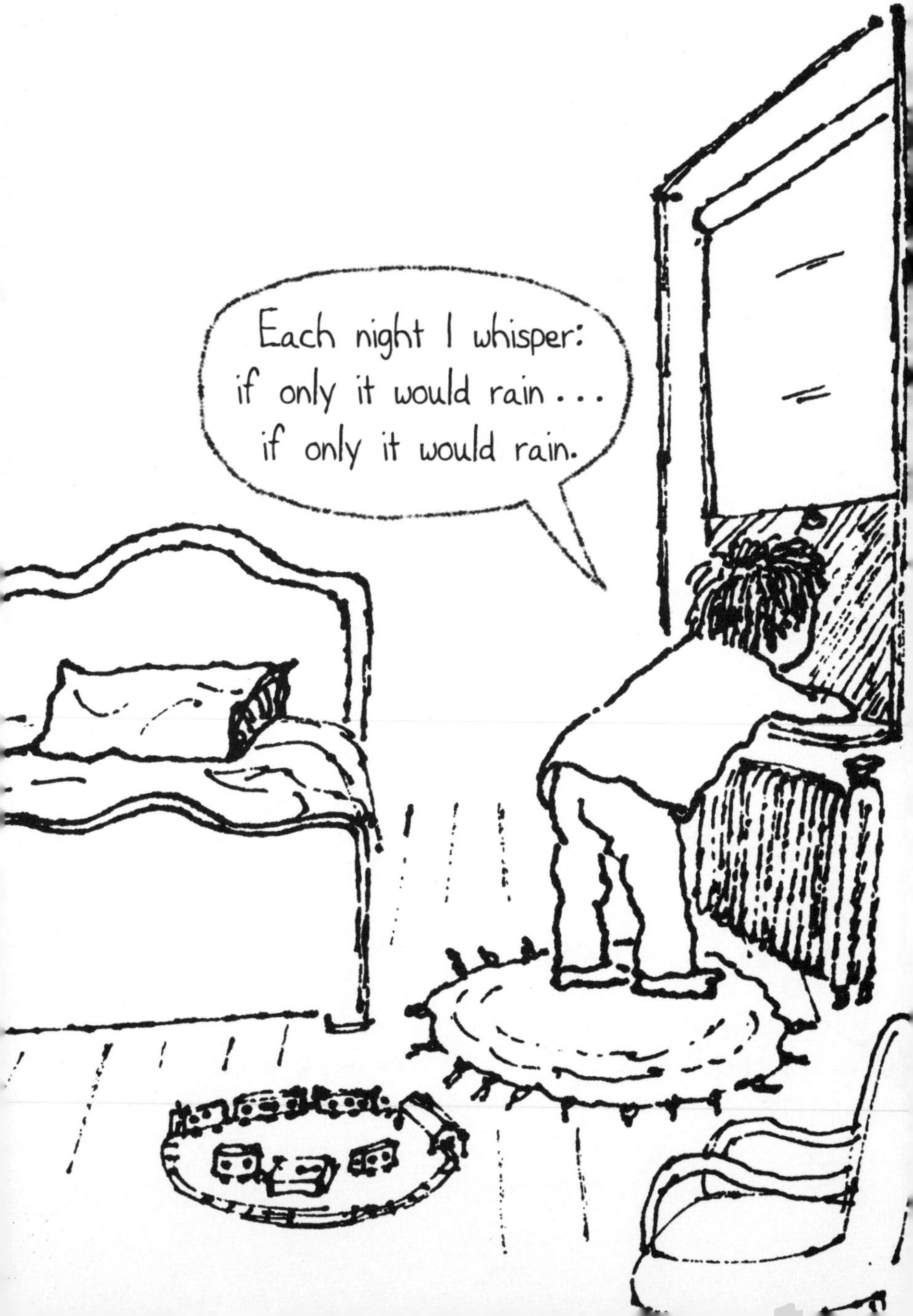
Each night I whisper: if only it would rain . . . if only it would rain.

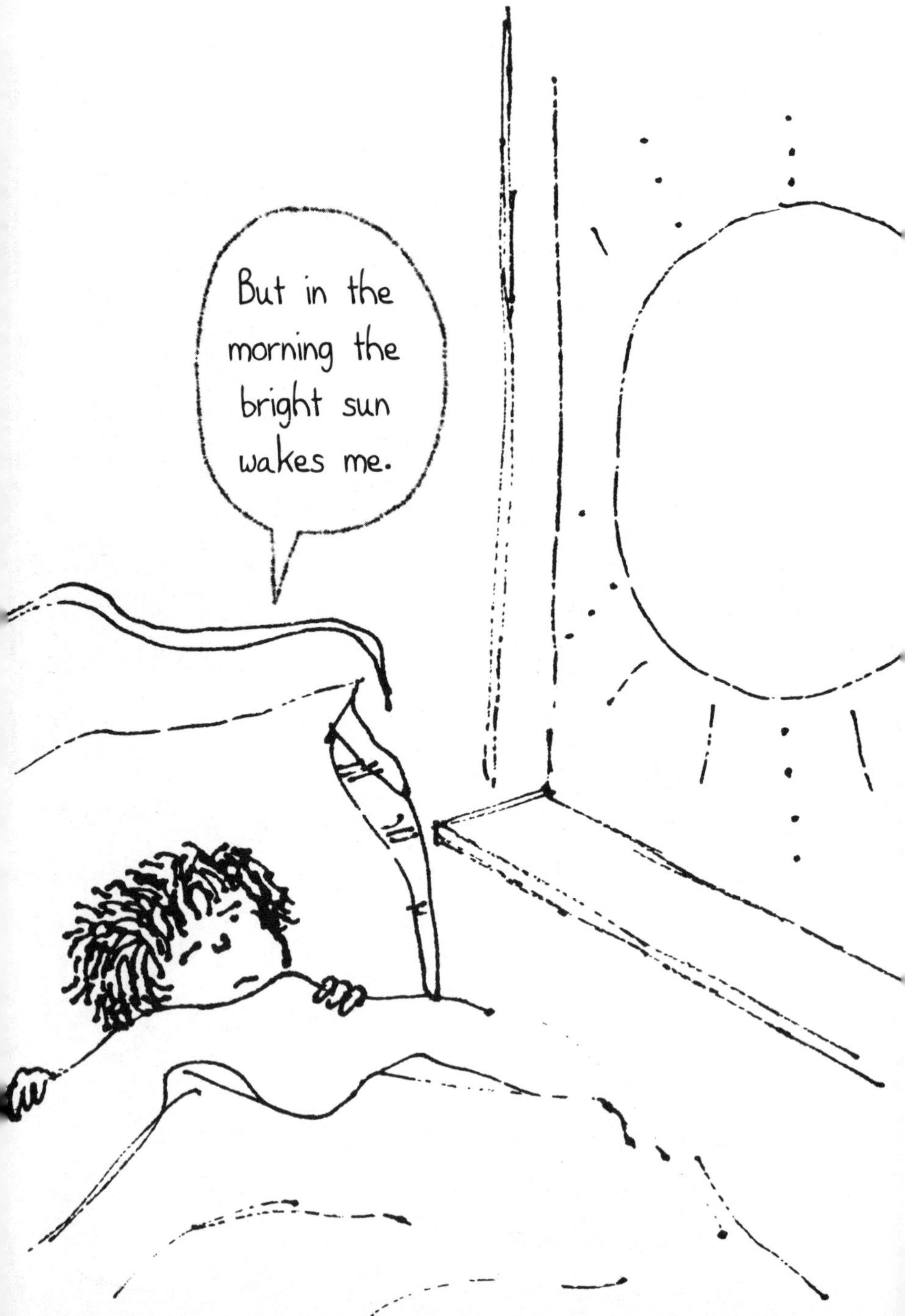
But in the morning the bright sun wakes me.

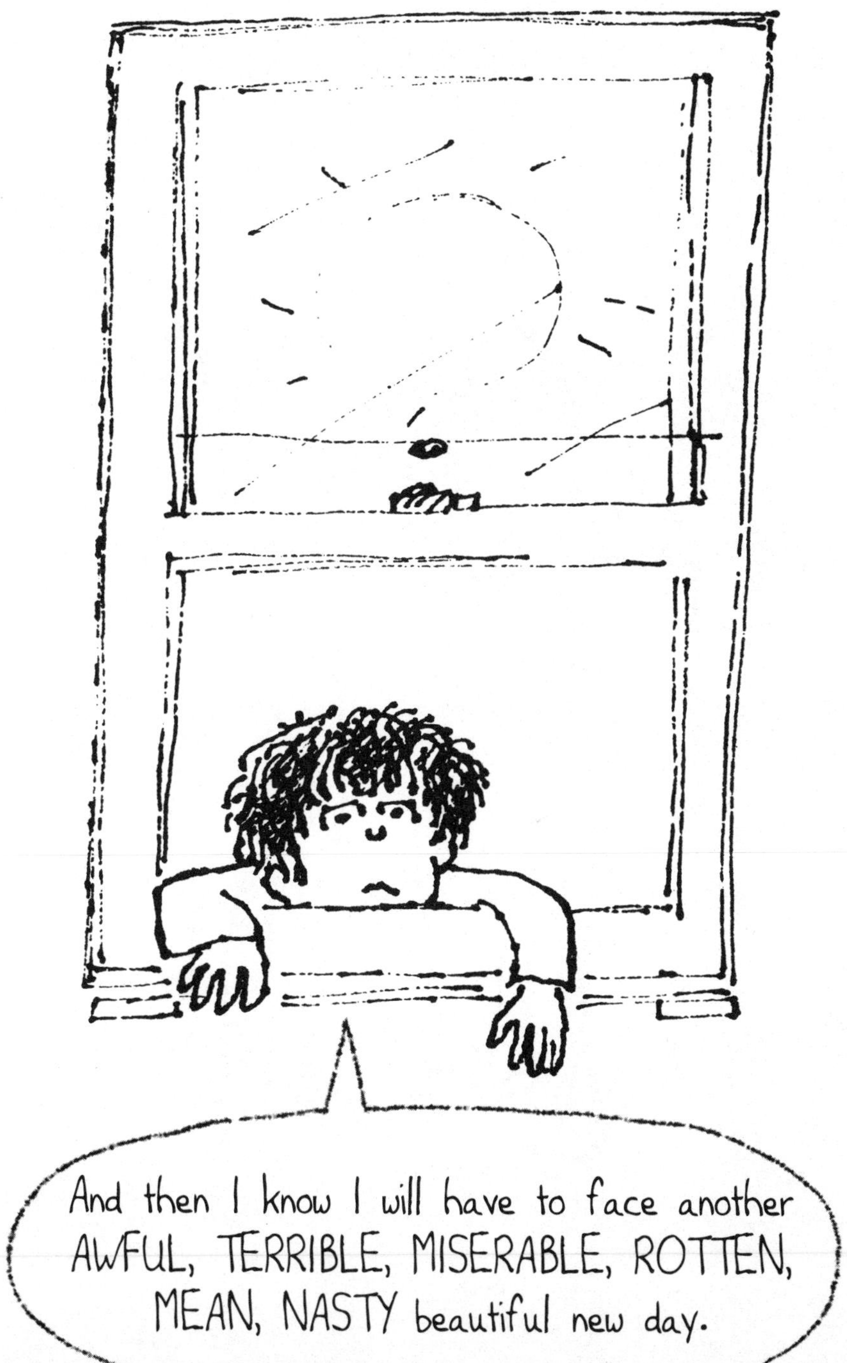

And then I know I will have to face another AWFUL, TERRIBLE, MISERABLE, ROTTEN, MEAN, NASTY beautiful new day.

MY DIARY

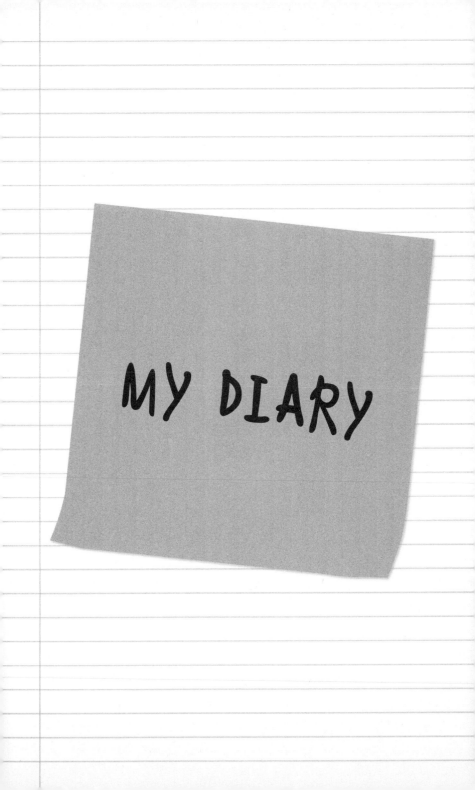

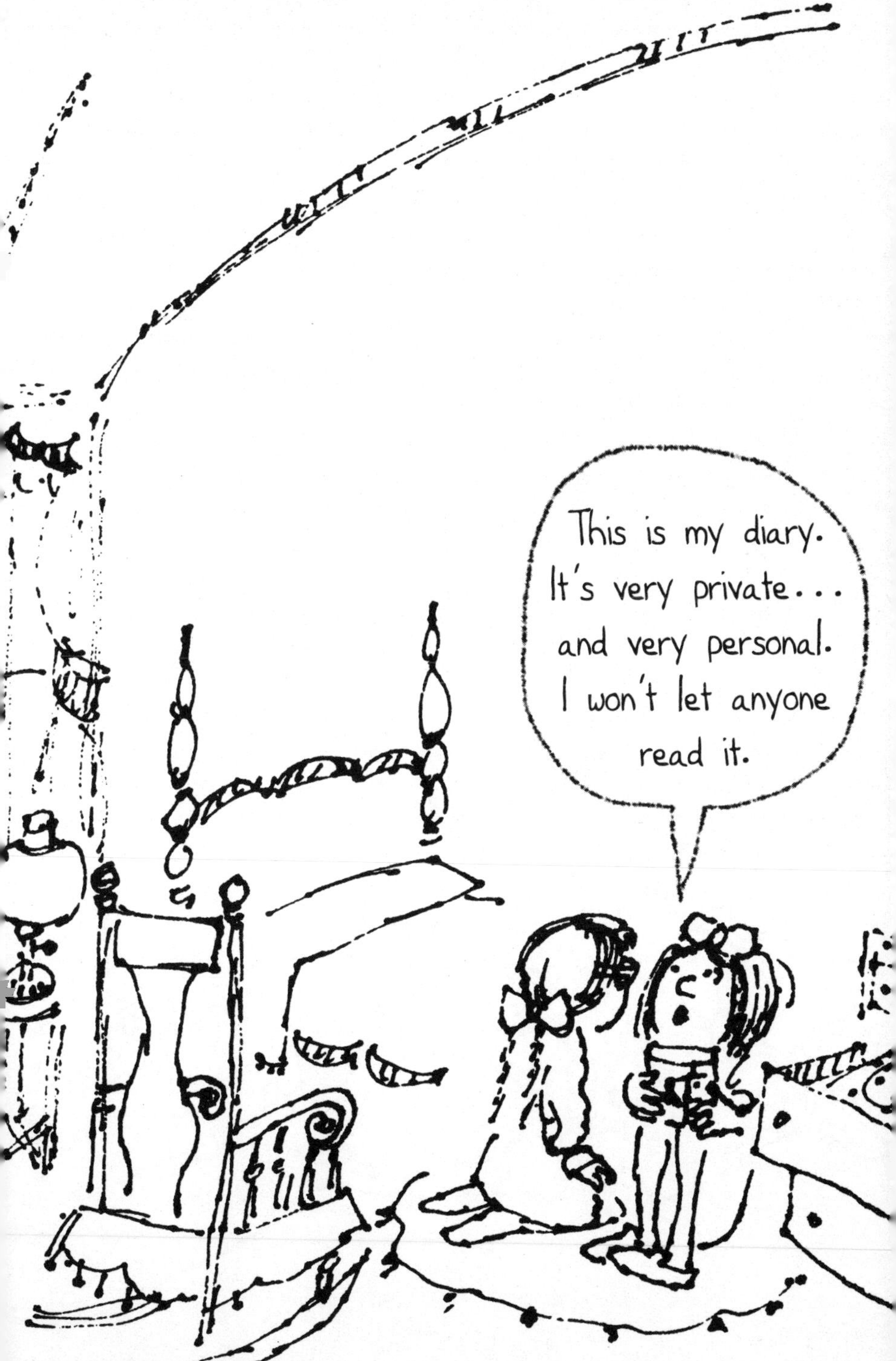
This is my diary. It's very private... and very personal. I won't let anyone read it.

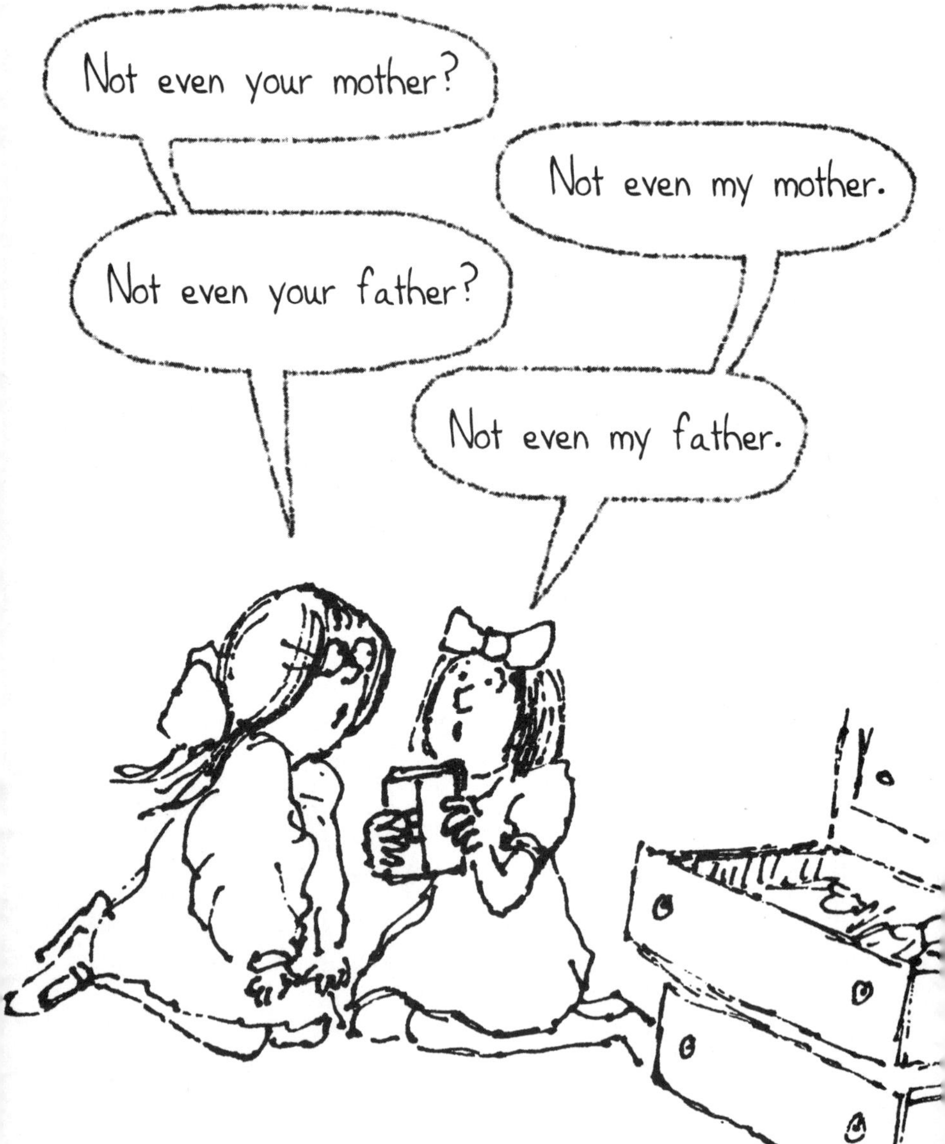
Not even your mother?
Not even my mother.
Not even your father?
Not even my father.

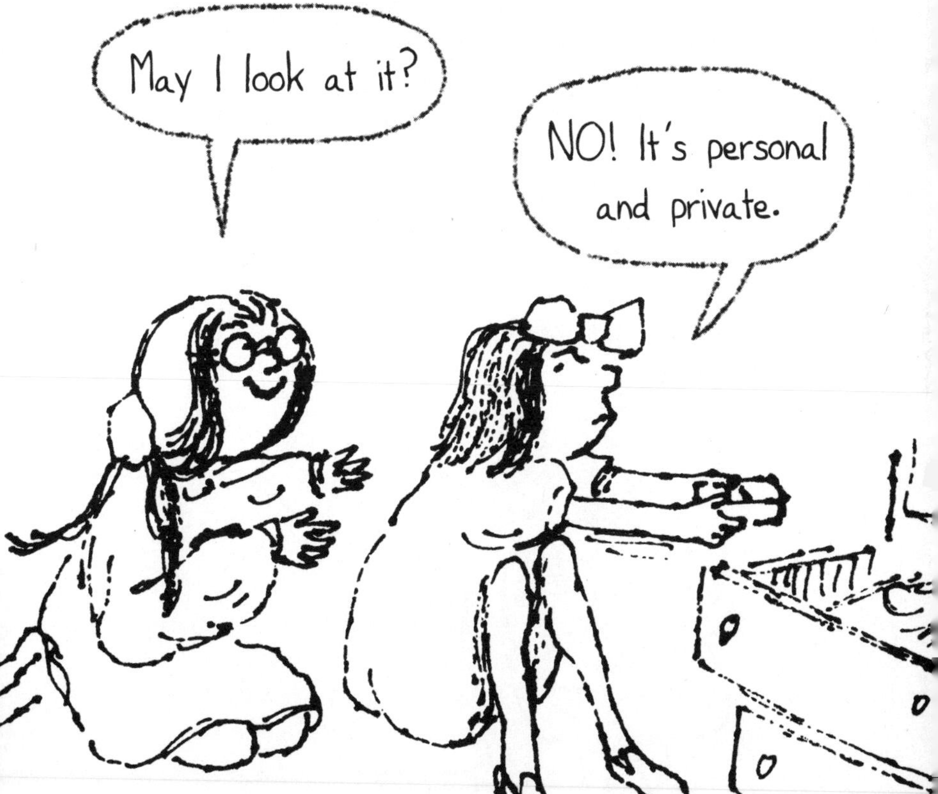
May I look at it?
NO! It's personal and private.

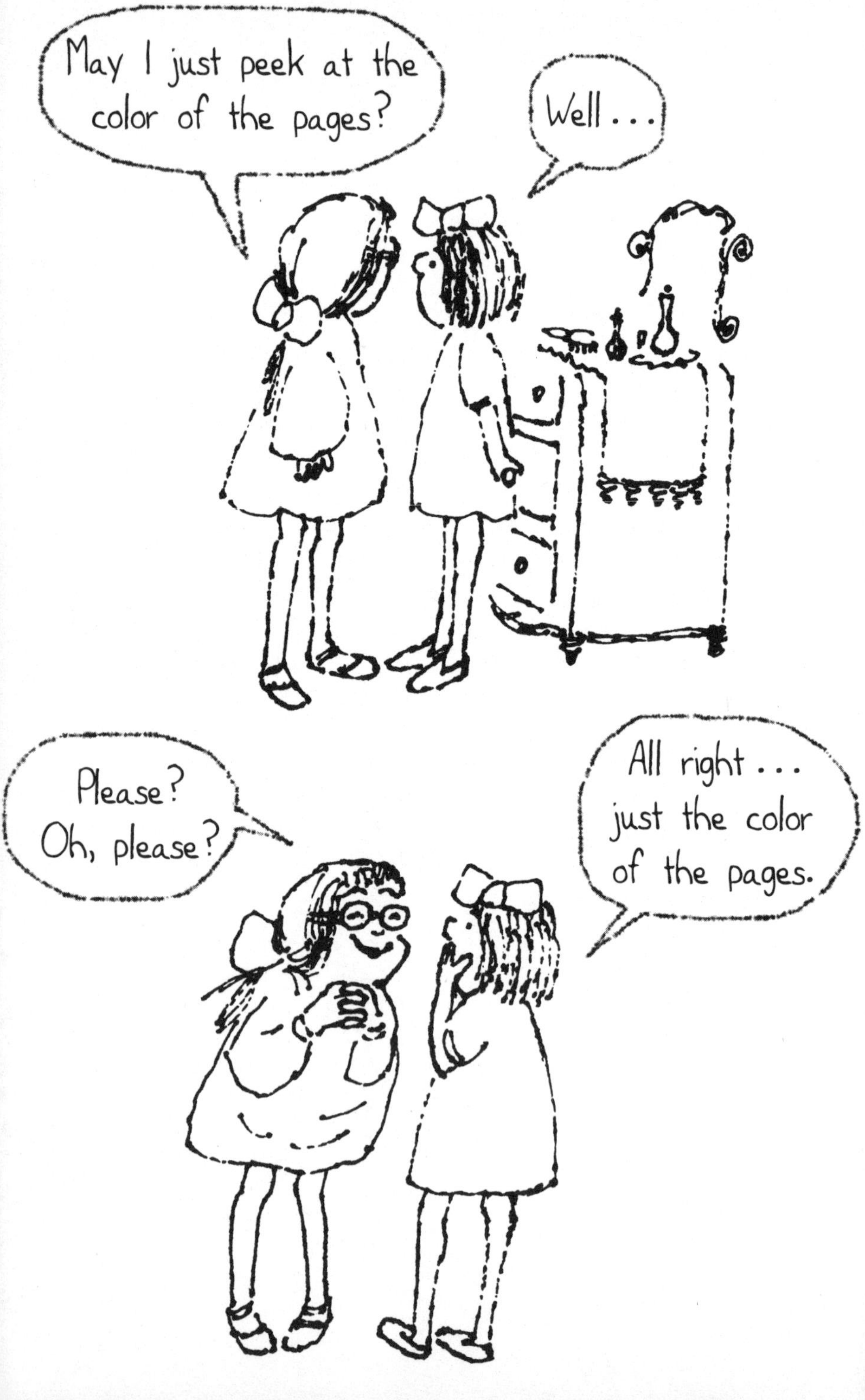
May I just peek at the color of the pages?
Well . . .
Please? Oh, please?
All right . . . just the color of the pages.

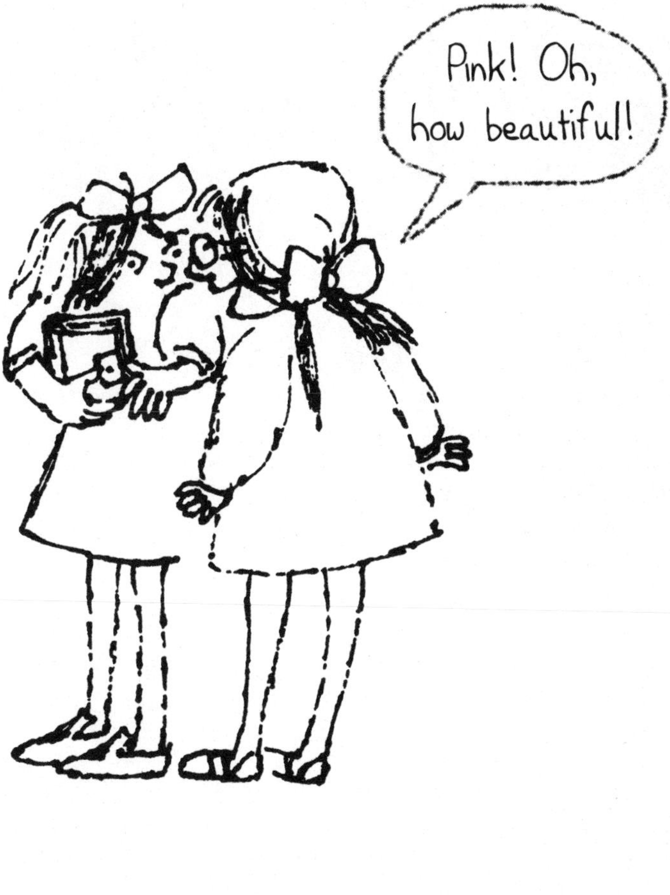
Pink! Oh, how beautiful!

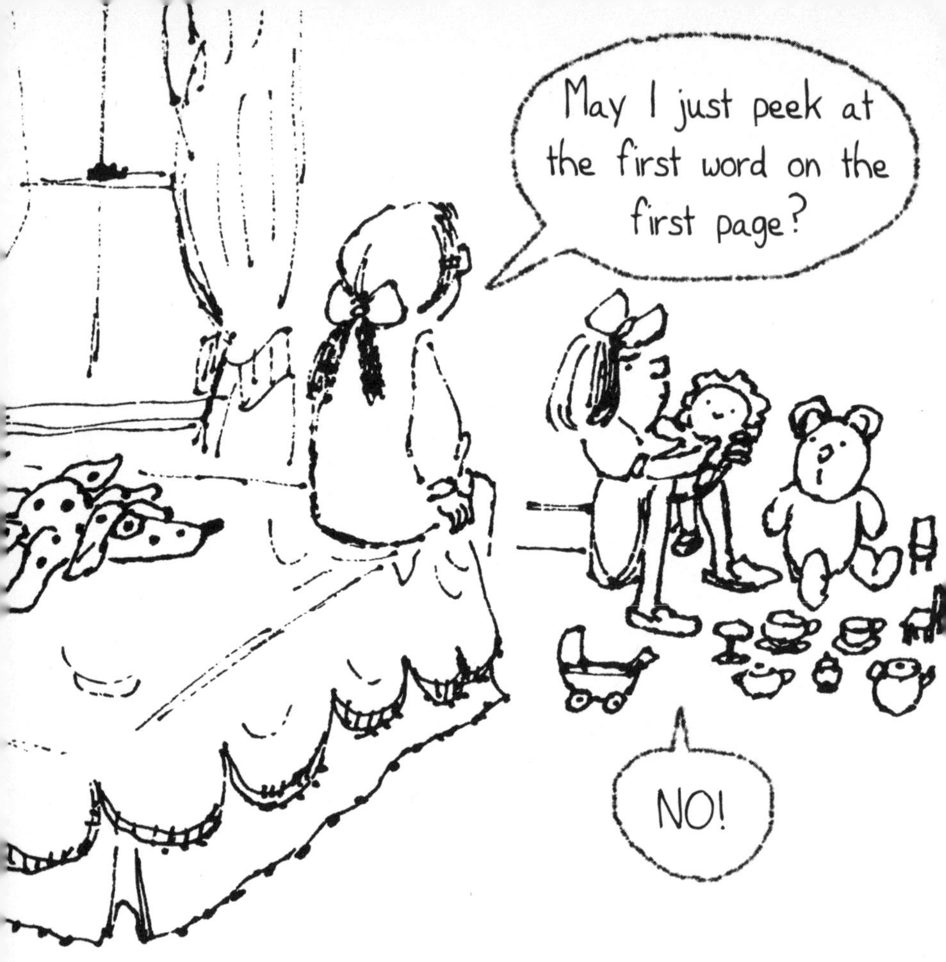
May I just peek at the first word on the first page?
NO!

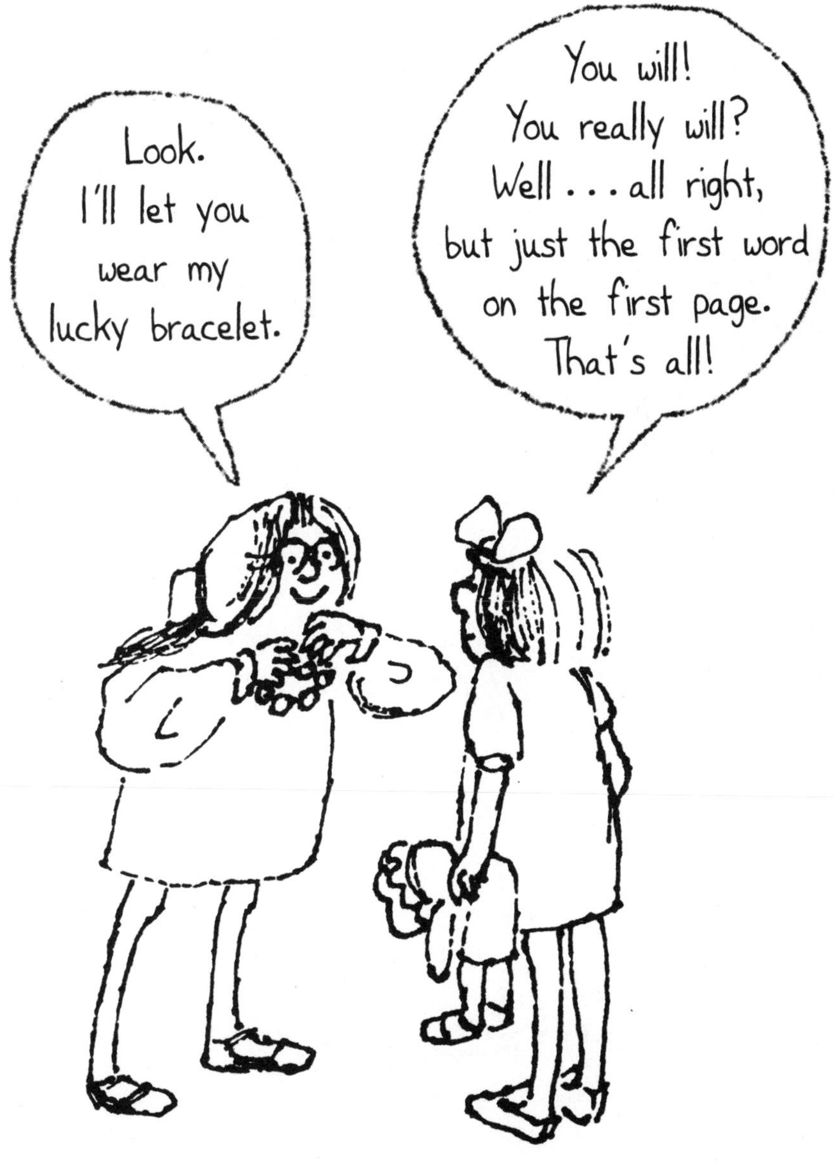
Look. I'll let you wear my lucky bracelet.
You will! You really will? Well . . . all right, but just the first word on the first page. That's all!

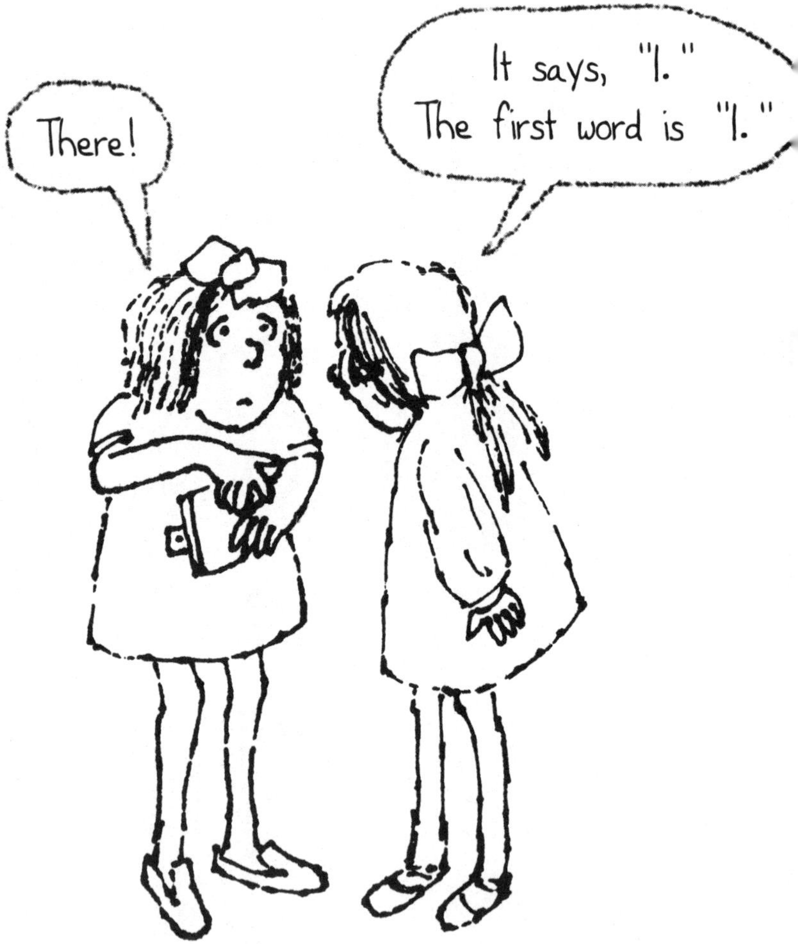
There!
It says, "I."
The first word is "I."

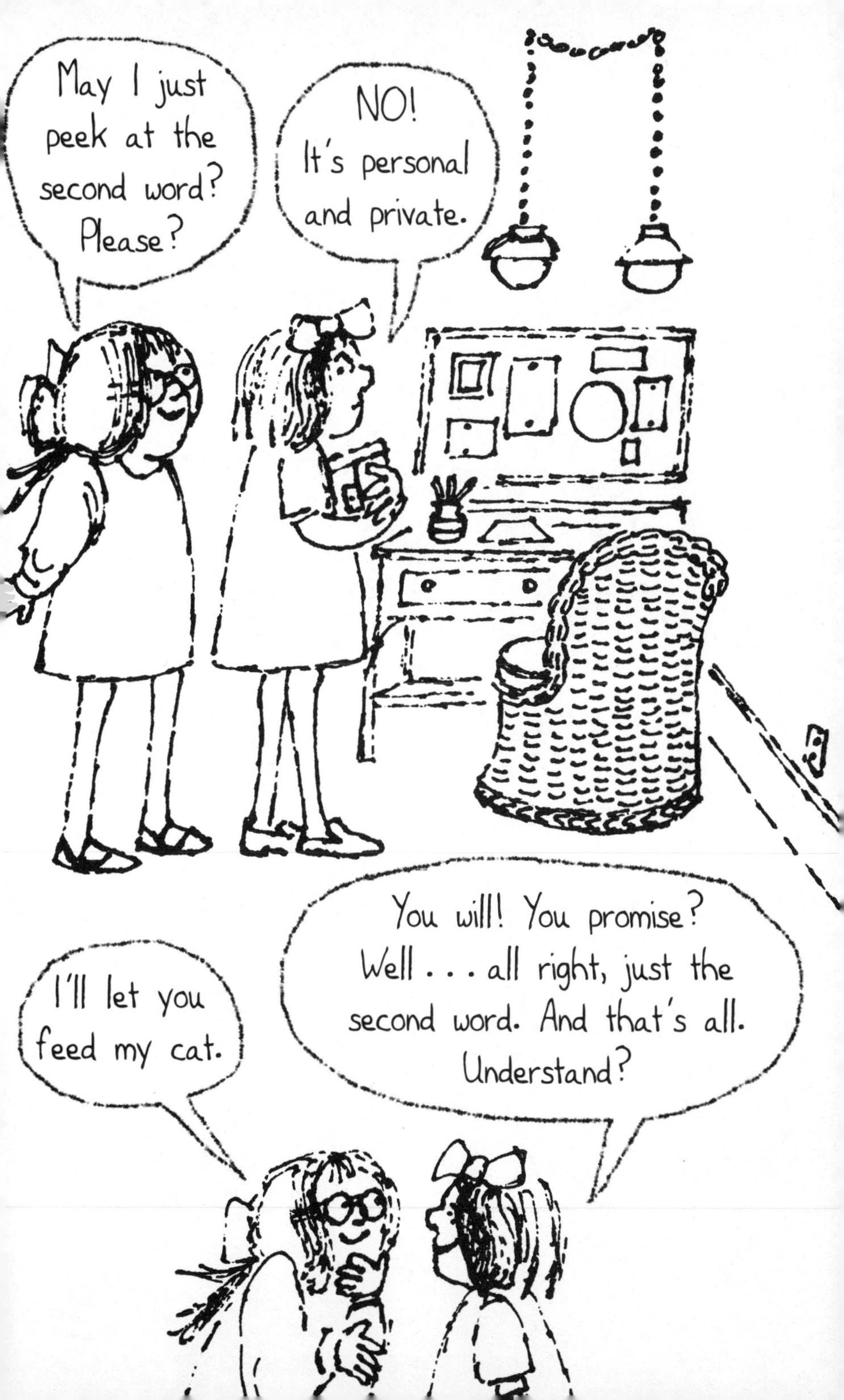
May I just peek at the second word? Please?
NO! It's personal and private.
I'll let you feed my cat.
You will! You promise? Well . . . all right, just the second word. And that's all. Understand?

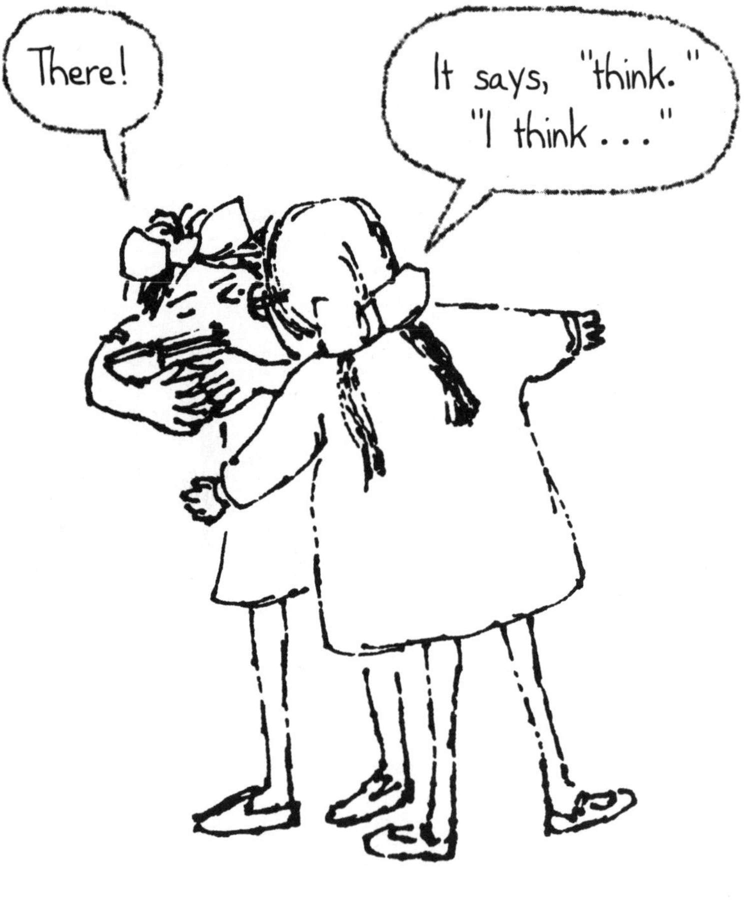
There!
It says, "think." "I think . . ."

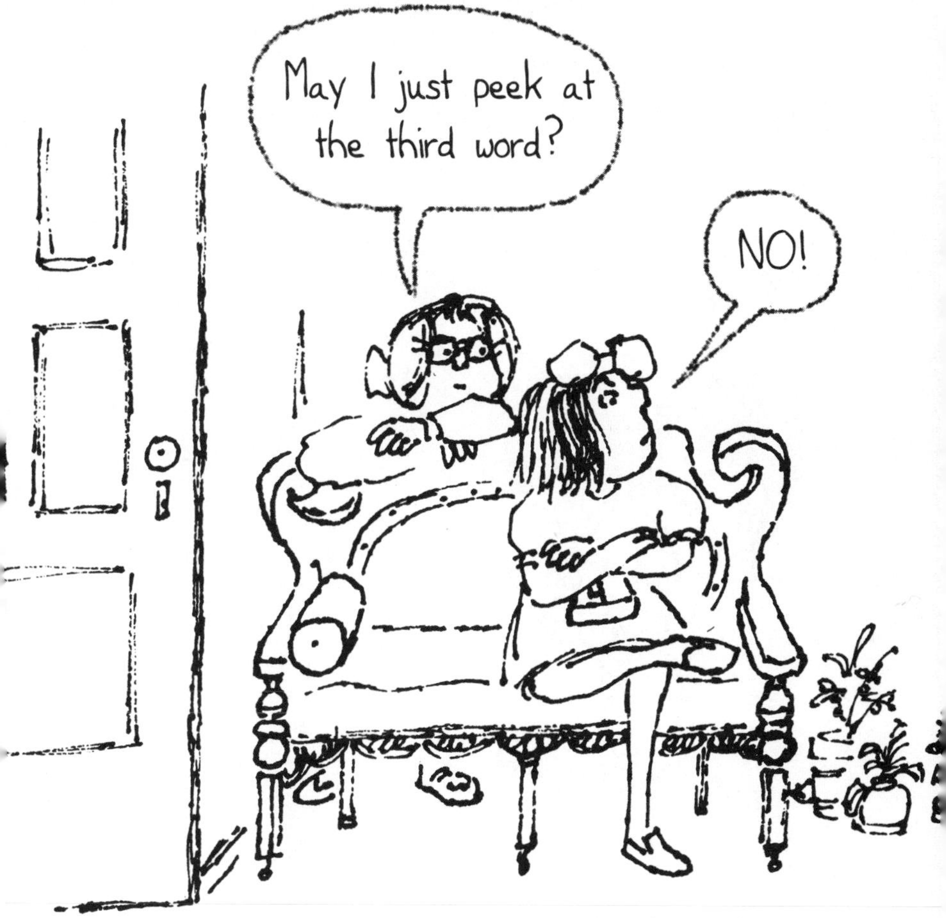
May I just peek at the third word?
NO!

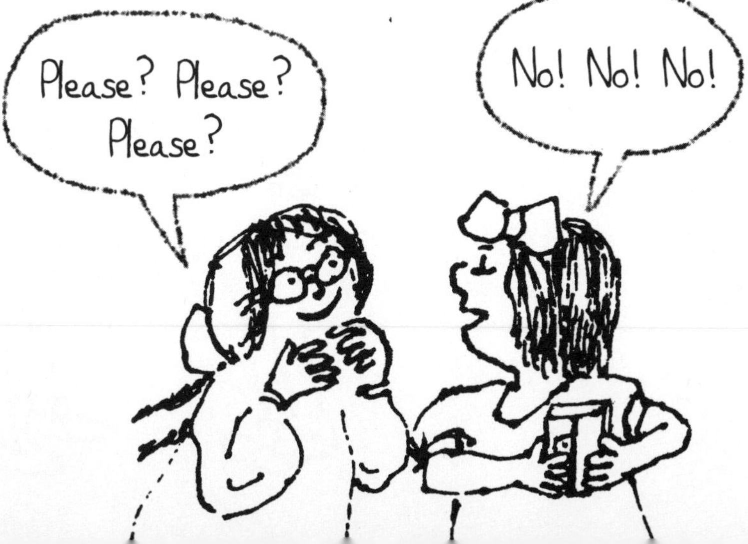
Please? Please? Please?
No! No! No!

I'll let you wear my good-luck charm. The one my Aunt Grace sent from Atlantic City.
You will!
All right . . . just the third word. AND THAT'S ALL! THAT IS ALL! UNDERSTAND!

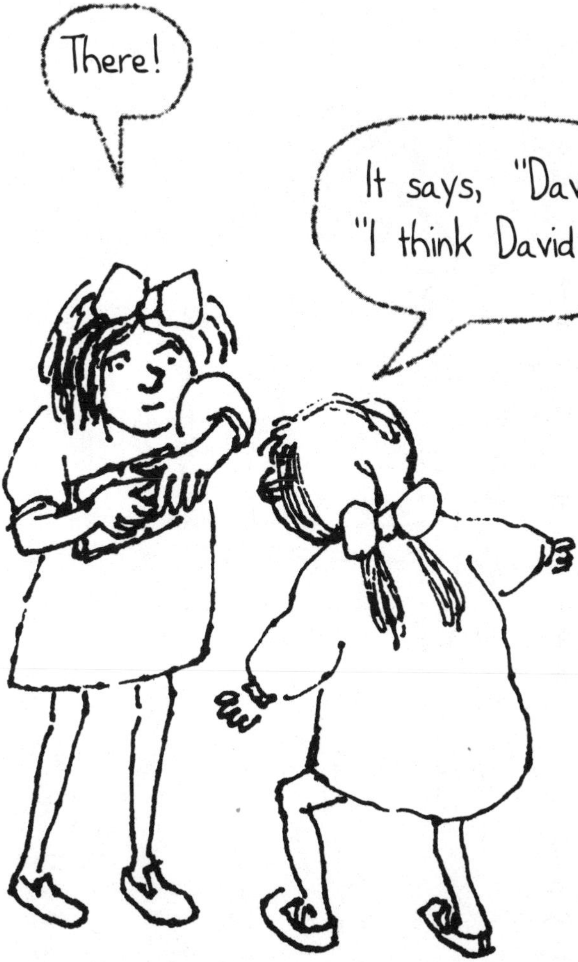
There!
It says, "David."
"I think David . . ."

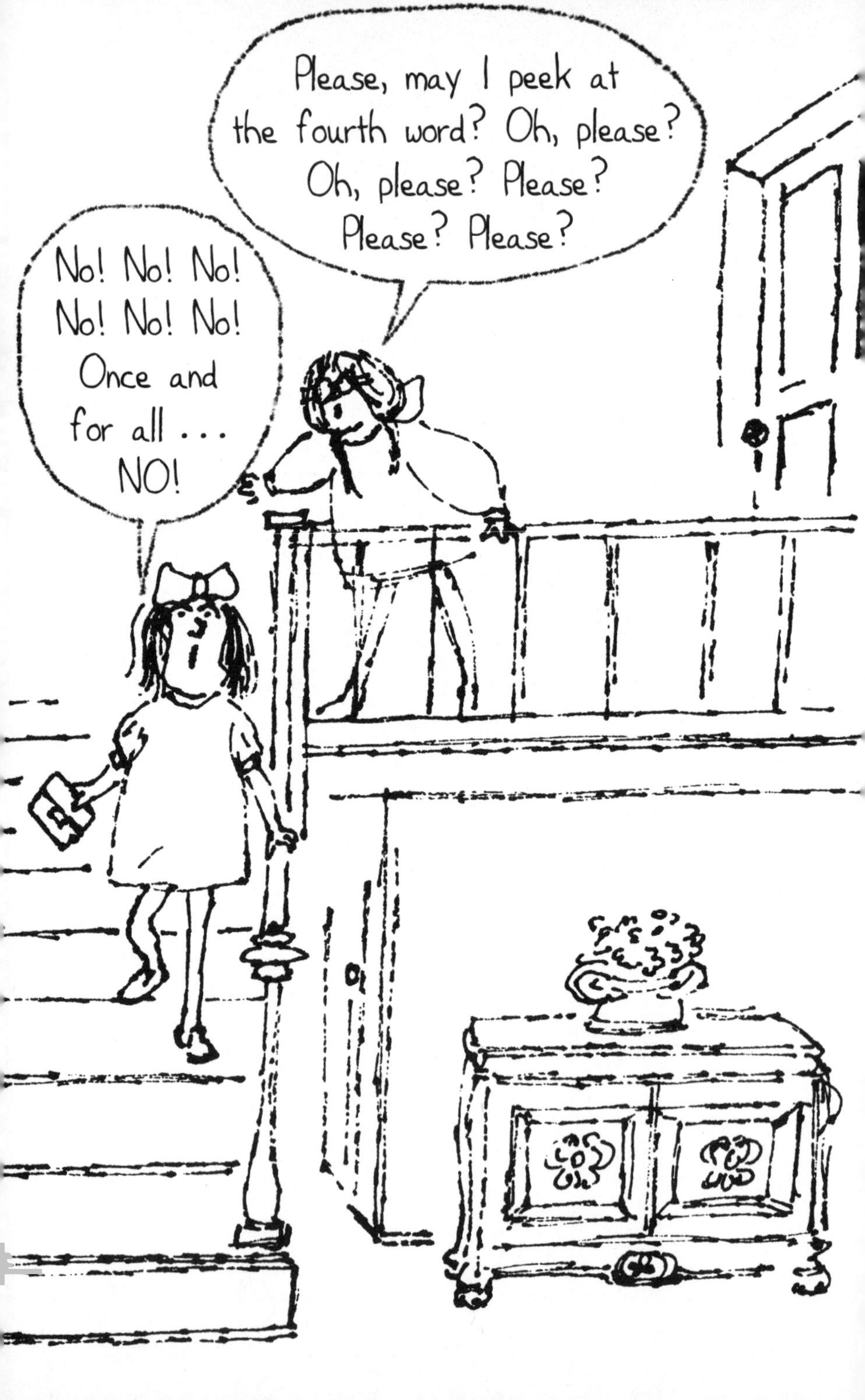
Please, may I peek at the fourth word? Oh, please? Oh, please? Please? Please? Please?
No! No! No! No! No! No! Once and for all . . . NO!

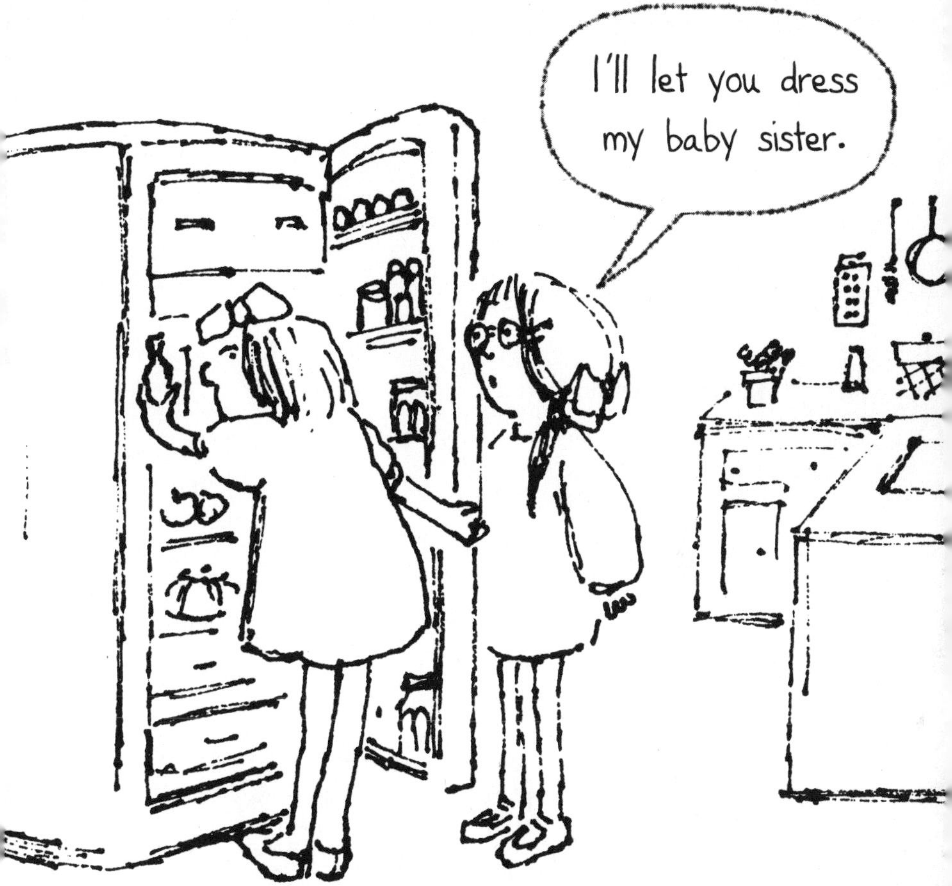
I'll let you dress my baby sister.

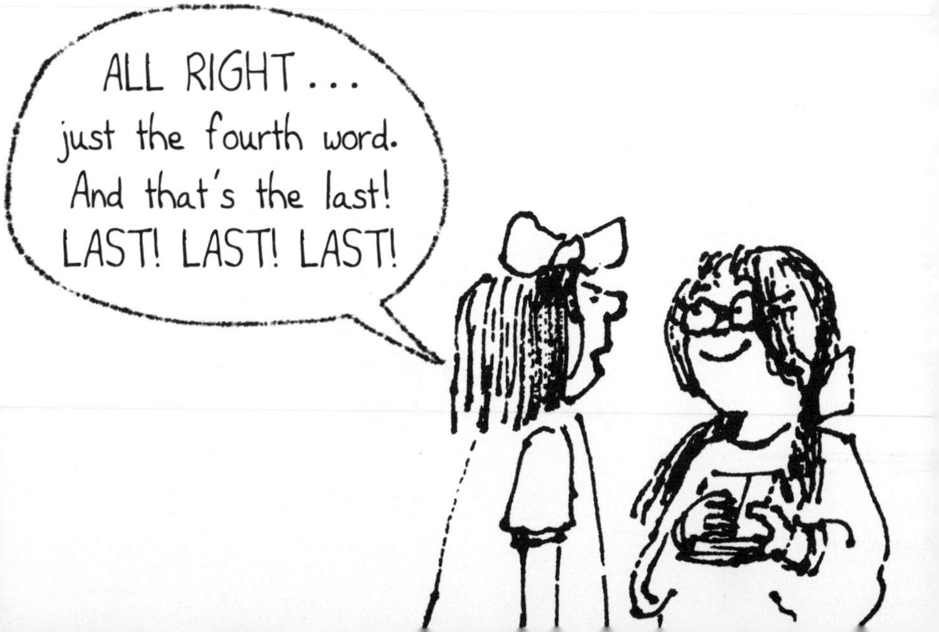
ALL RIGHT . . . just the fourth word. And that's the last! LAST! LAST! LAST!

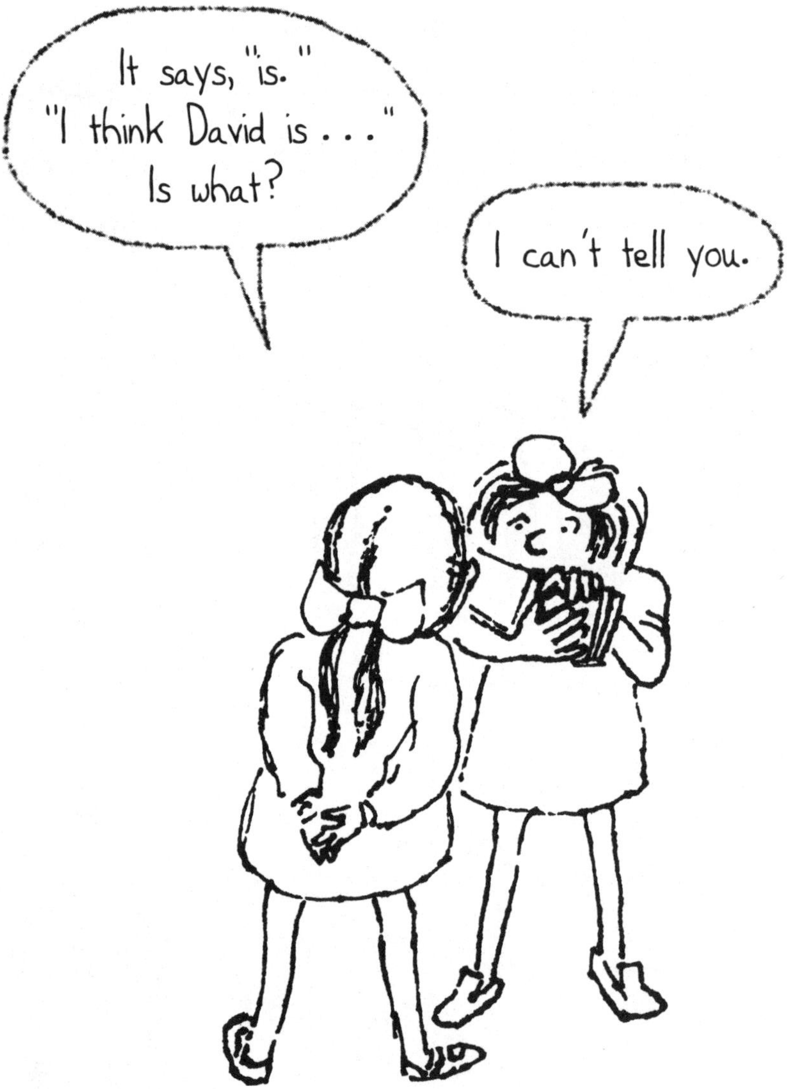
It says, "is."
"I think David is . . ."
Is what?
I can't tell you.

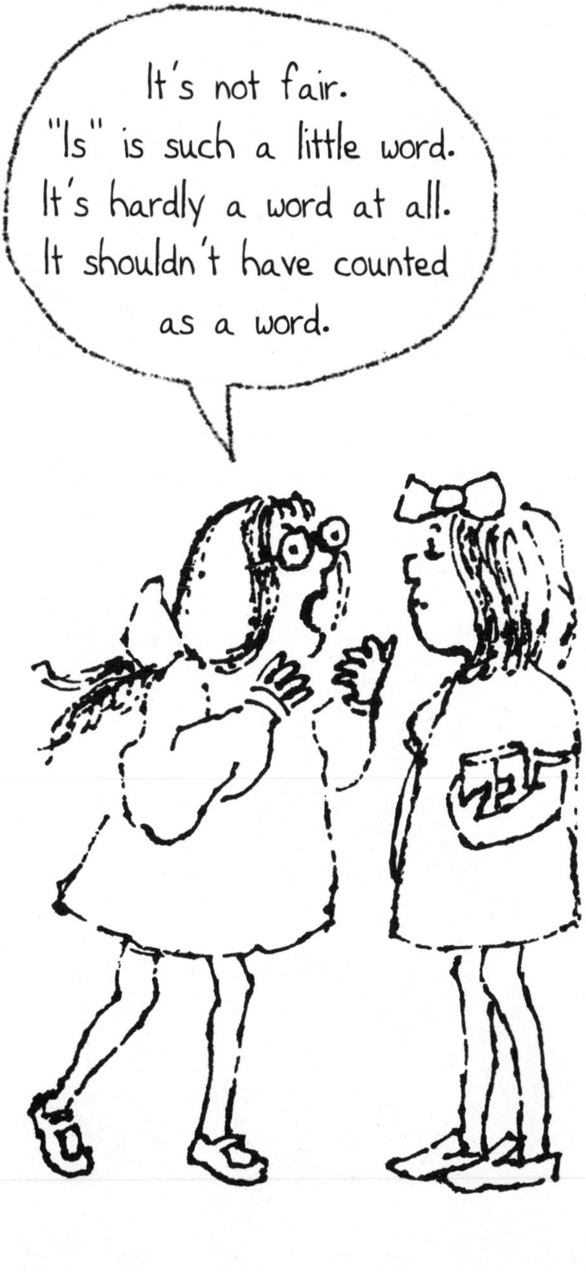
It's not fair.
"Is" is such a little word.
It's hardly a word at all.
It shouldn't have counted
as a word.

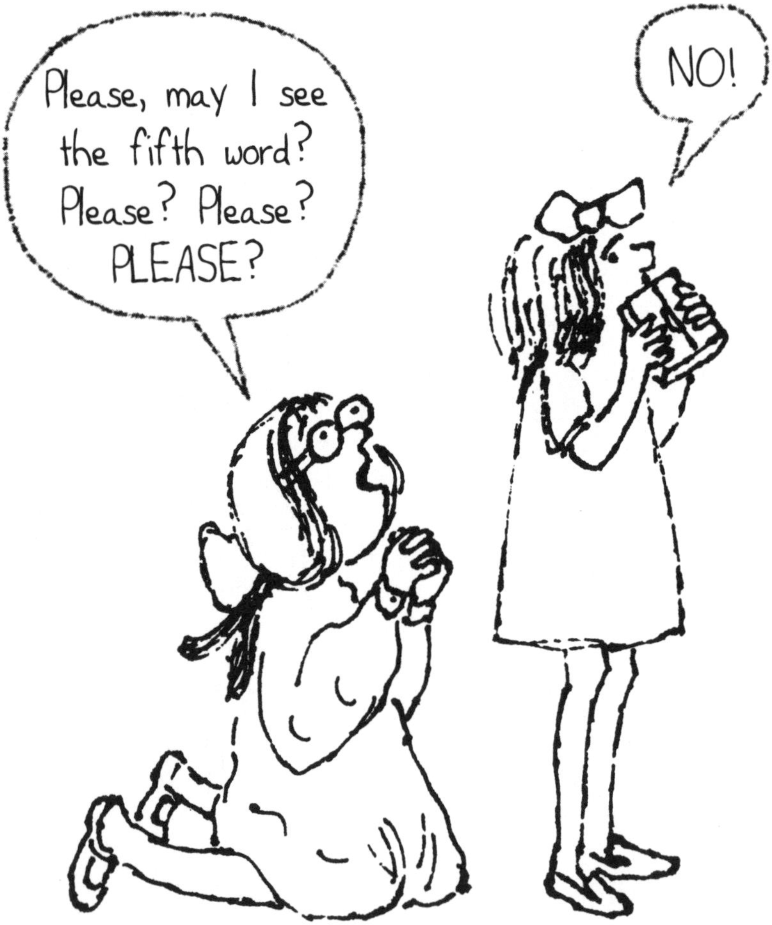
Please, may I see the fifth word? Please? Please? PLEASE?
NO!

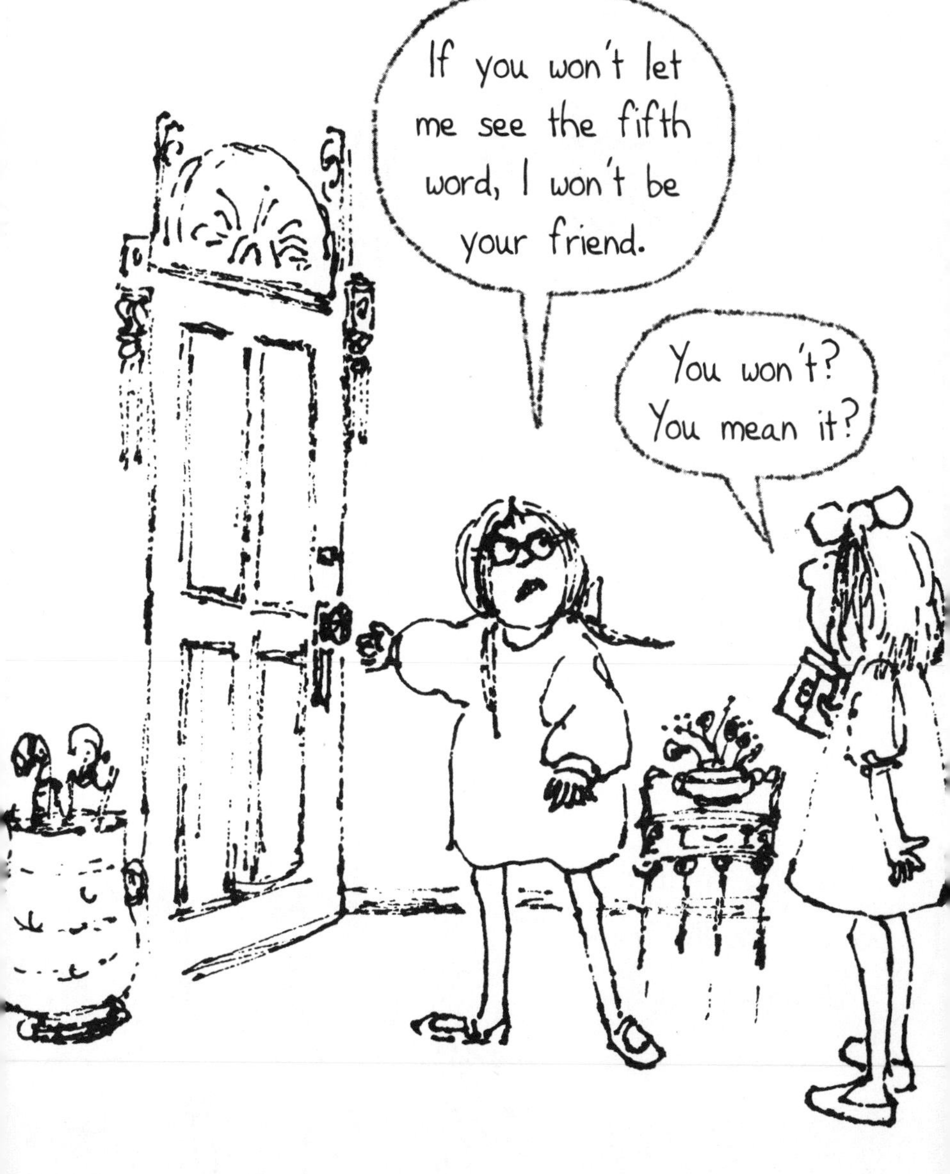
If you won't let me see the fifth word, I won't be your friend.
You won't? You mean it?

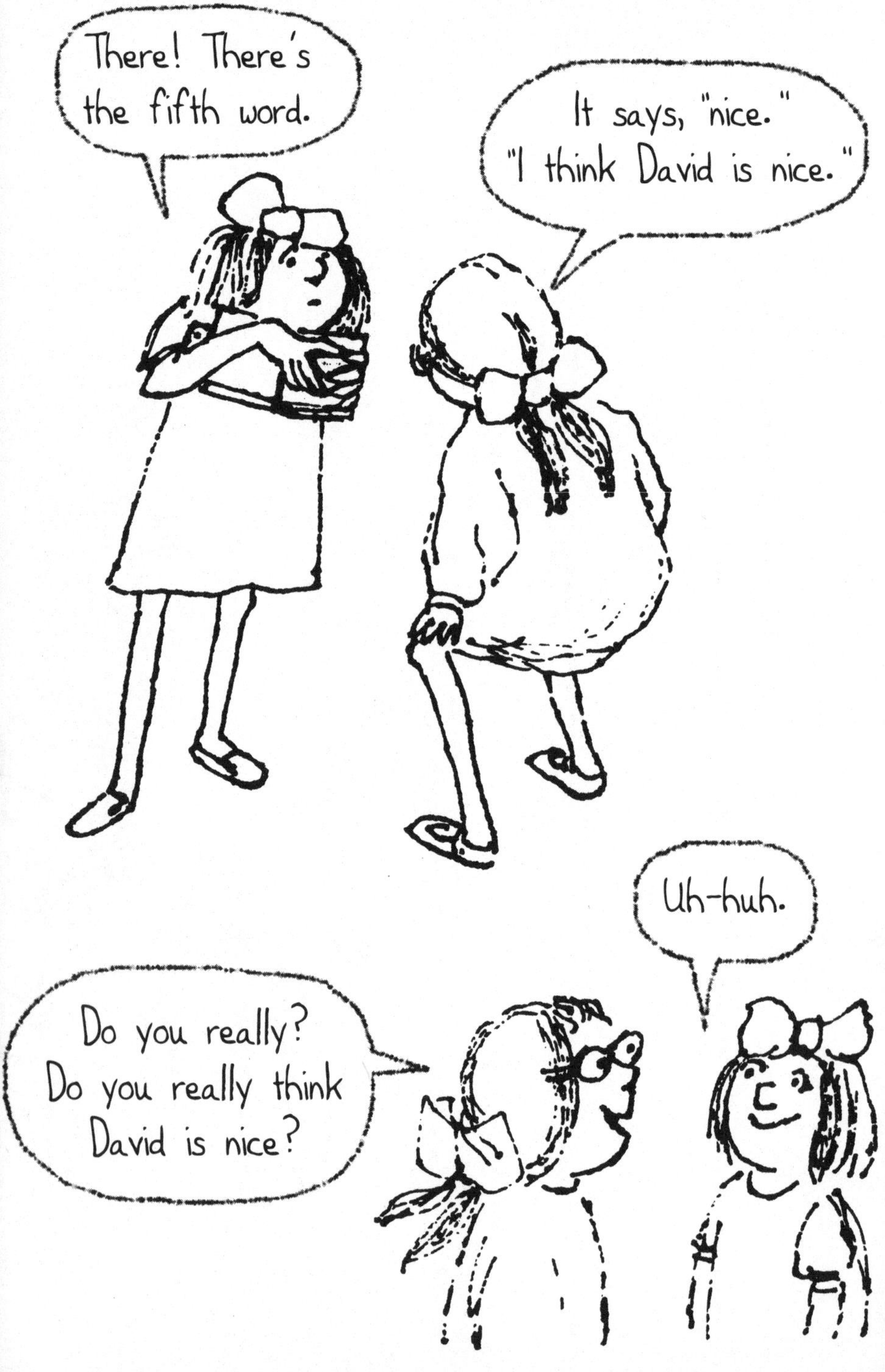
There! There's the fifth word.
It says, "nice." "I think David is nice."
Uh-huh.
Do you really? Do you really think David is nice?

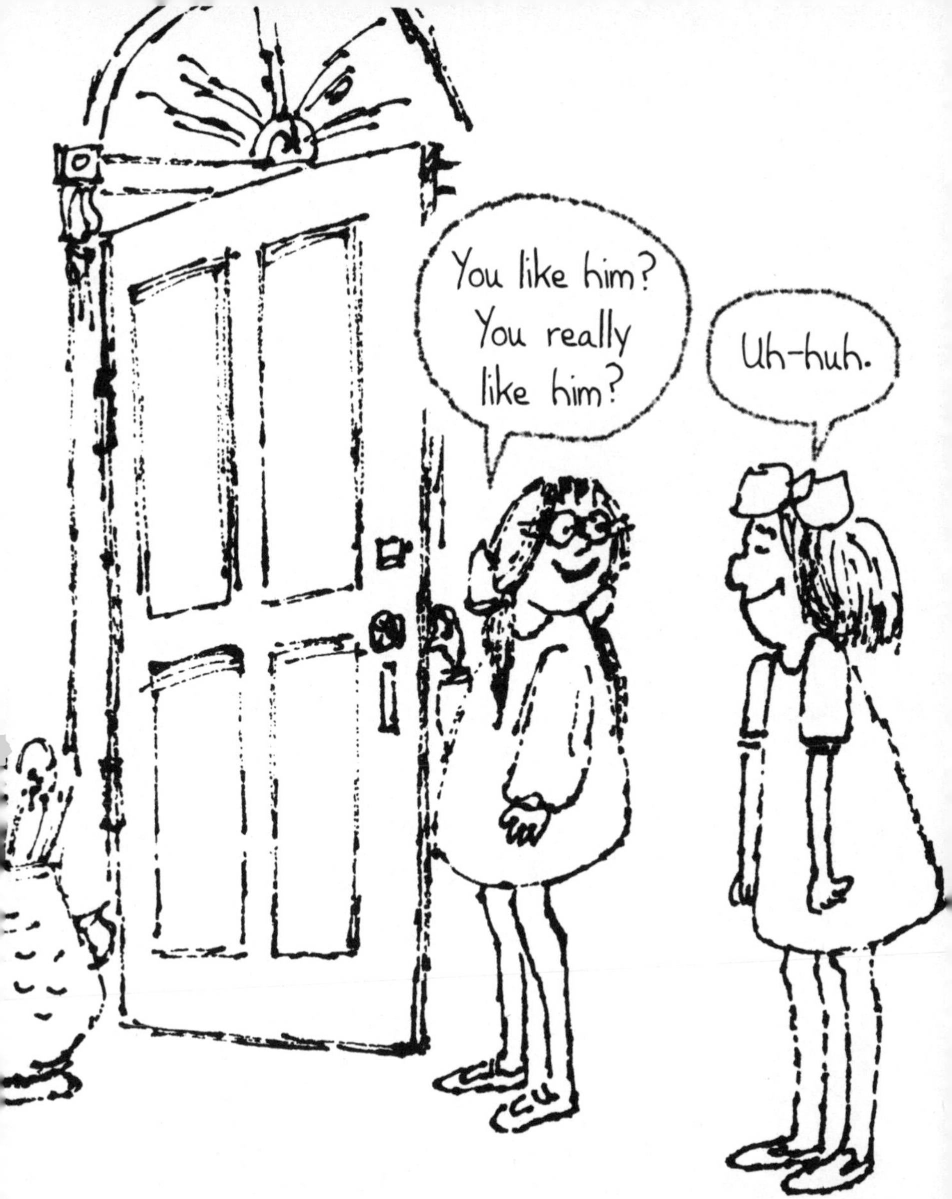
You like him? You really like him?
Uh-huh.

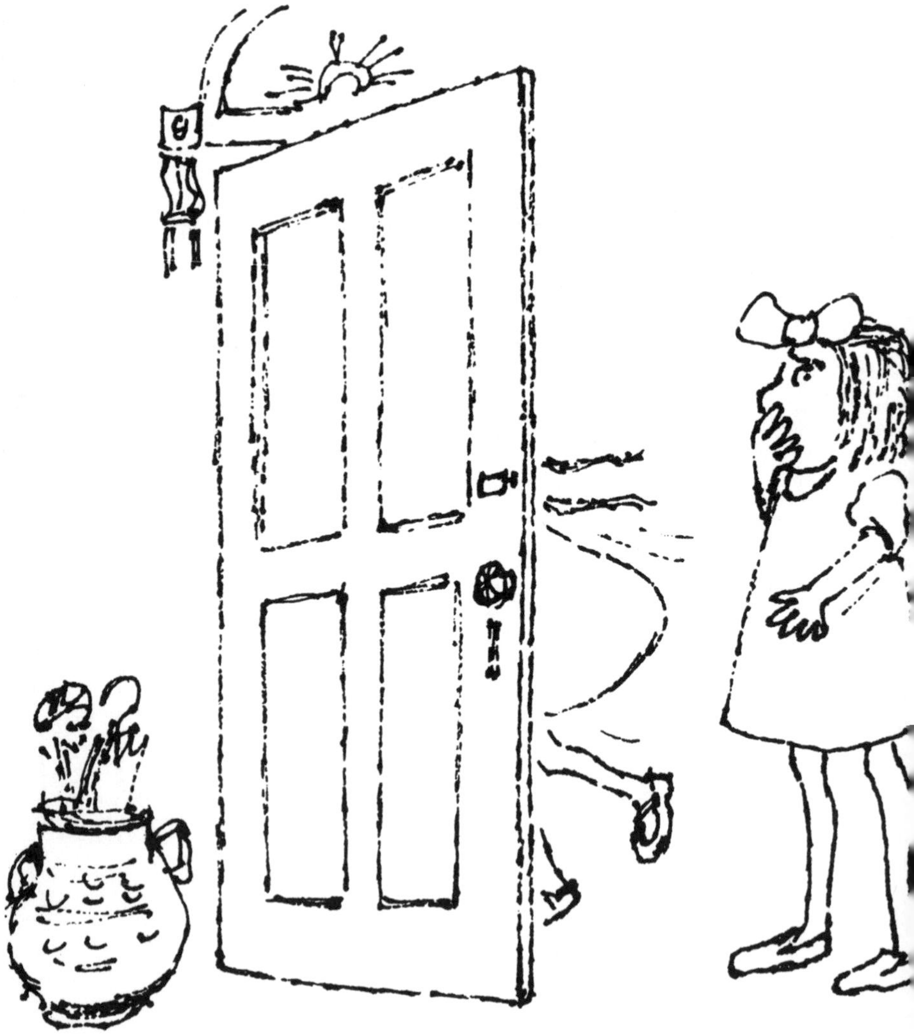

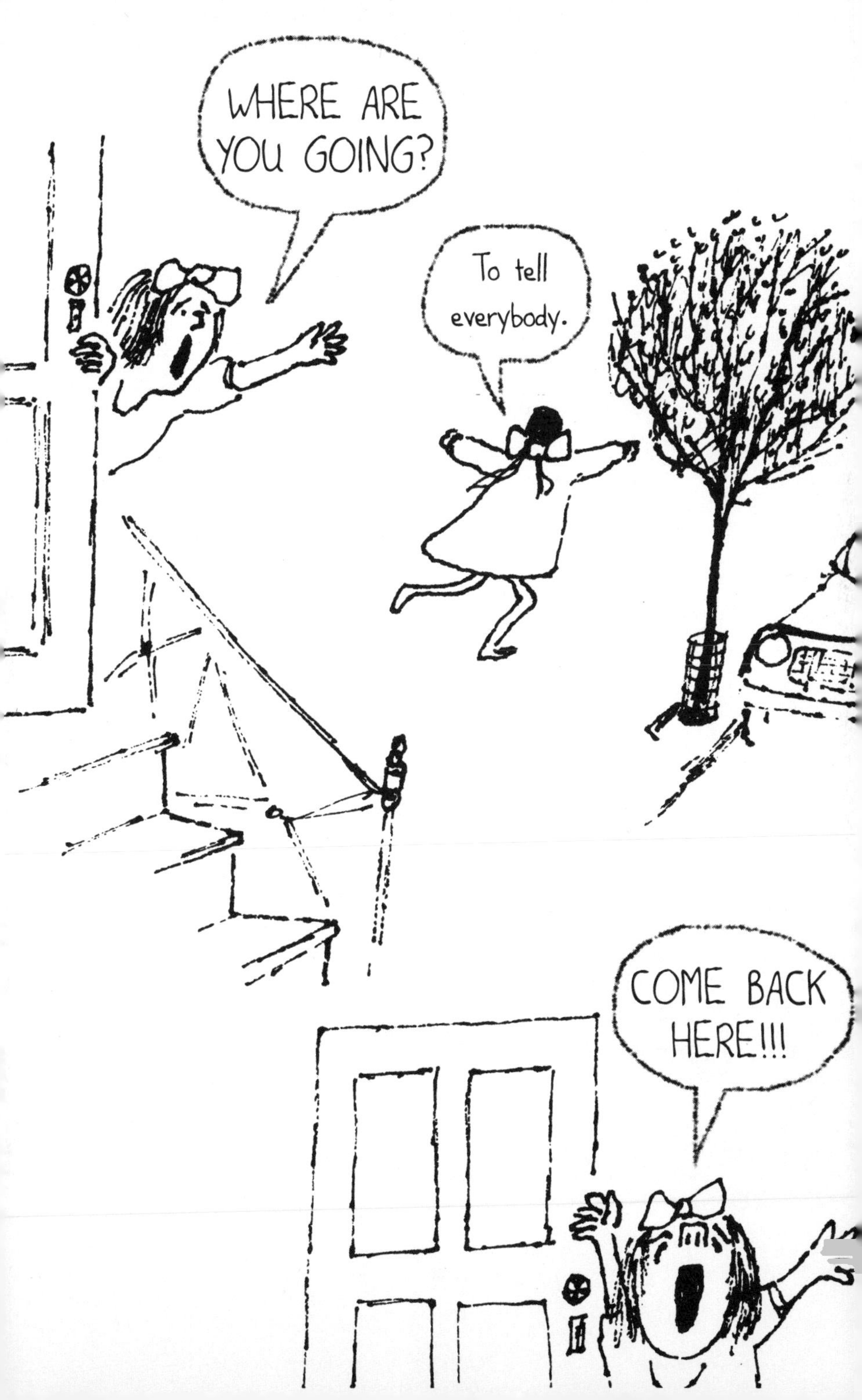
WHERE ARE YOU GOING?
To tell everybody.
COME BACK HERE!!!

SITTING UP STRAIGHT

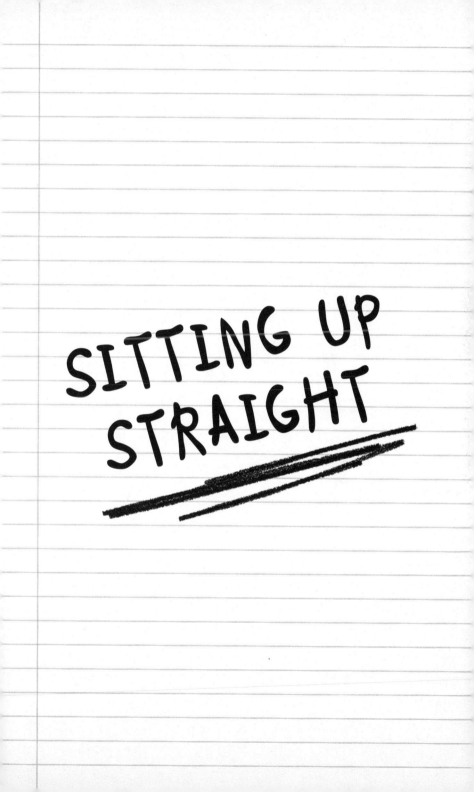

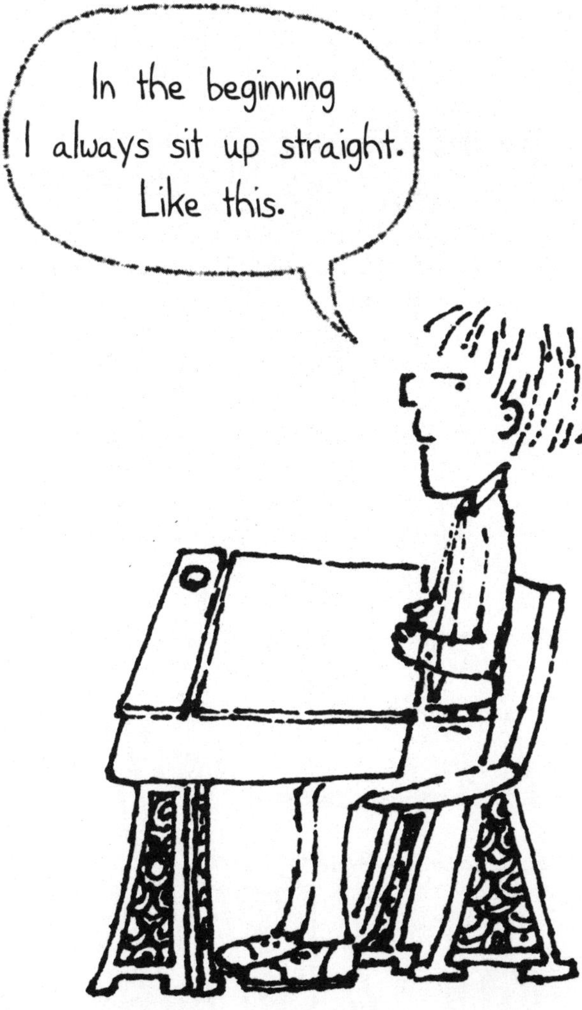
In the beginning I always sit up straight. Like this.

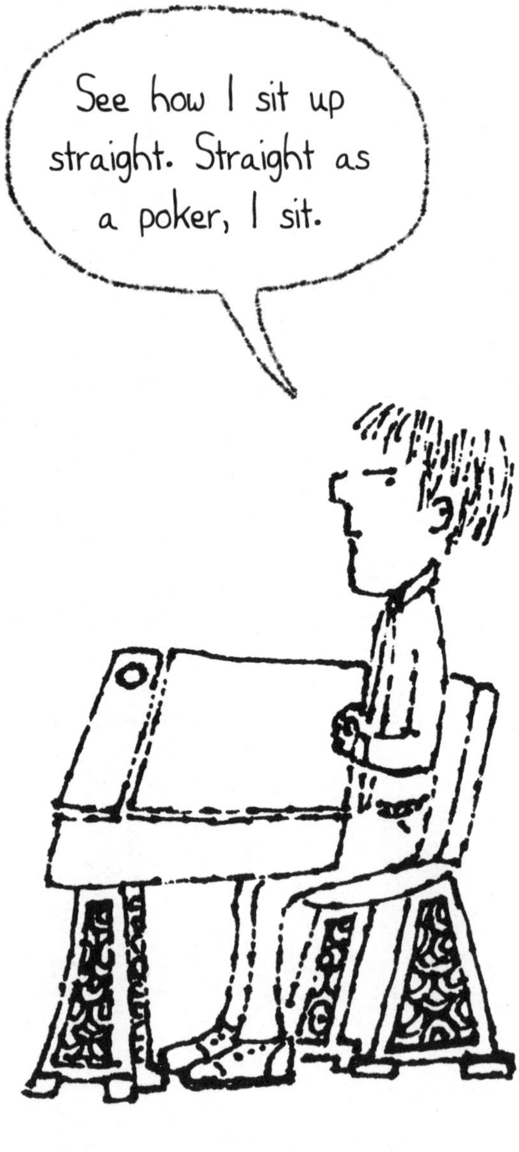
See how I sit up straight. Straight as a poker, I sit.

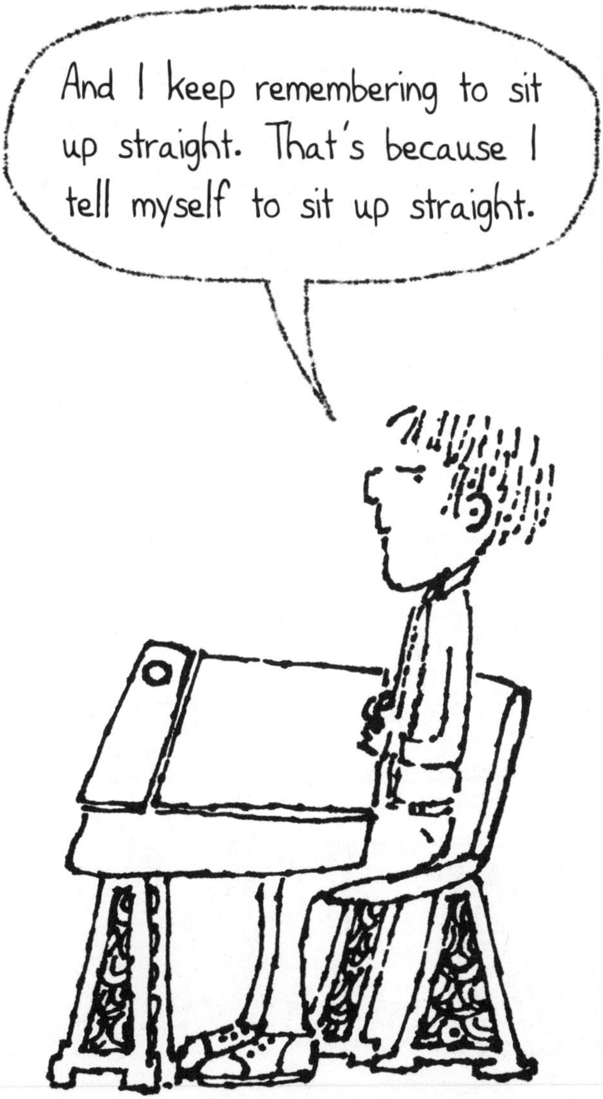
And I keep remembering to sit up straight. That's because I tell myself to sit up straight.

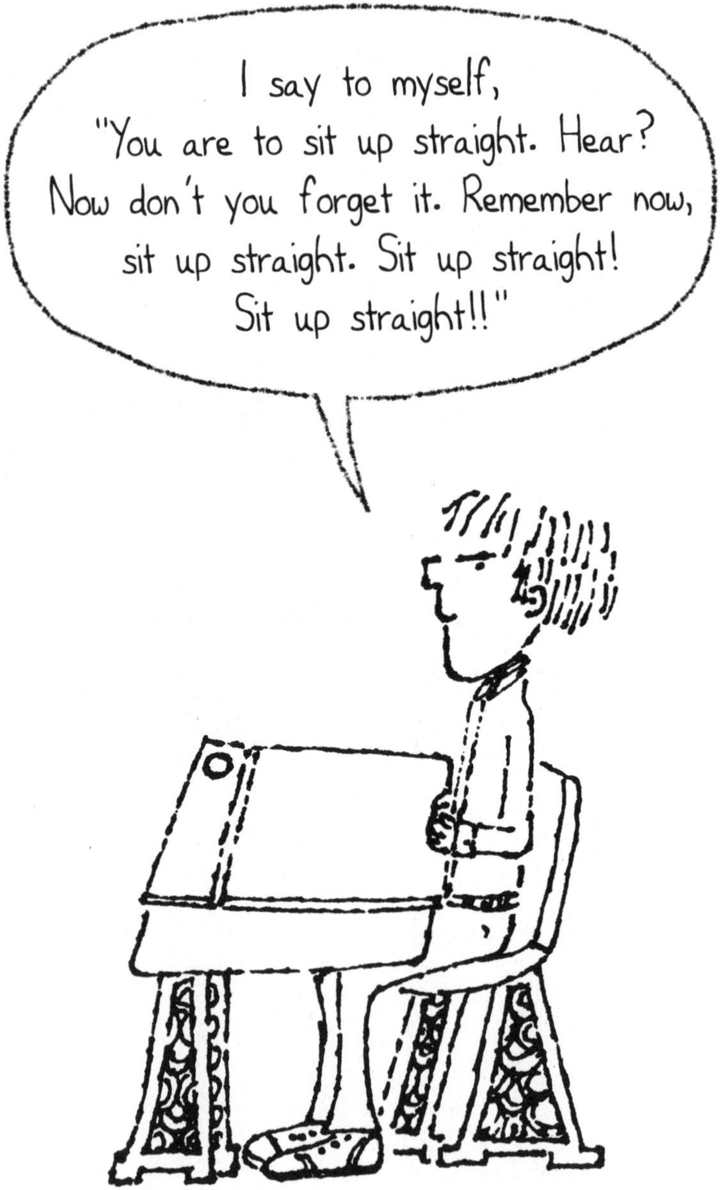
I say to myself,
"You are to sit up straight. Hear?
Now don't you forget it. Remember now,
sit up straight. Sit up straight!
Sit up straight!!"

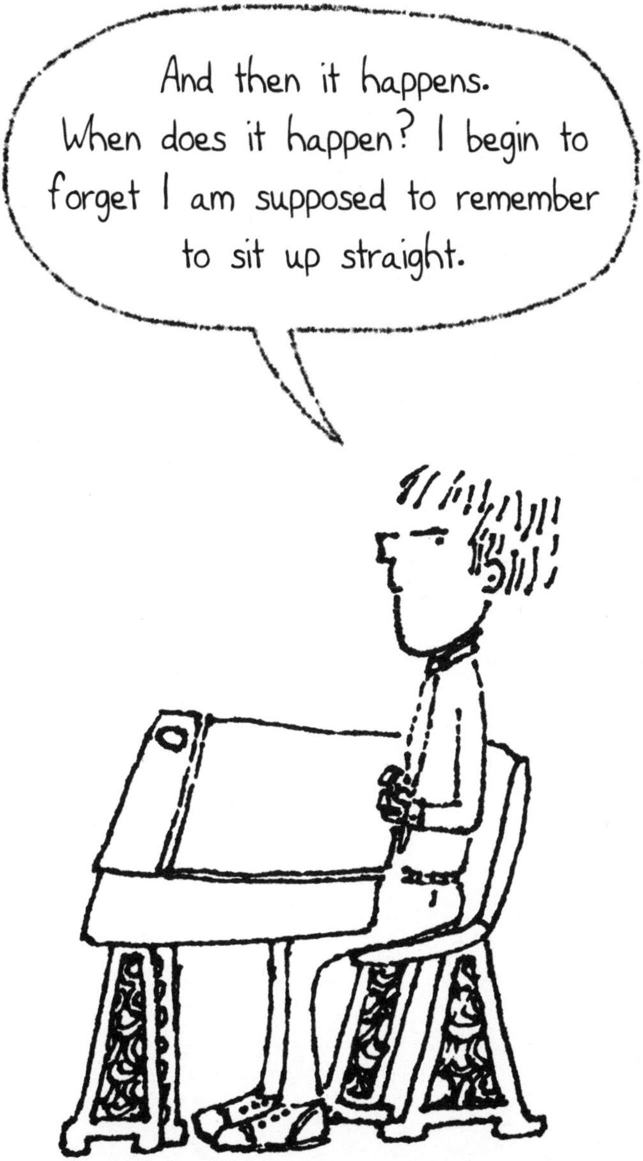
And then it happens. When does it happen? I begin to forget I am supposed to remember to sit up straight.

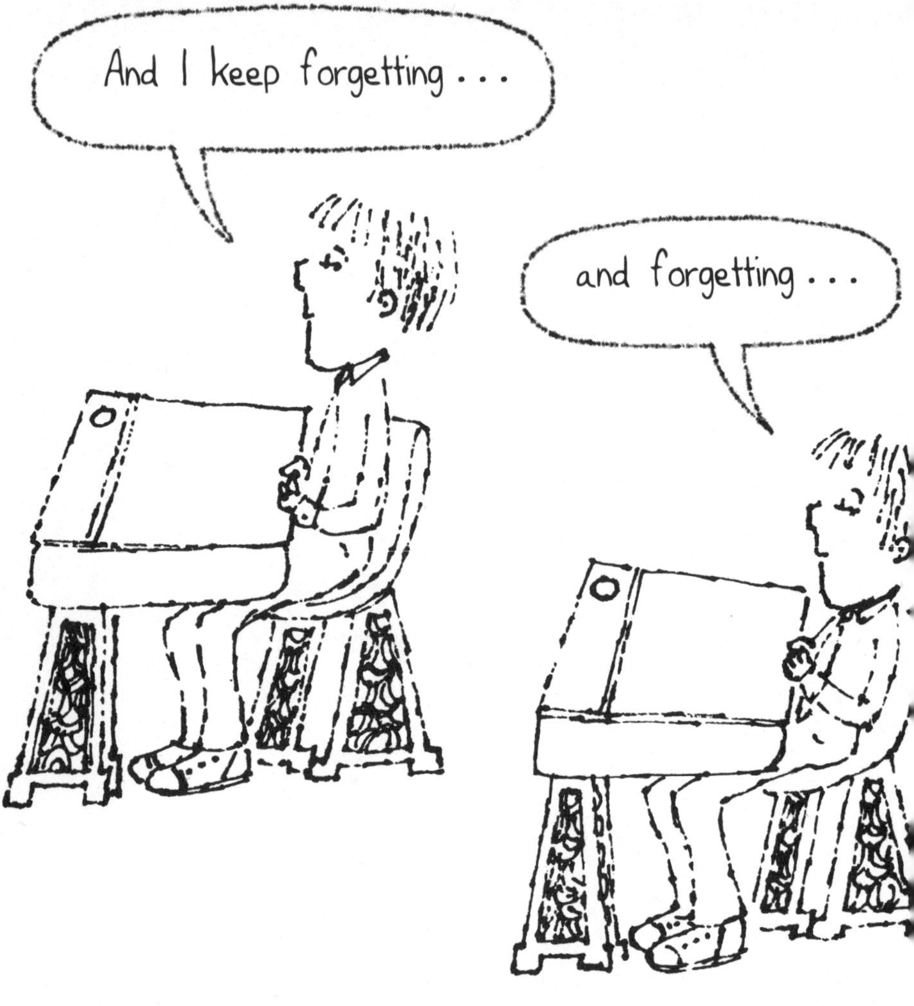
And I keep forgetting . . .
and forgetting . . .

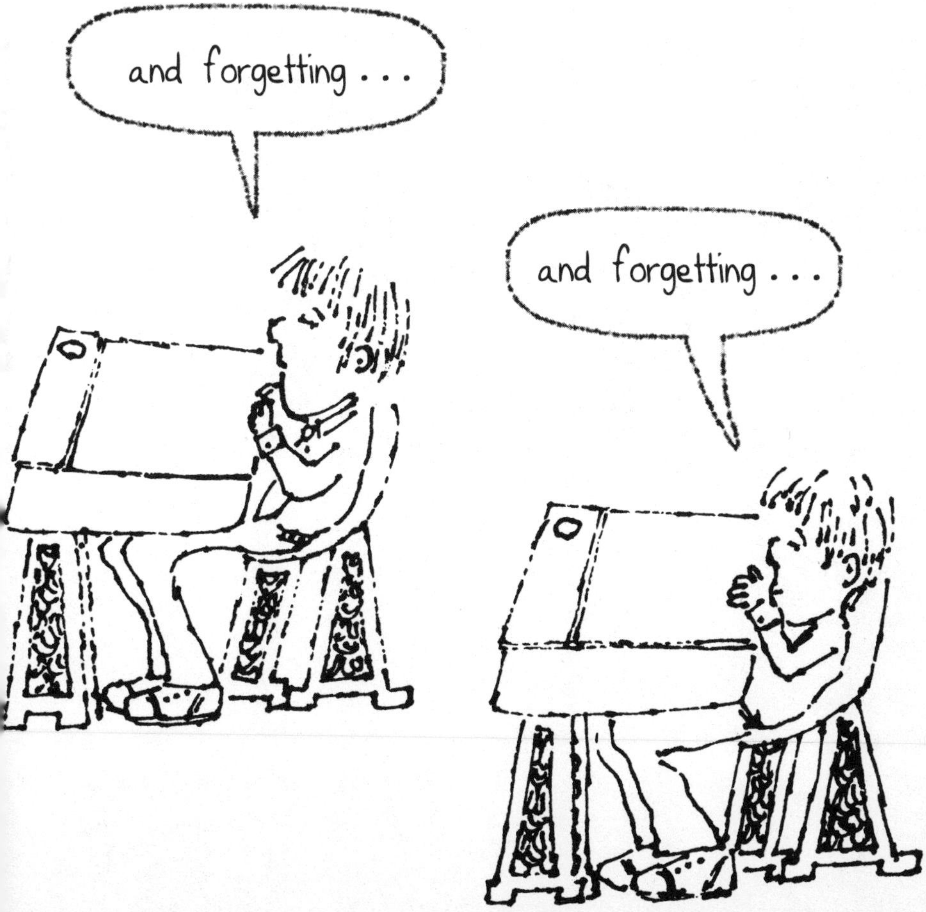
and forgetting . . .
and forgetting . . .

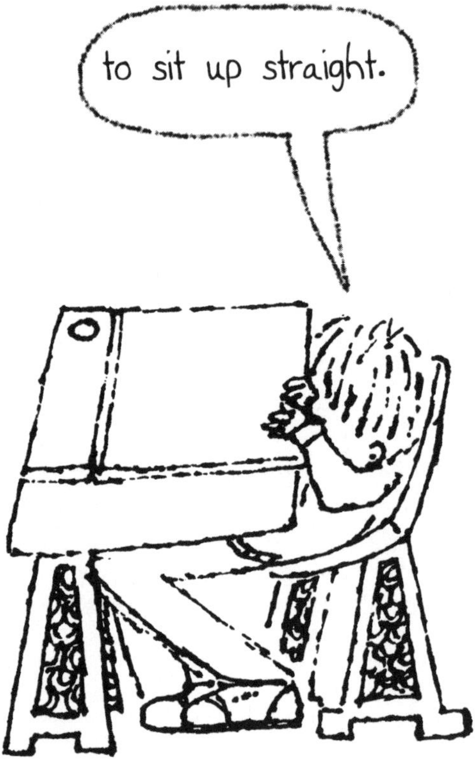
to sit up straight.

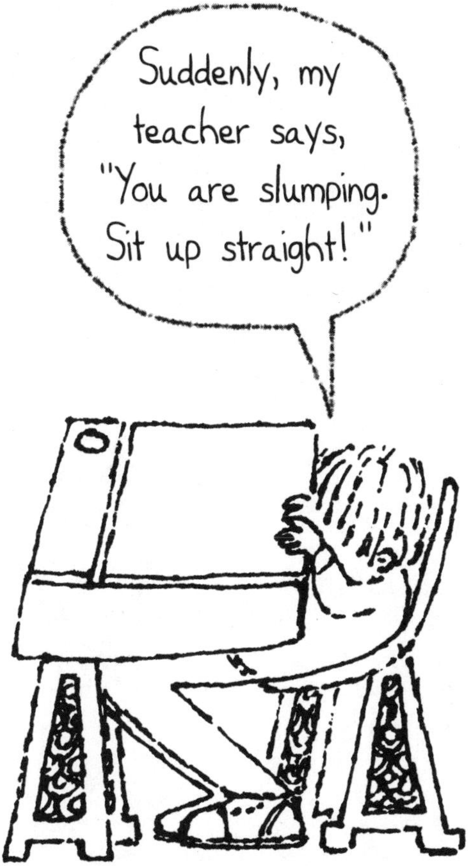
Suddenly, my teacher says, "You are slumping. Sit up straight!"

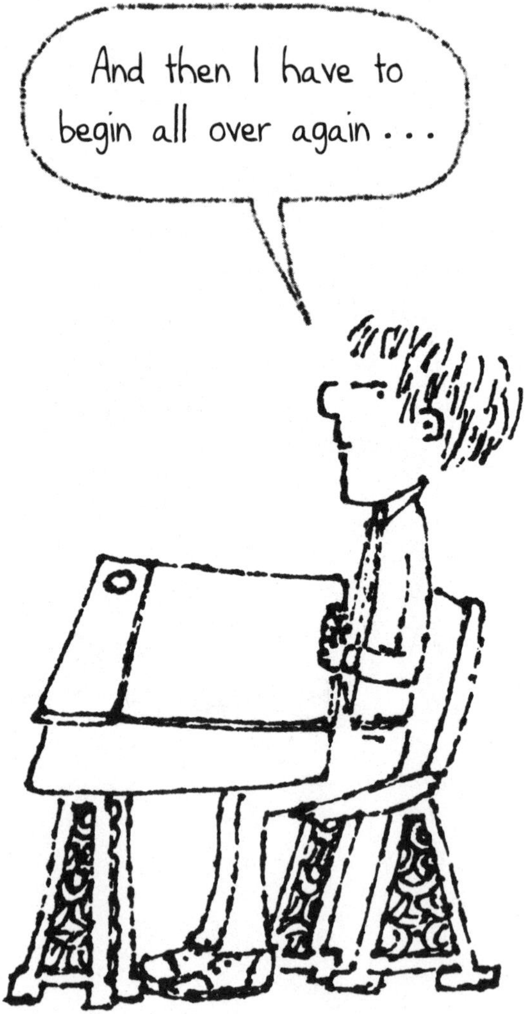
And then I have to begin all over again . . .

to remember
to sit up straight . . .
to sit up straight . . .
to sit up straight.

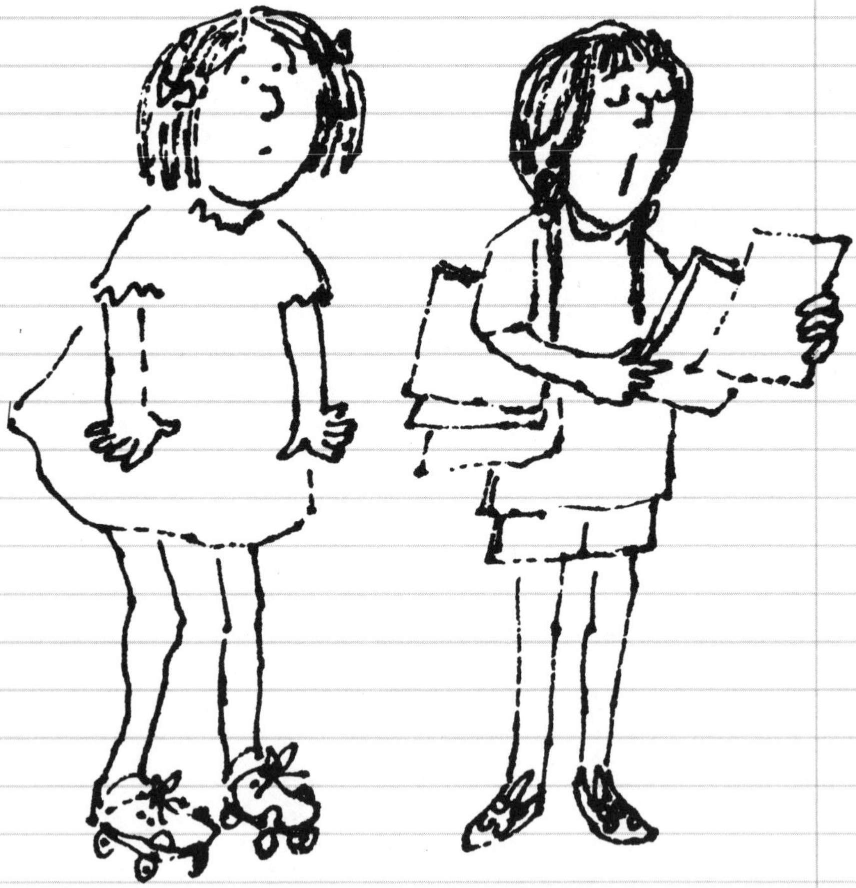

TEN BEST

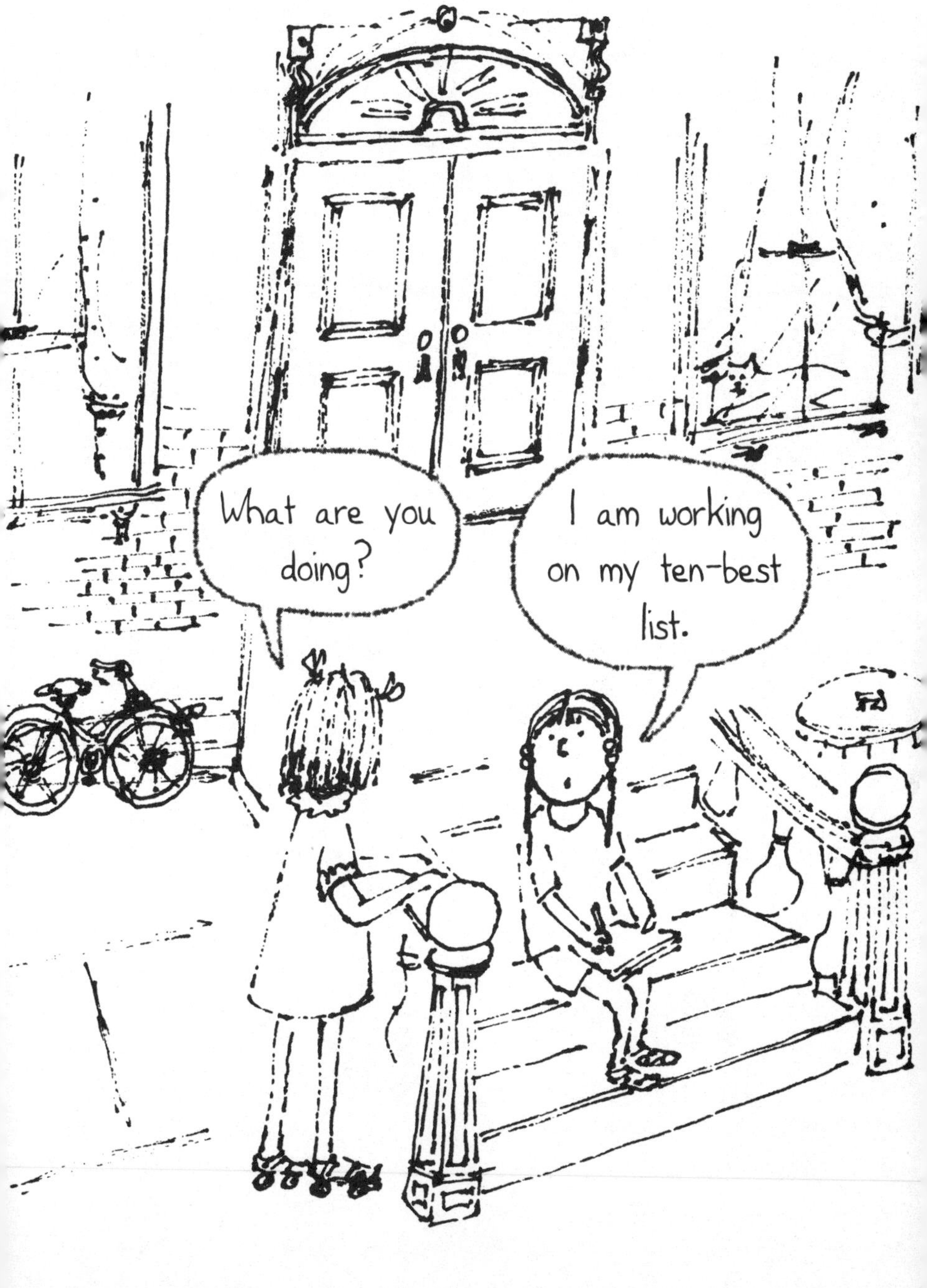
What are you doing?
I am working on my ten-best list.

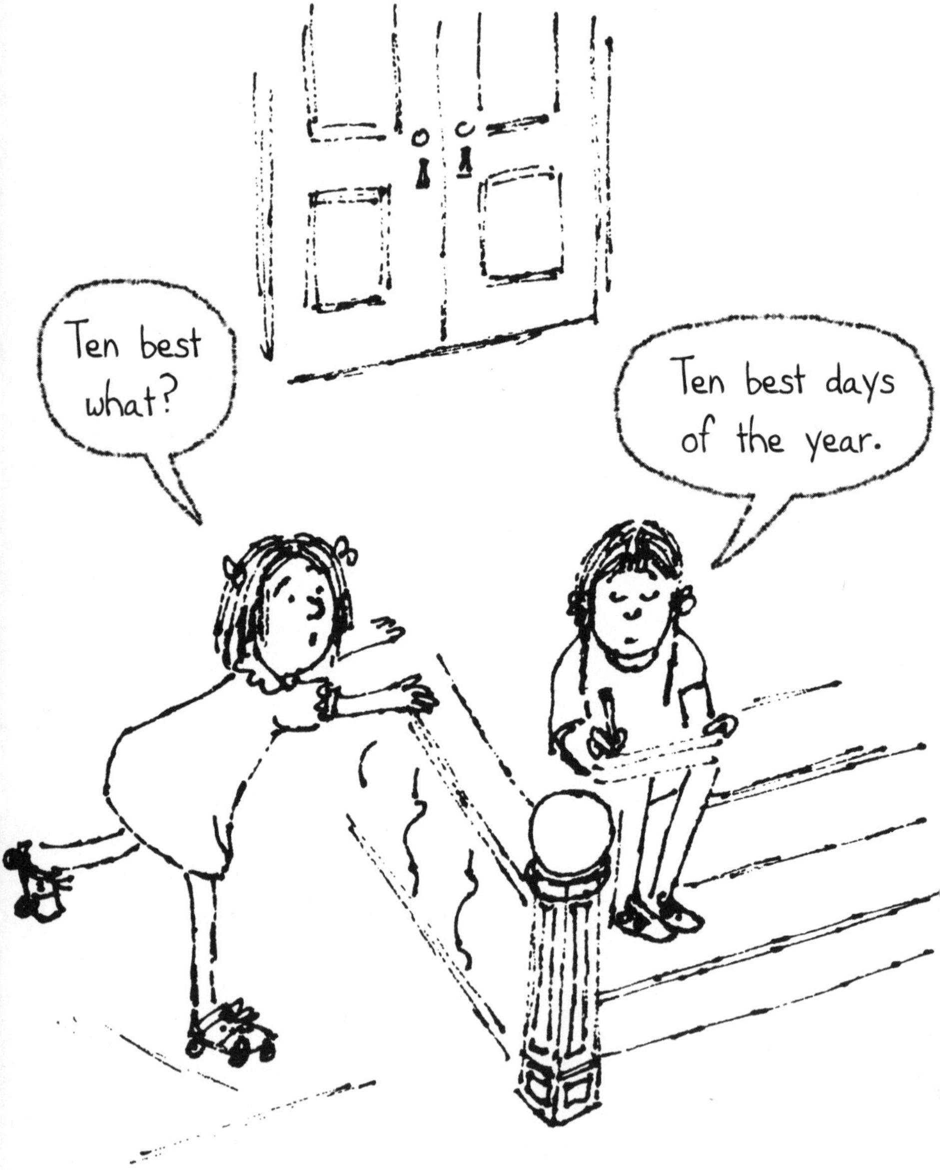
Ten best what?
Ten best days of the year.

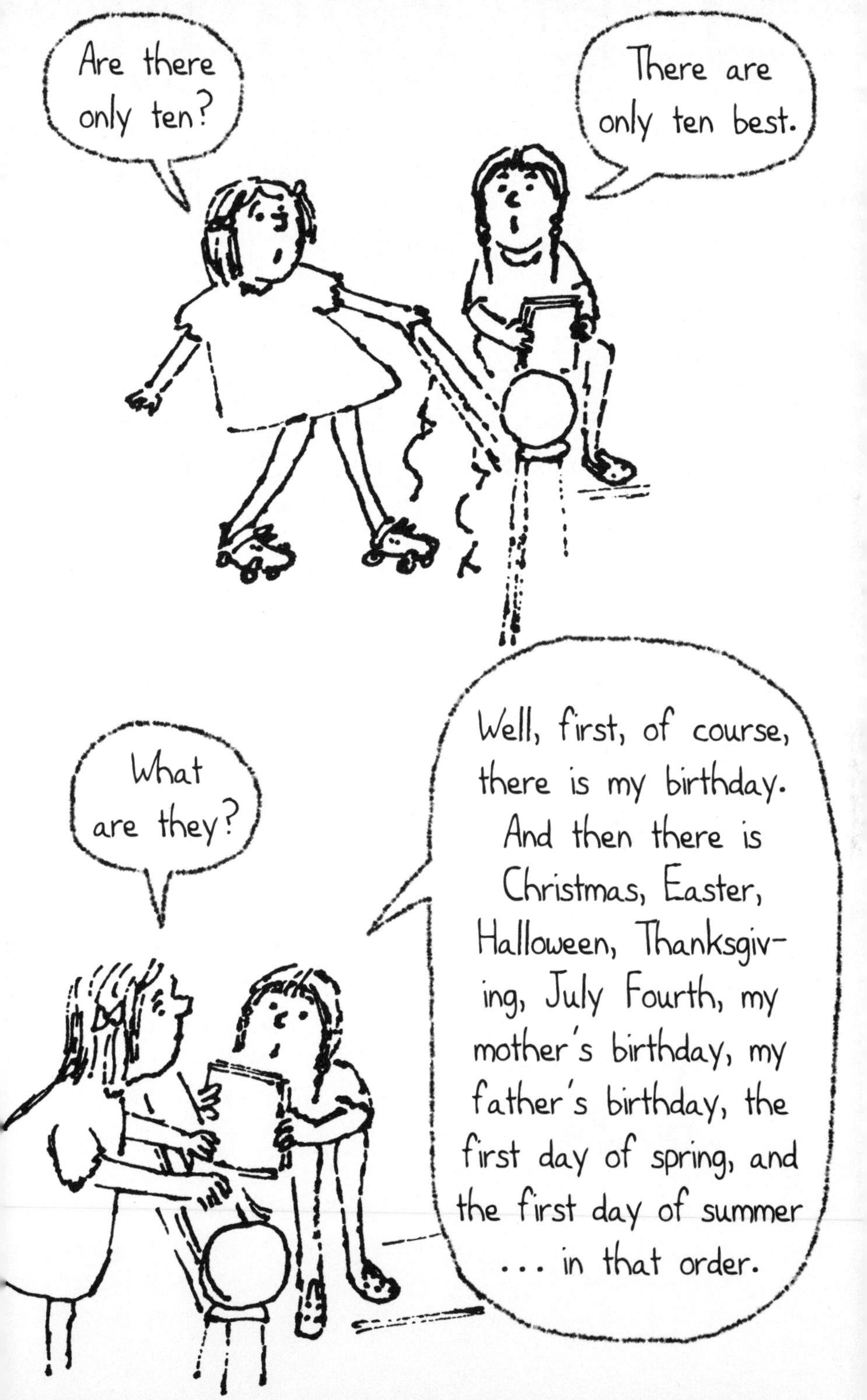
Are there only ten?
There are only ten best.
What are they?
Well, first, of course, there is my birthday. And then there is Christmas, Easter, Halloween, Thanksgiving, July Fourth, my mother's birthday, my father's birthday, the first day of spring, and the first day of summer ... in that order.

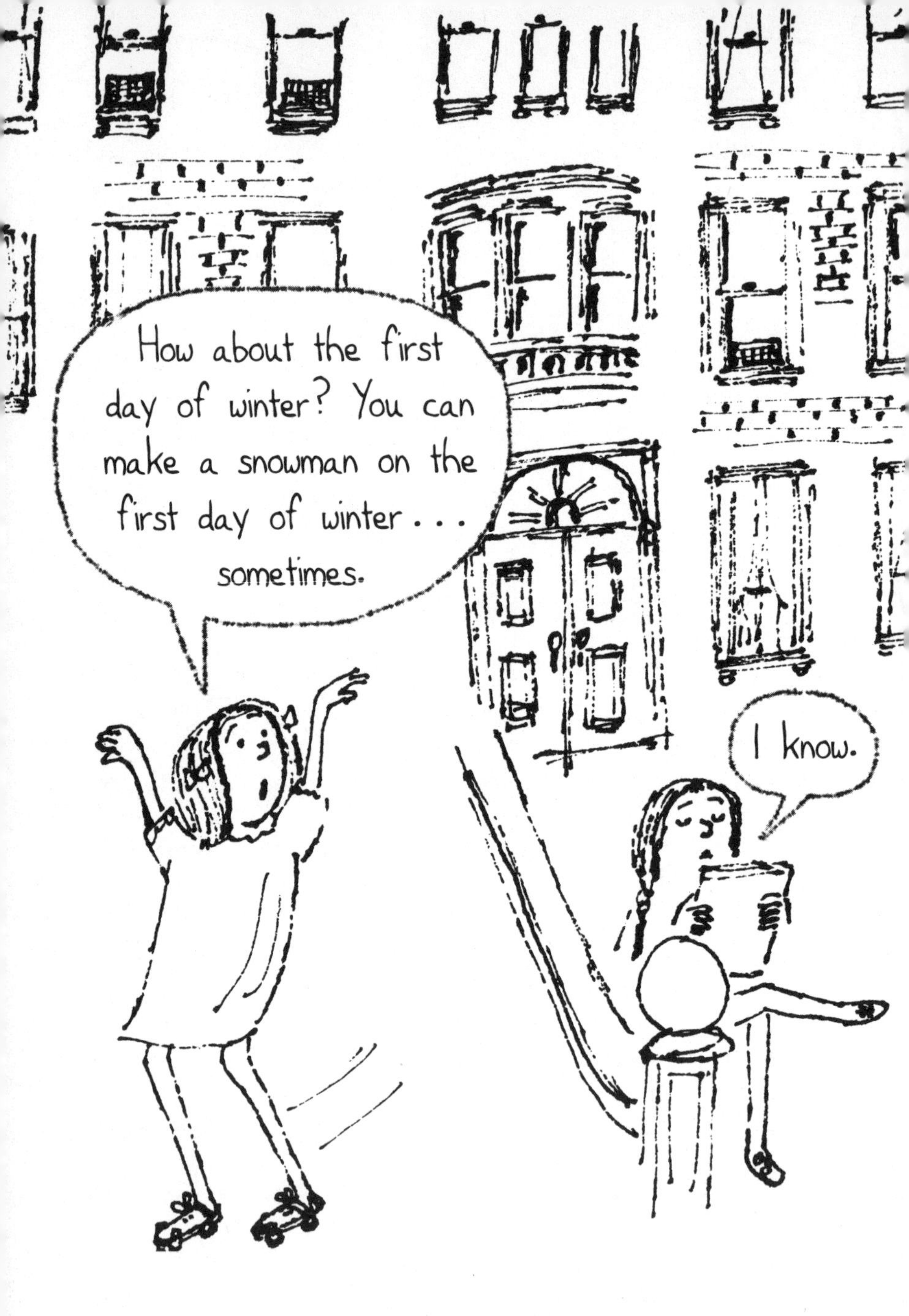
How about the first day of winter? You can make a snowman on the first day of winter . . . sometimes.
I know.

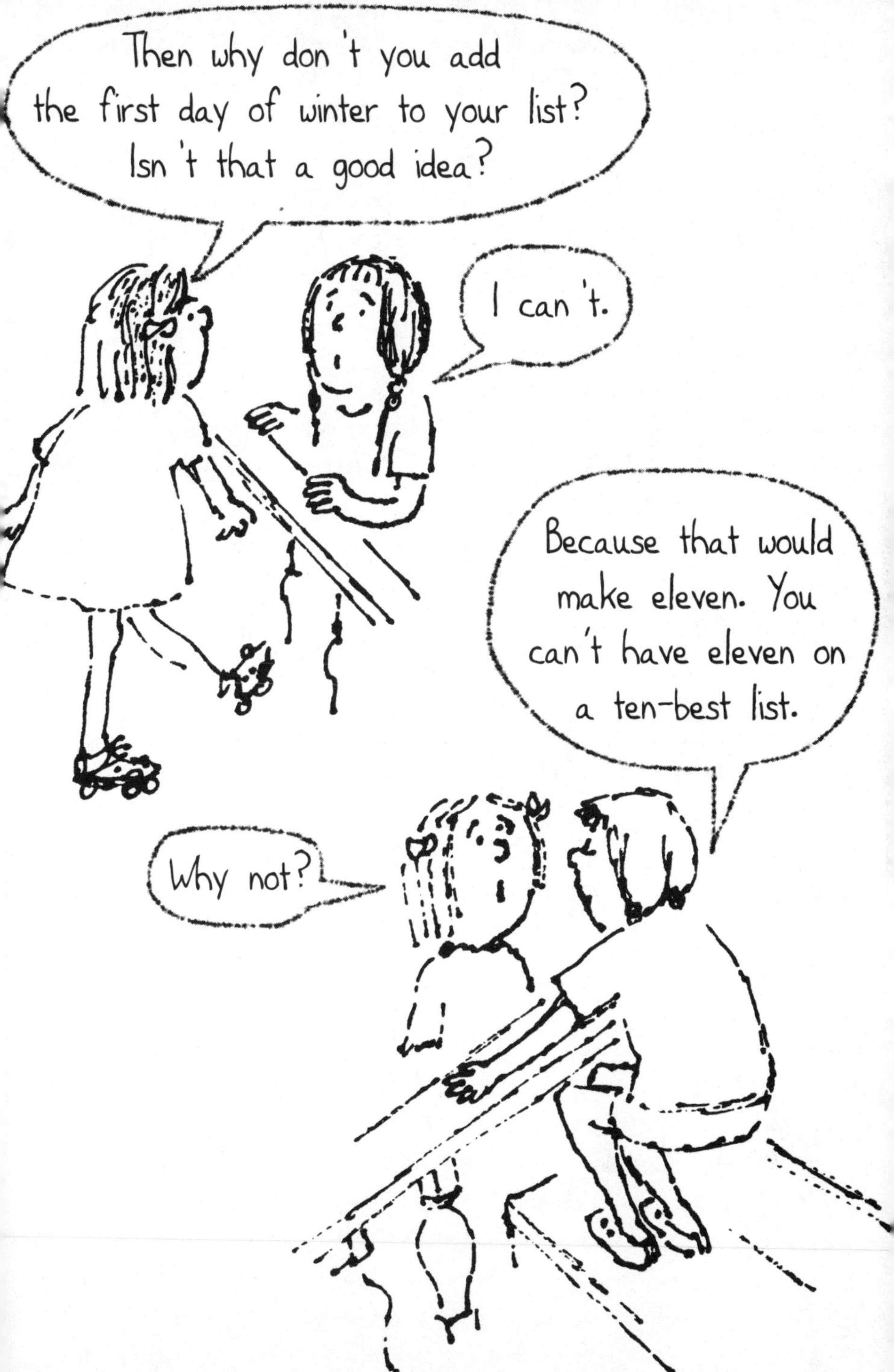
Then why don't you add the first day of winter to your list? Isn't that a good idea?
I can't.
Why not?
Because that would make eleven. You can't have eleven on a ten-best list.

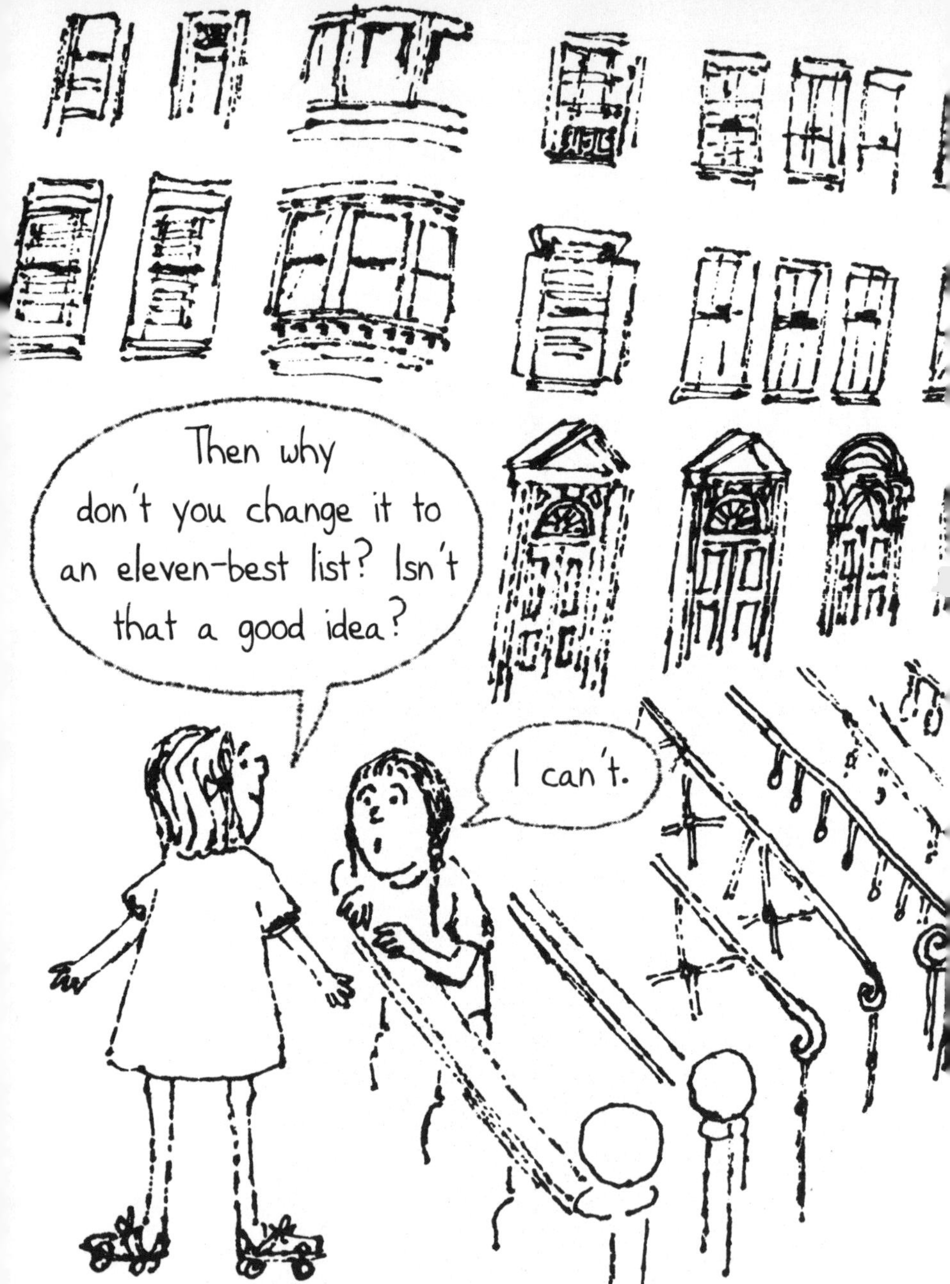
Then why don't you change it to an eleven-best list? Isn't that a good idea?
I can't.

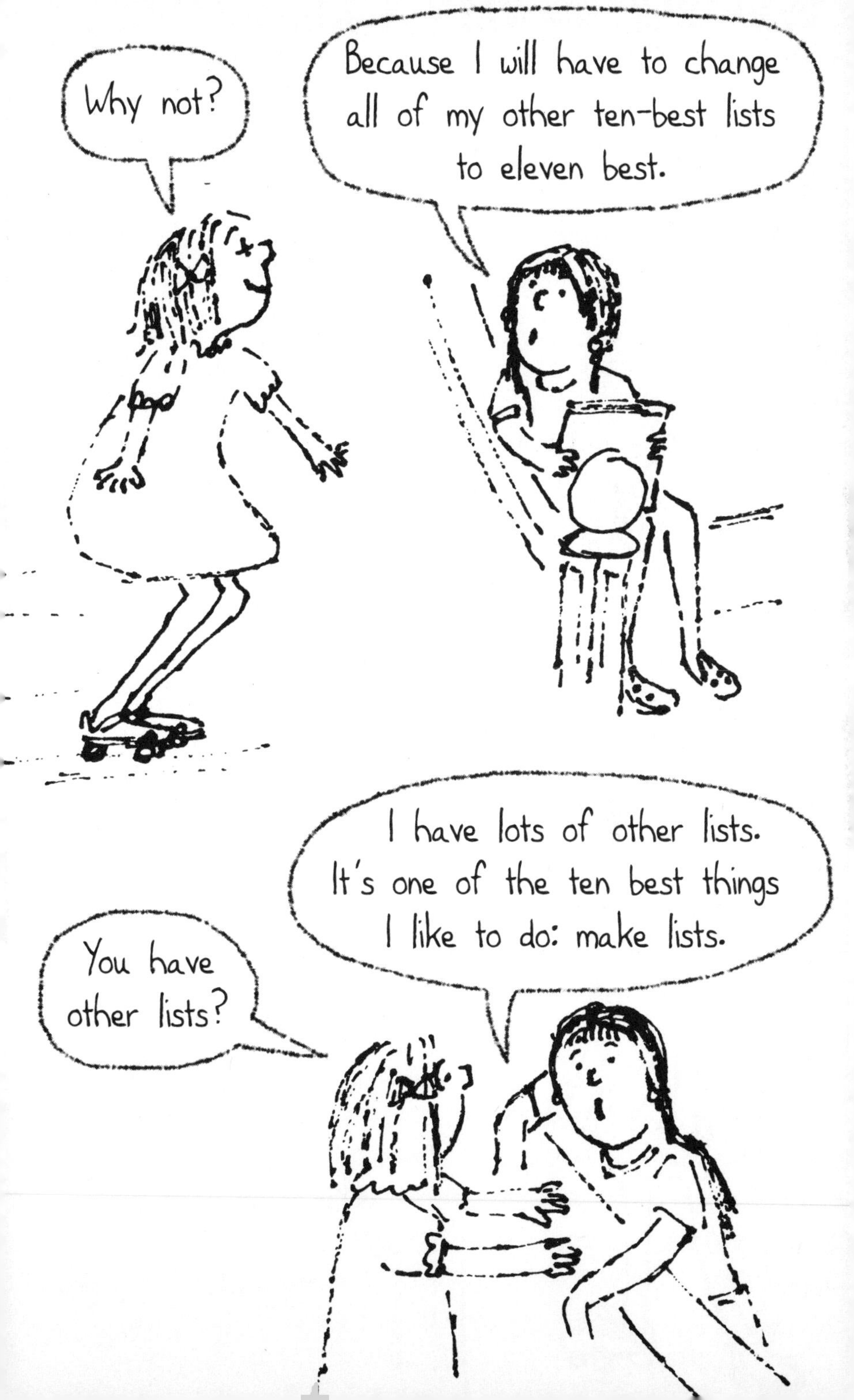
Why not?
Because I will have to change all of my other ten-best lists to eleven best.
You have other lists?
I have lots of other lists. It's one of the ten best things I like to do: make lists.

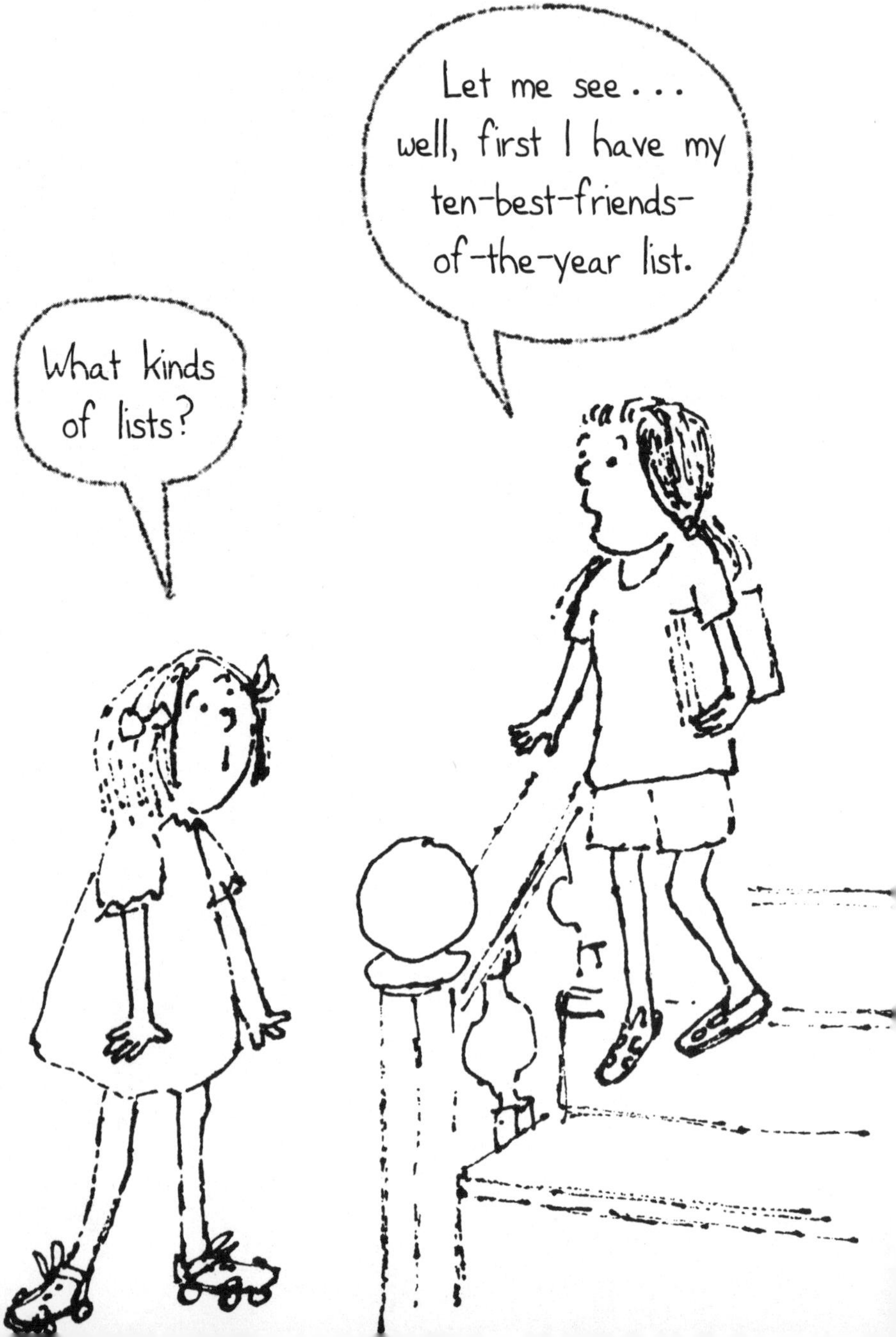
Let me see . . . well, first I have my ten-best-friends-of-the-year list.
What kinds of lists?

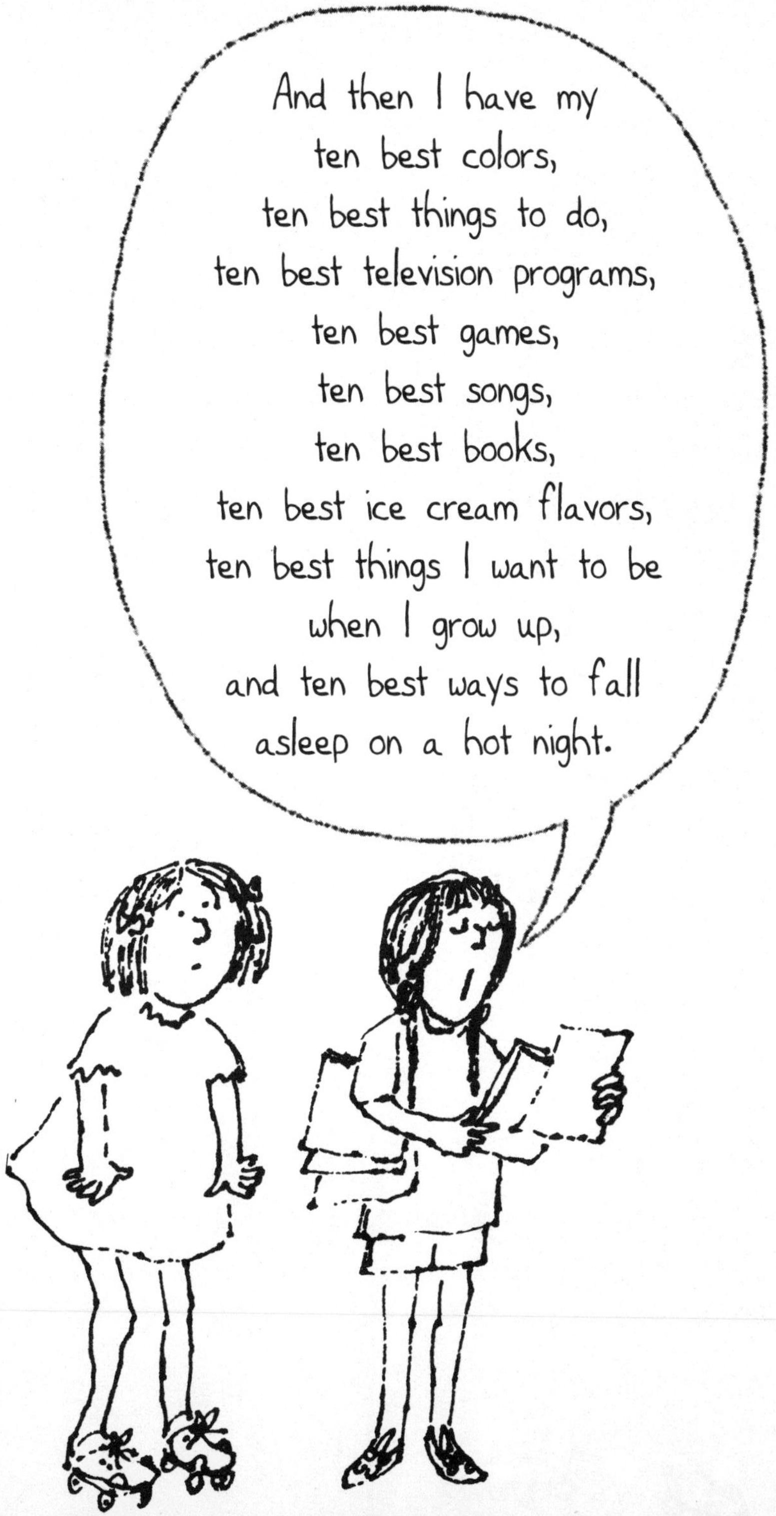
And then I have my
ten best colors,
ten best things to do,
ten best television programs,
ten best games,
ten best songs,
ten best books,
ten best ice cream flavors,
ten best things I want to be
when I grow up,
and ten best ways to fall
asleep on a hot night.

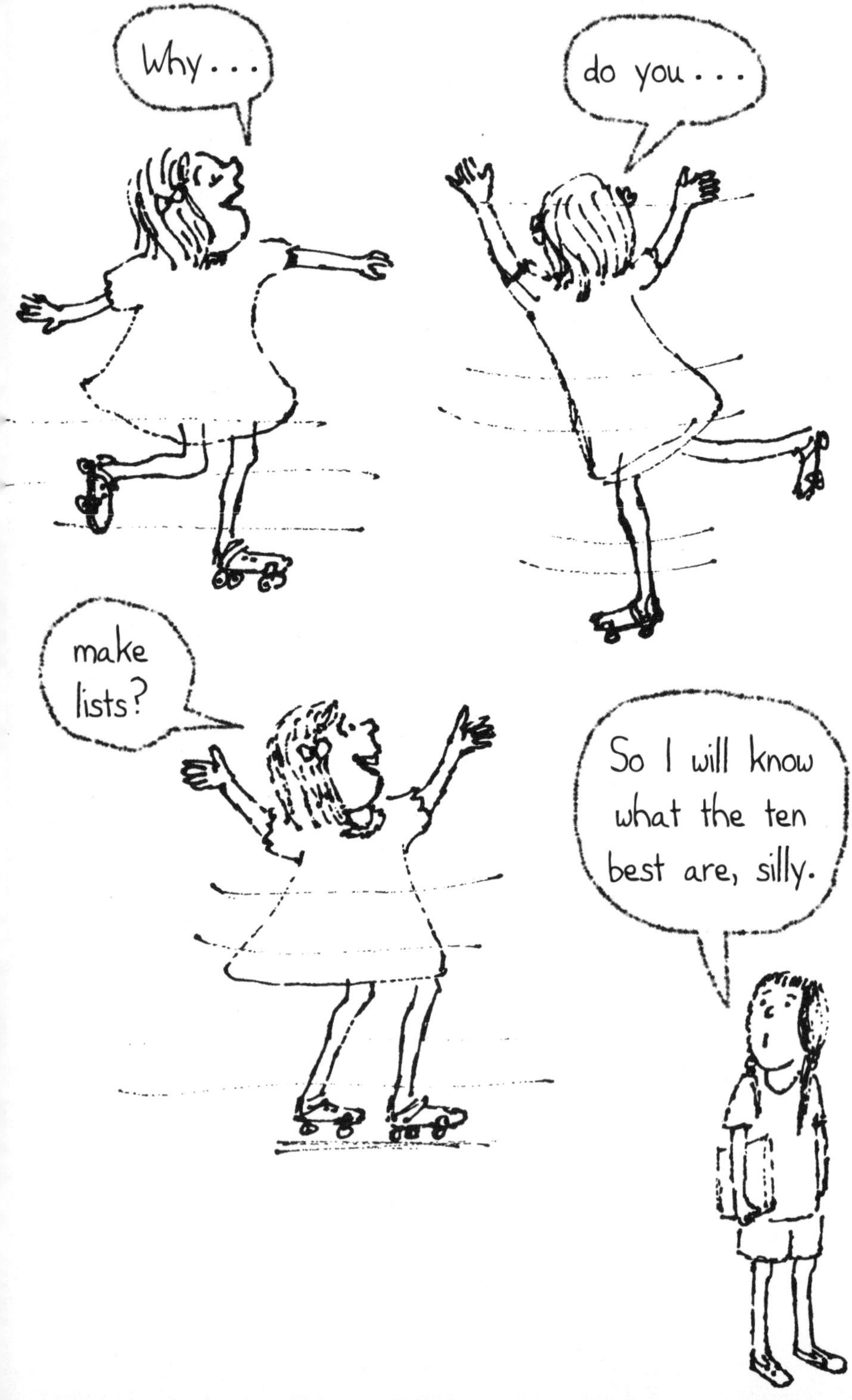
Why...
do you...
make lists?
So I will know what the ten best are, silly.

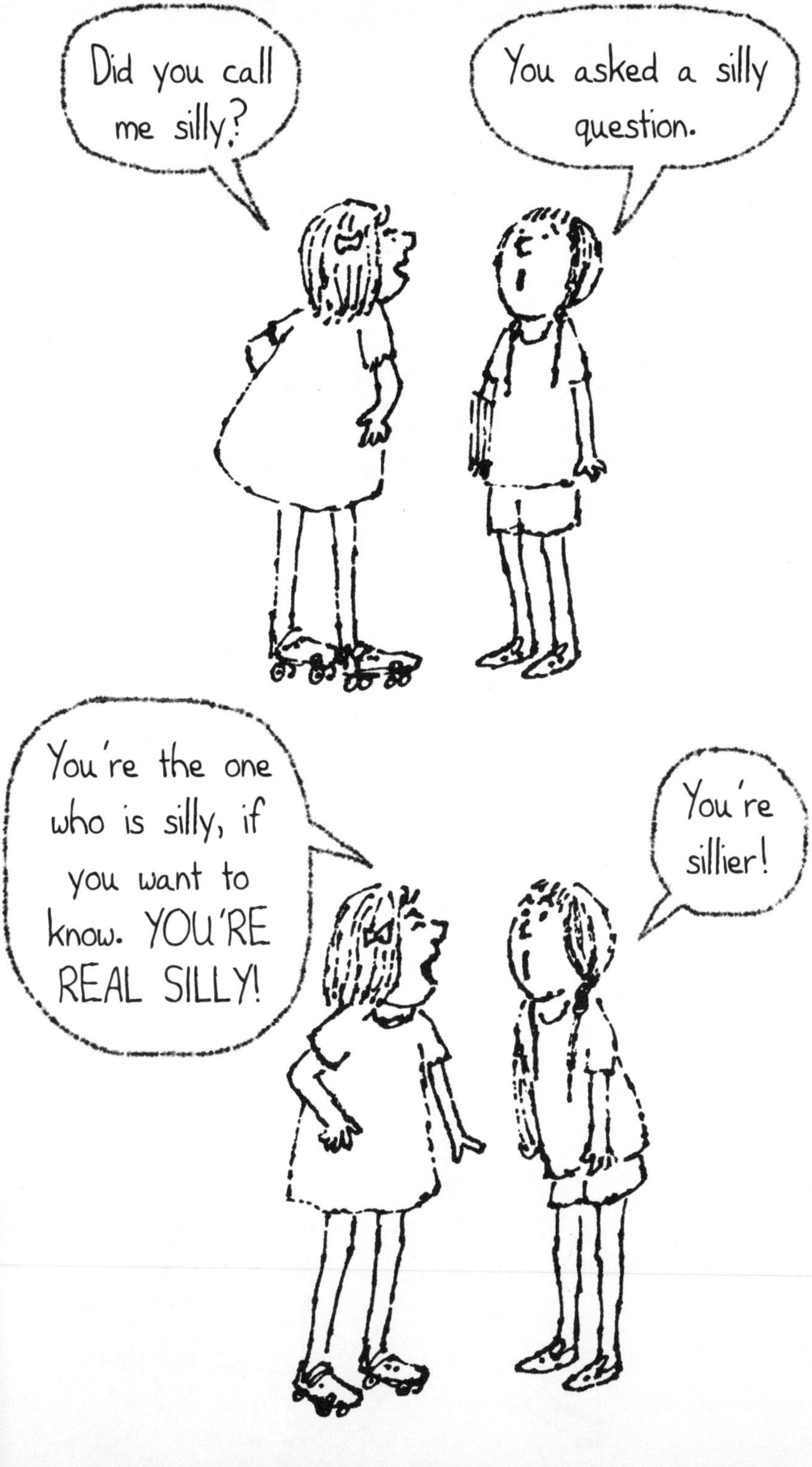
Did you call me silly?
You asked a silly question.
You're the one who is silly, if you want to know. YOU'RE REAL SILLY!
You're sillier!

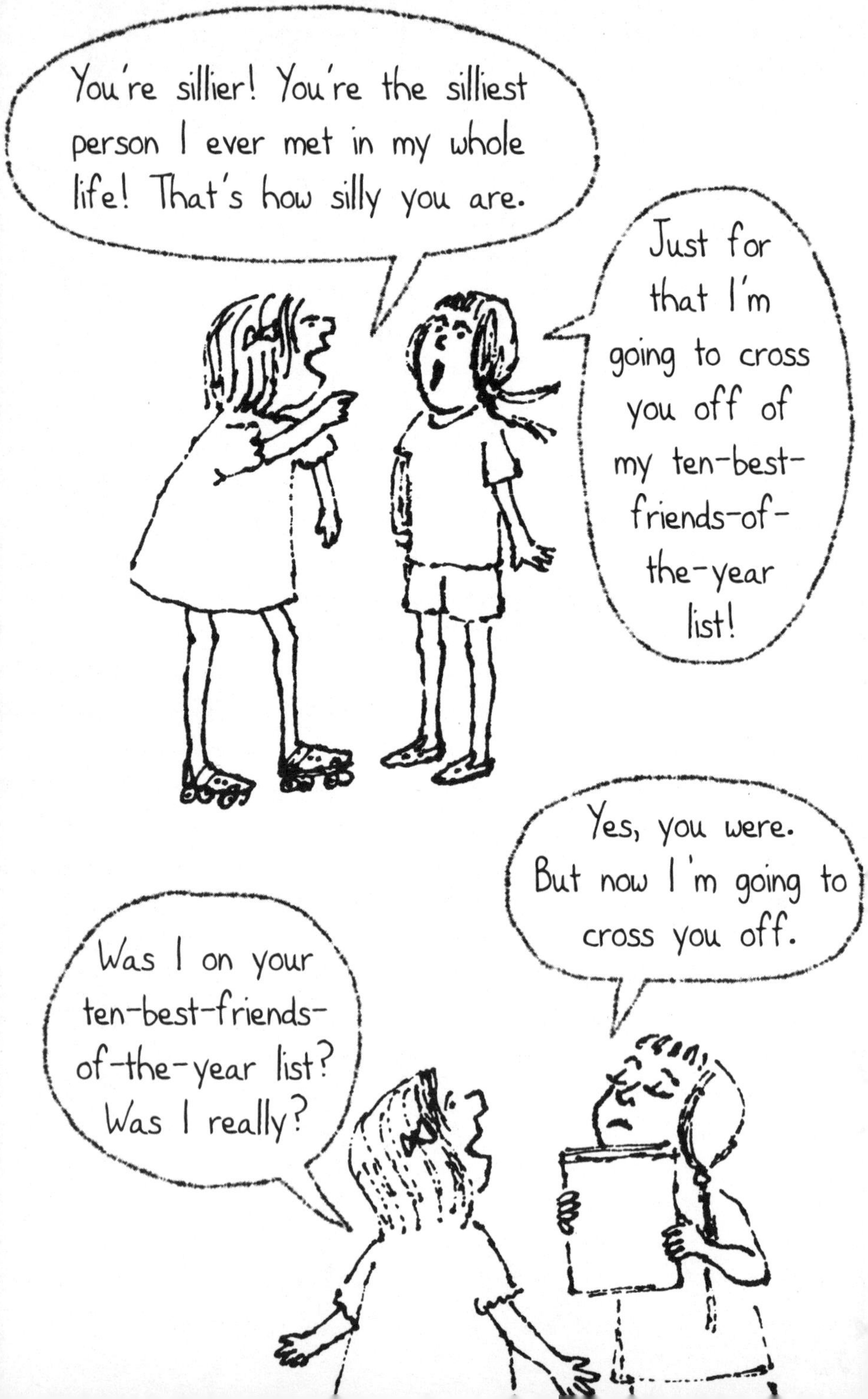
You're sillier! You're the silliest person I ever met in my whole life! That's how silly you are.
Just for that I'm going to cross you off of my ten-best-friends-of-the-year list!
Yes, you were. But now I'm going to cross you off.
Was I on your ten-best-friends-of-the-year list? Was I really?

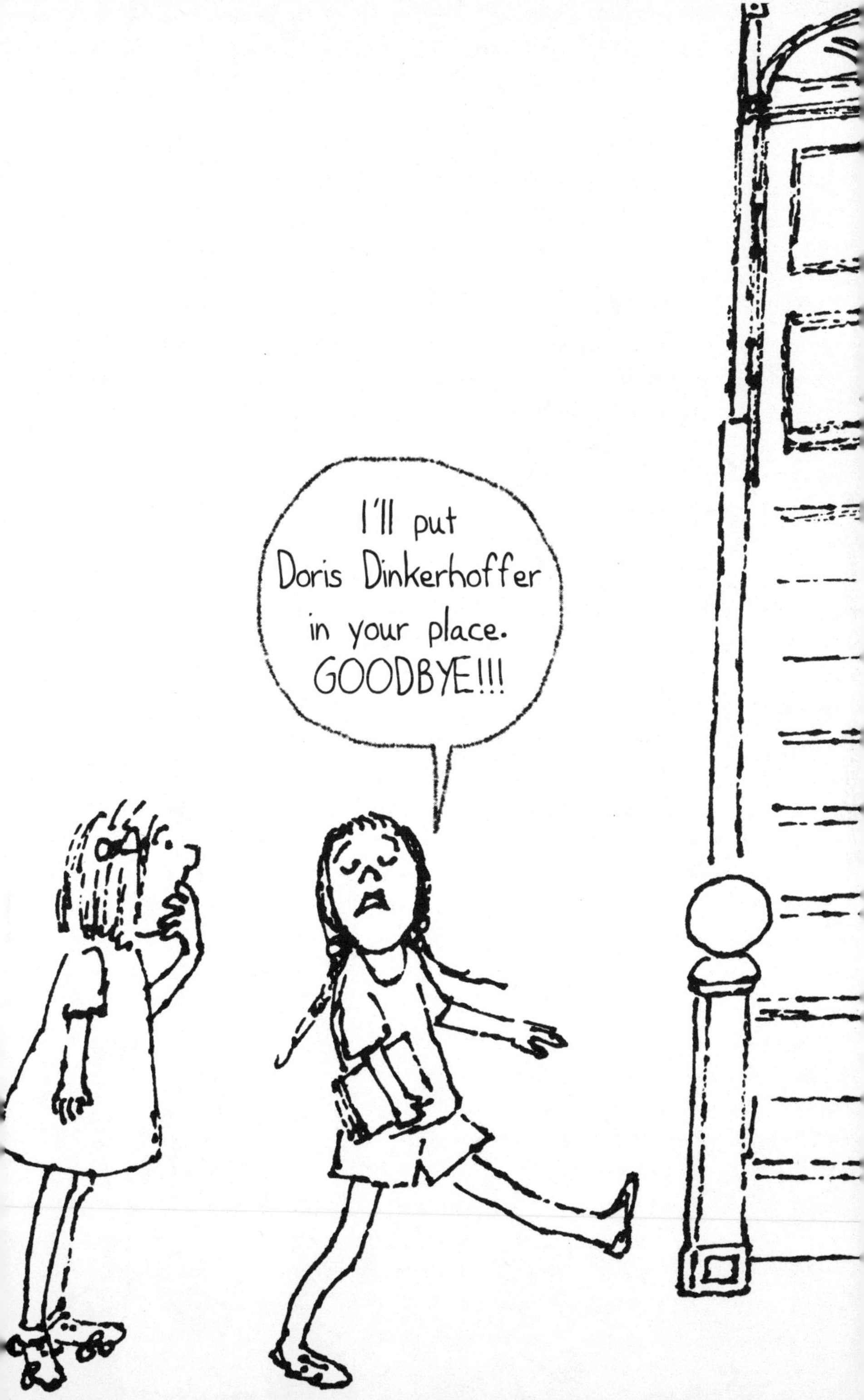
I'll put
Doris Dinkerhoffer
in your place.
GOODBYE!!!

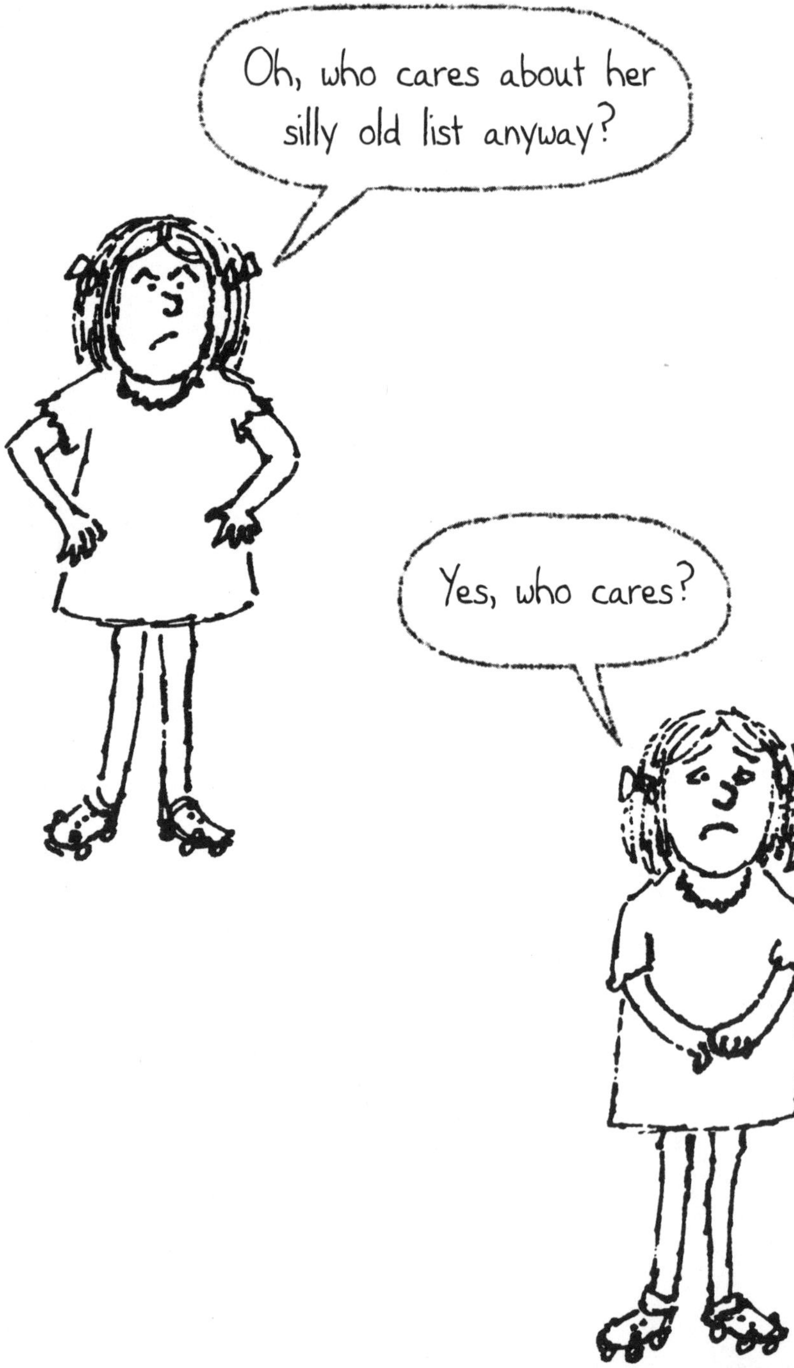
Oh, who cares about her silly old list anyway?
Yes, who cares?

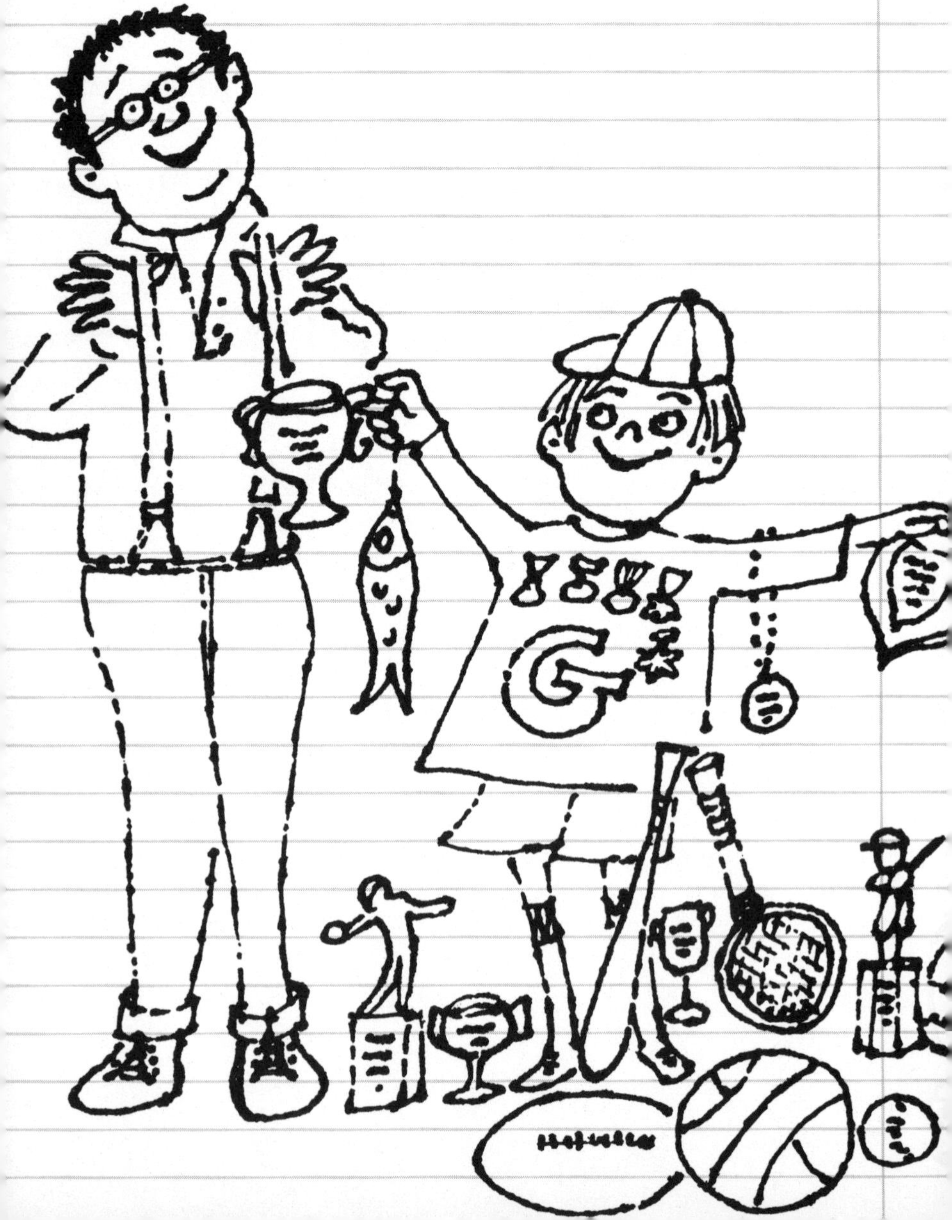

PETER PERFECT

The Story of a Perfect Boy

YOUR NAME IS PETER PERFECT AND YOU ARE THE PERFECT BOY.

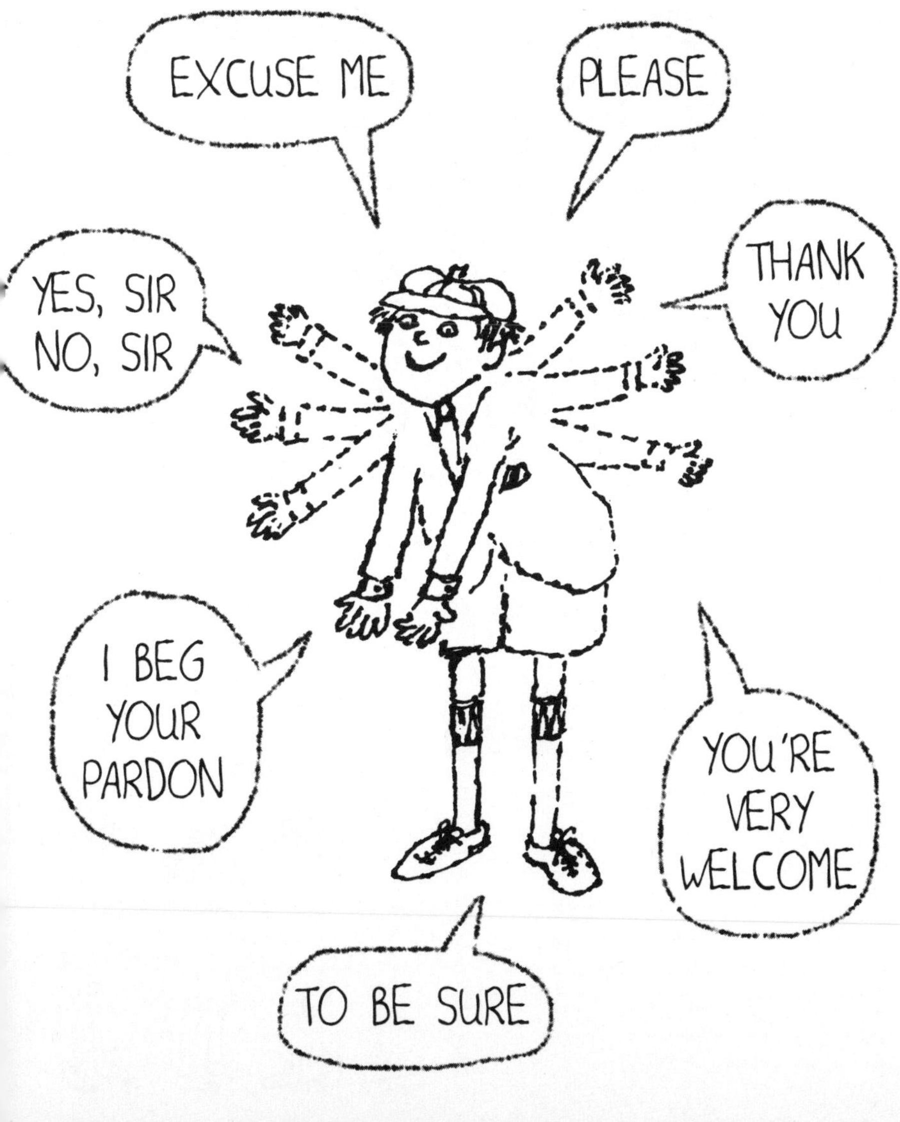
EXCUSE ME
PLEASE
YES, SIR NO, SIR
THANK YOU
I BEG YOUR PARDON
YOU'RE VERY WELCOME
TO BE SURE

YOUR MOTHER IS PROUD OF YOU.

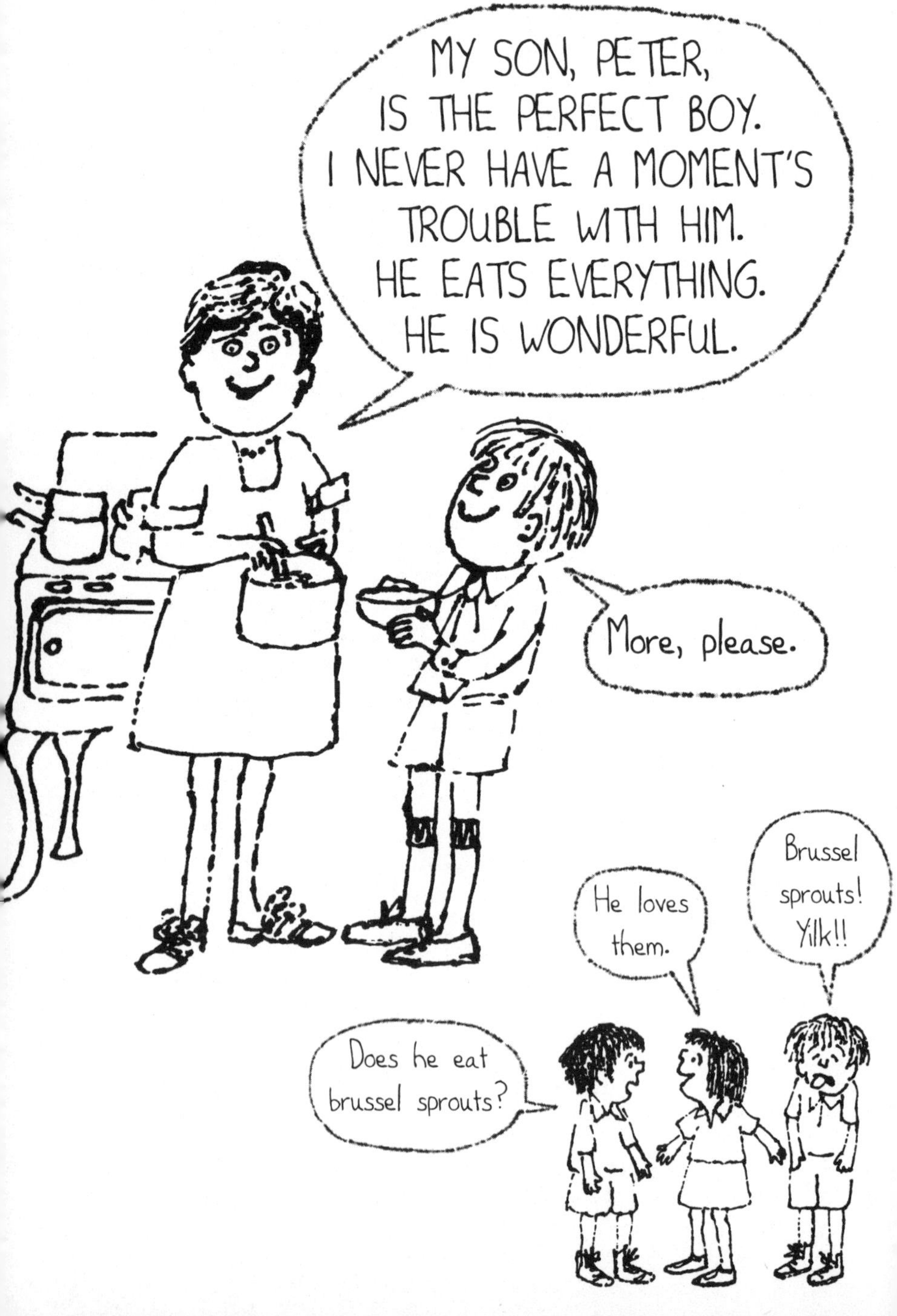
MY SON, PETER, IS THE PERFECT BOY. I NEVER HAVE A MOMENT'S TROUBLE WITH HIM. HE EATS EVERYTHING. HE IS WONDERFUL.
More, please.
Does he eat brussel sprouts?
He loves them.
Brussel sprouts! Yilk!!

YOUR FATHER IS PROUD OF YOU.

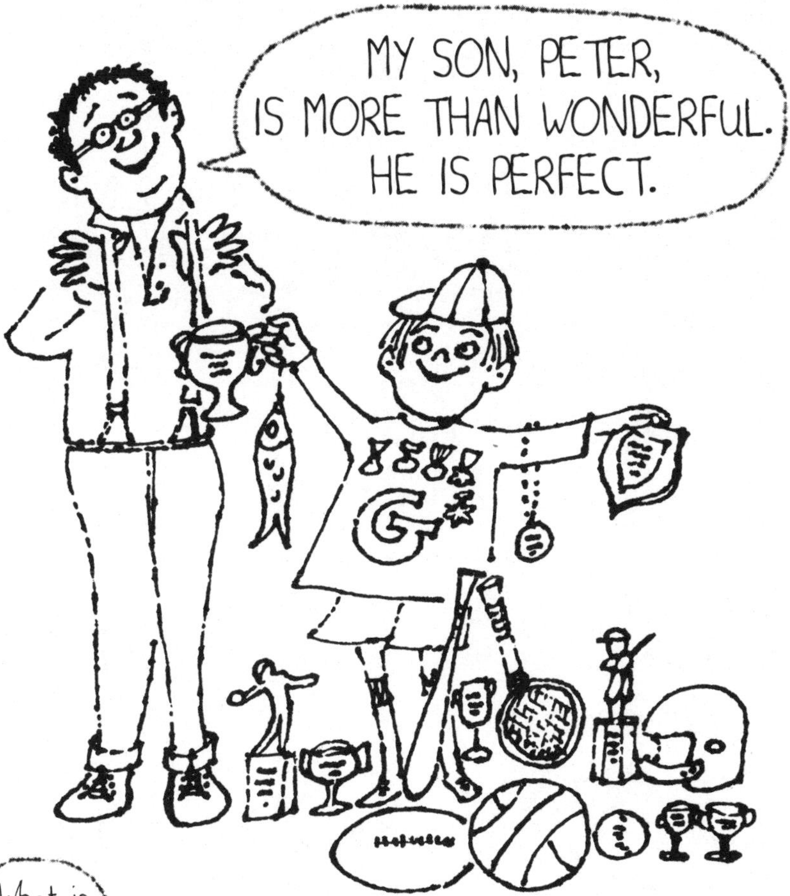
MY SON, PETER, IS MORE THAN WONDERFUL. HE IS PERFECT.

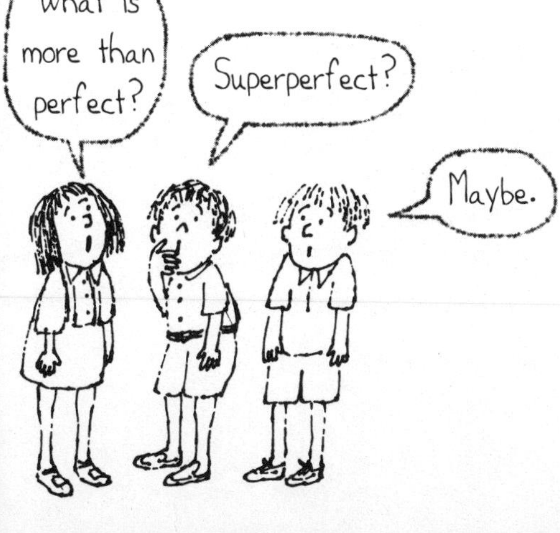
What is more than perfect?
Superperfect?
Maybe.

YOUR TEACHER IS PROUD OF YOU.

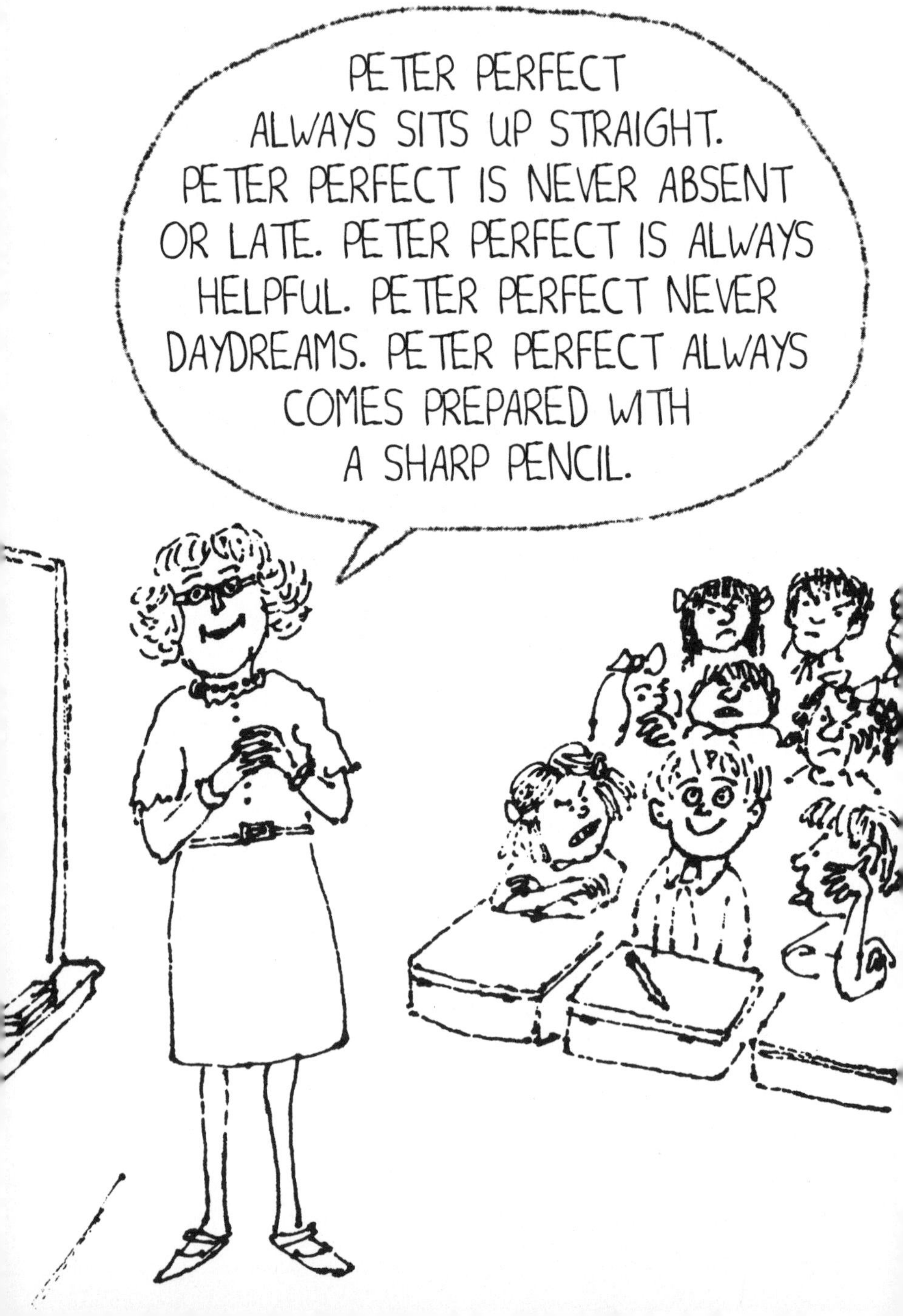
PETER PERFECT ALWAYS SITS UP STRAIGHT. PETER PERFECT IS NEVER ABSENT OR LATE. PETER PERFECT IS ALWAYS HELPFUL. PETER PERFECT NEVER DAYDREAMS. PETER PERFECT ALWAYS COMES PREPARED WITH A SHARP PENCIL.

This morning I had a pencil with a point. Now I have a pencil without a point.
Does that make you pointless?

PEOPLE, EVERYWHERE, ARE TALKING ABOUT YOU, PETER PERFECT.

DID YOU KNOW THAT PETER PERFECT HAS NEVER . . .

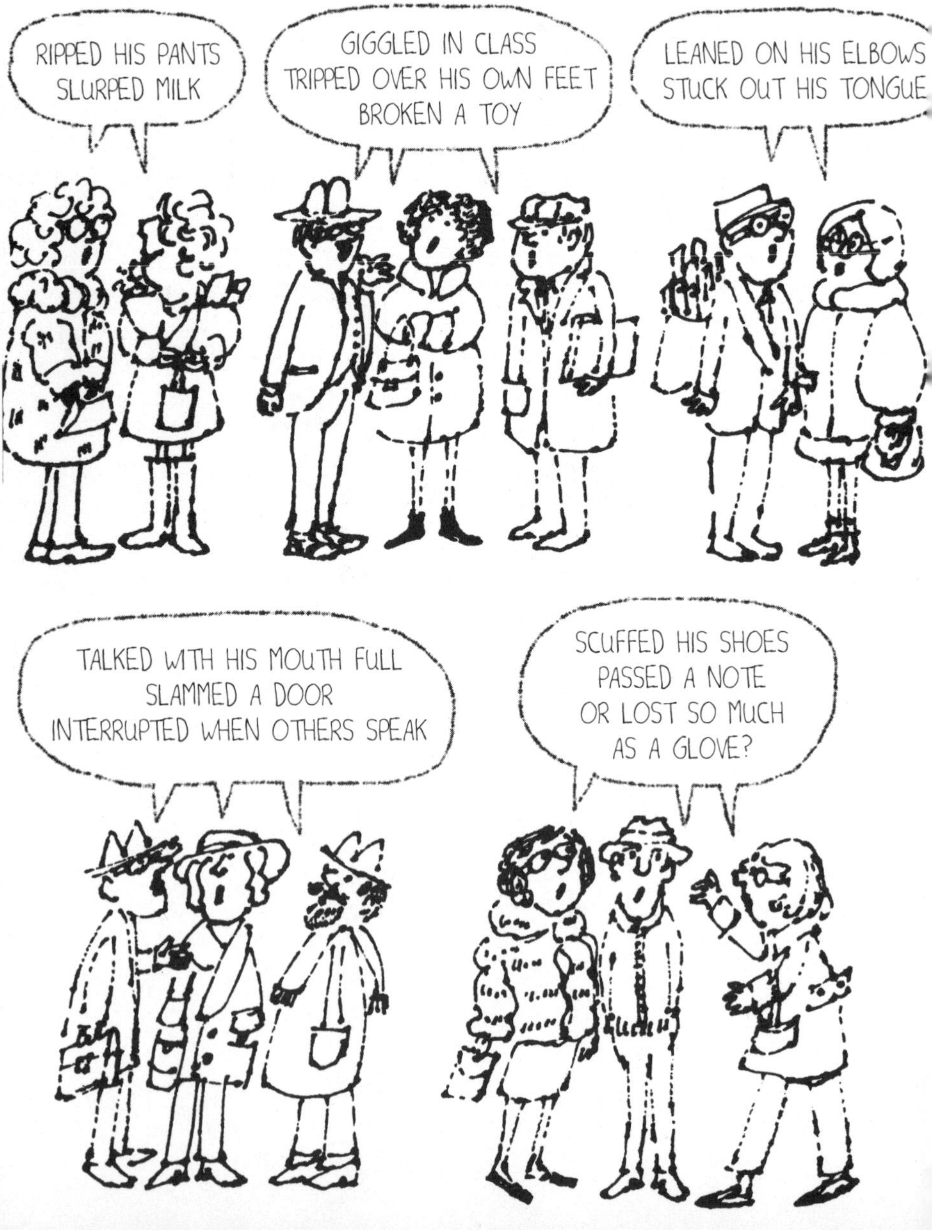
RIPPED HIS PANTS
SLURPED MILK
GIGGLED IN CLASS
TRIPPED OVER HIS OWN FEET
BROKEN A TOY
LEANED ON HIS ELBOWS
STUCK OUT HIS TONGUE
TALKED WITH HIS MOUTH FULL
SLAMMED A DOOR
INTERRUPTED WHEN OTHERS SPEAK
SCUFFED HIS SHOES
PASSED A NOTE
OR LOST SO MUCH
AS A GLOVE?

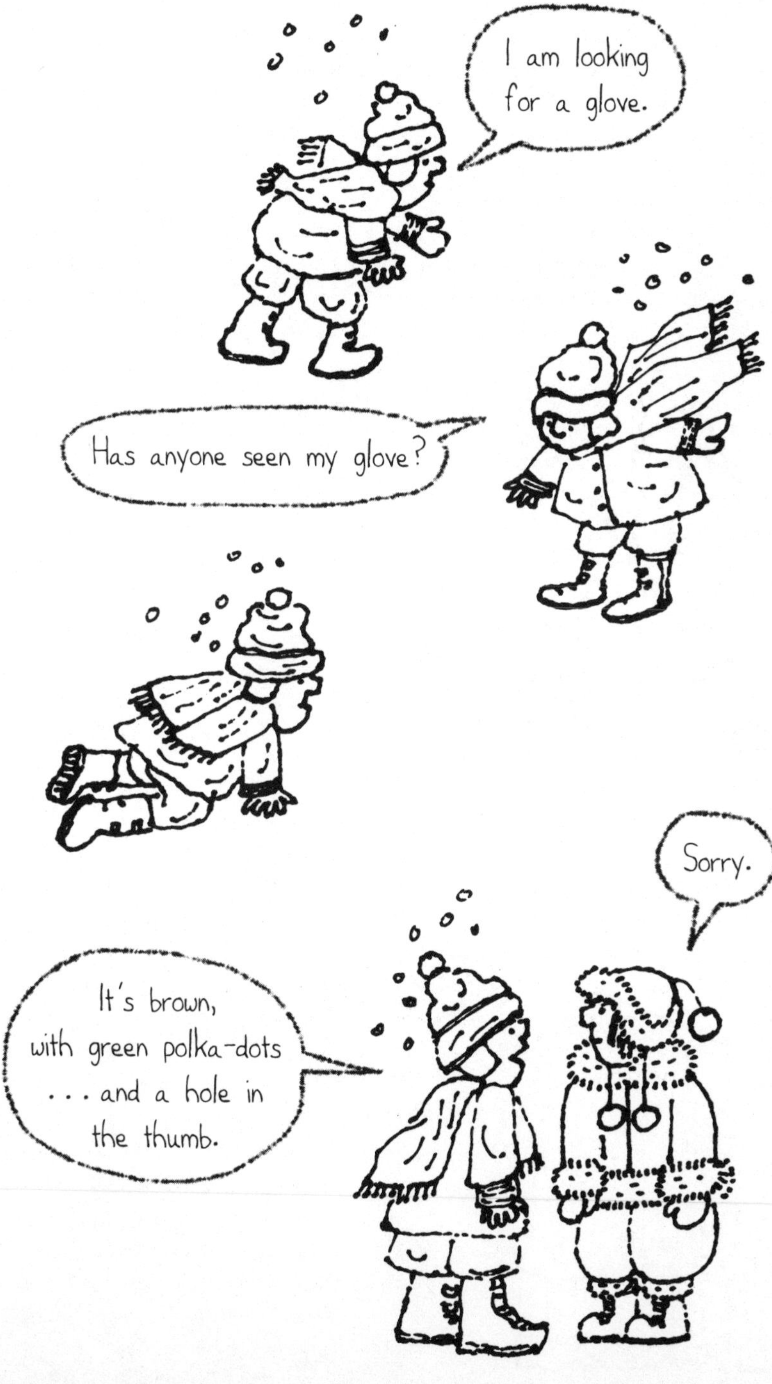
I am looking for a glove.
Has anyone seen my glove?
Sorry.
It's brown, with green polka-dots . . . and a hole in the thumb.

MOTHERS MAKE AN EXAMPLE OF YOU.

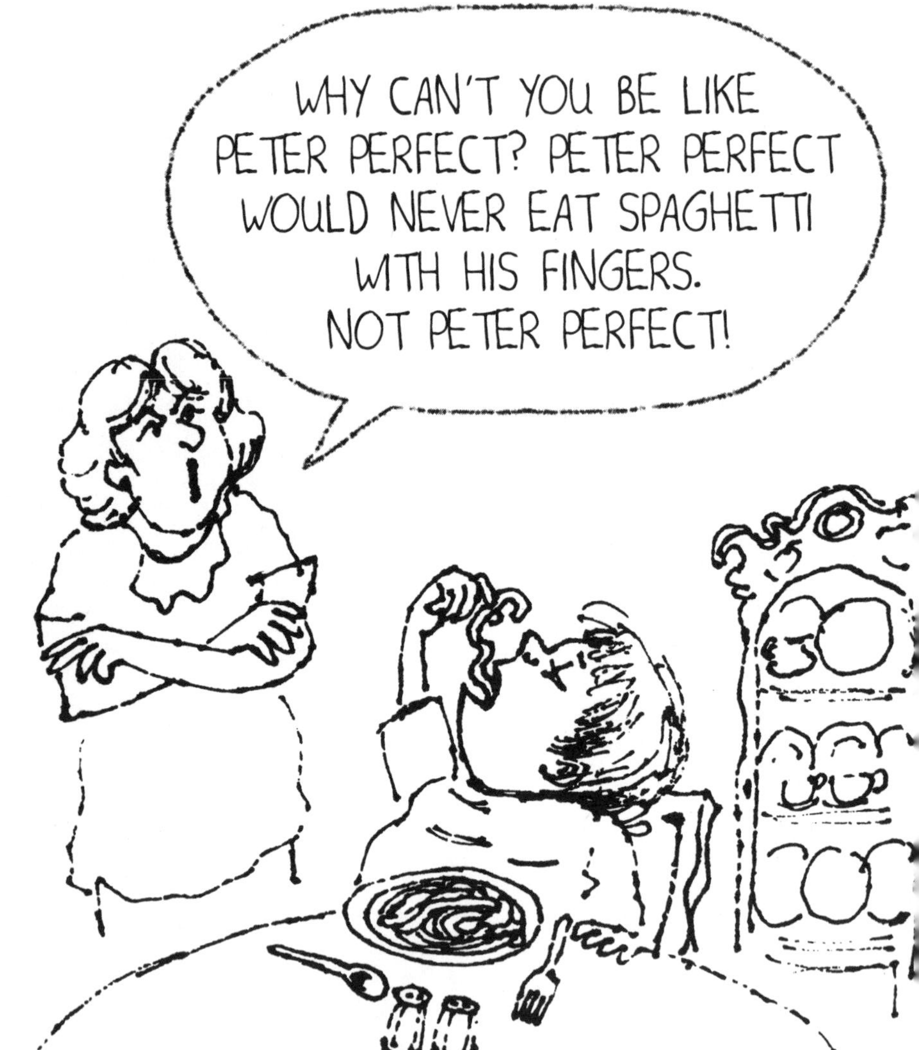
WHY CAN'T YOU BE LIKE PETER PERFECT? PETER PERFECT WOULD NEVER EAT SPAGHETTI WITH HIS FINGERS. NOT PETER PERFECT!

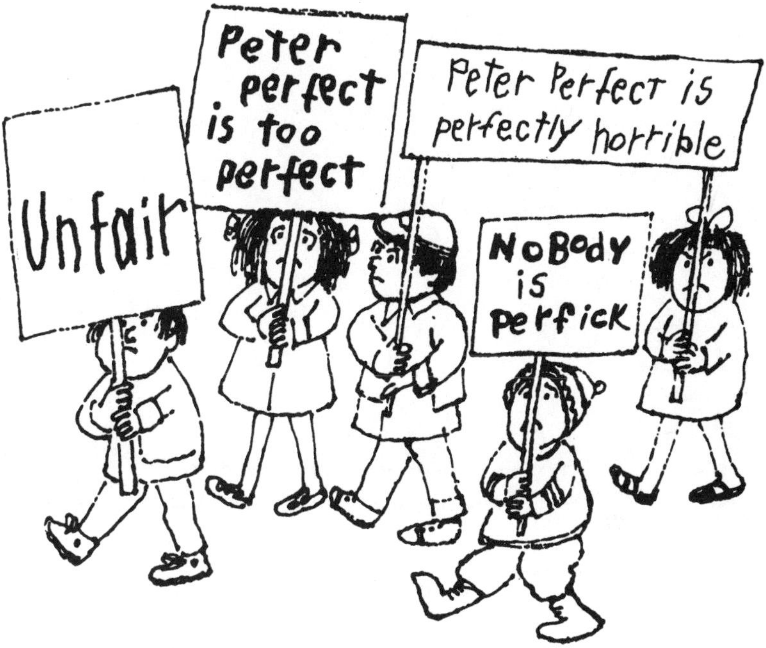
Unfair
Peter perfect is too perfect
Peter Perfect is perfectly horrible
NoBody is perfick

"WHEN MY SON, PETER PERFECT, TAKES A BATH, I NEVER HAVE TO REMIND HIM TO SCRUB BEHIND HIS EARS."

—HIS MOTHER

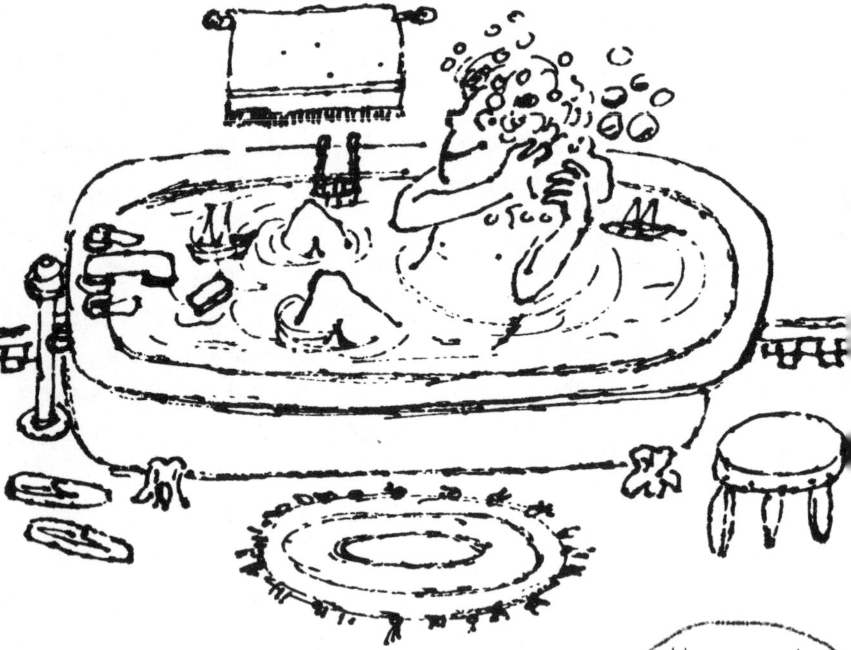

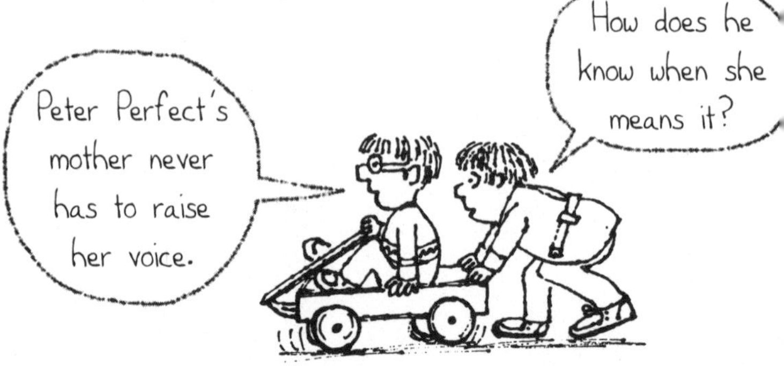
Peter Perfect's mother never has to raise her voice.
How does he know when she means it?

"PETER PERFECT HAS PERFECT MANNERS. HE NEVER DROPS CRUMBS ON HIS LAP."
—HIS GRANDMOTHER

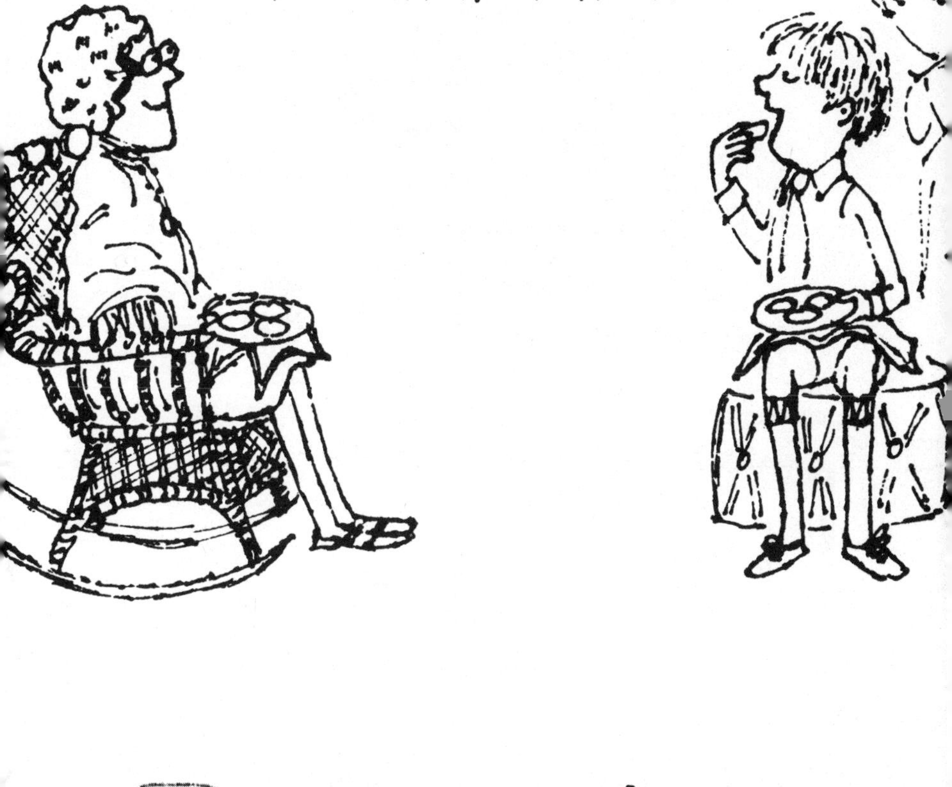

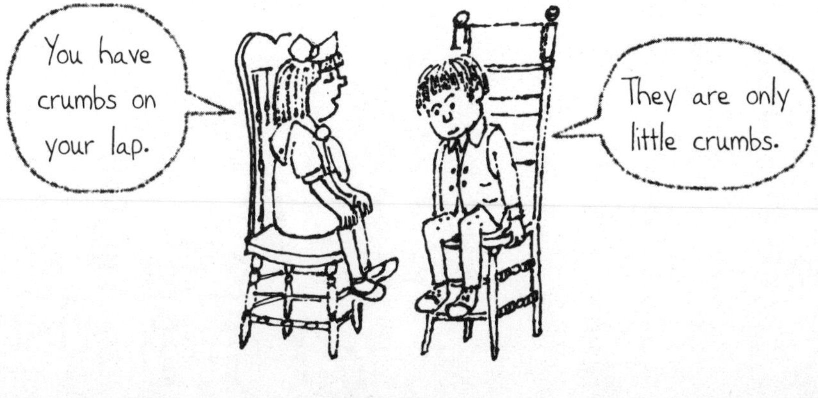
You have crumbs on your lap.
They are only little crumbs.

"PETER PERFECT'S STRAWS DO NOT GET BENT OR MUSHY AT THE ENDS."
—SODA FOUNTAIN MAN

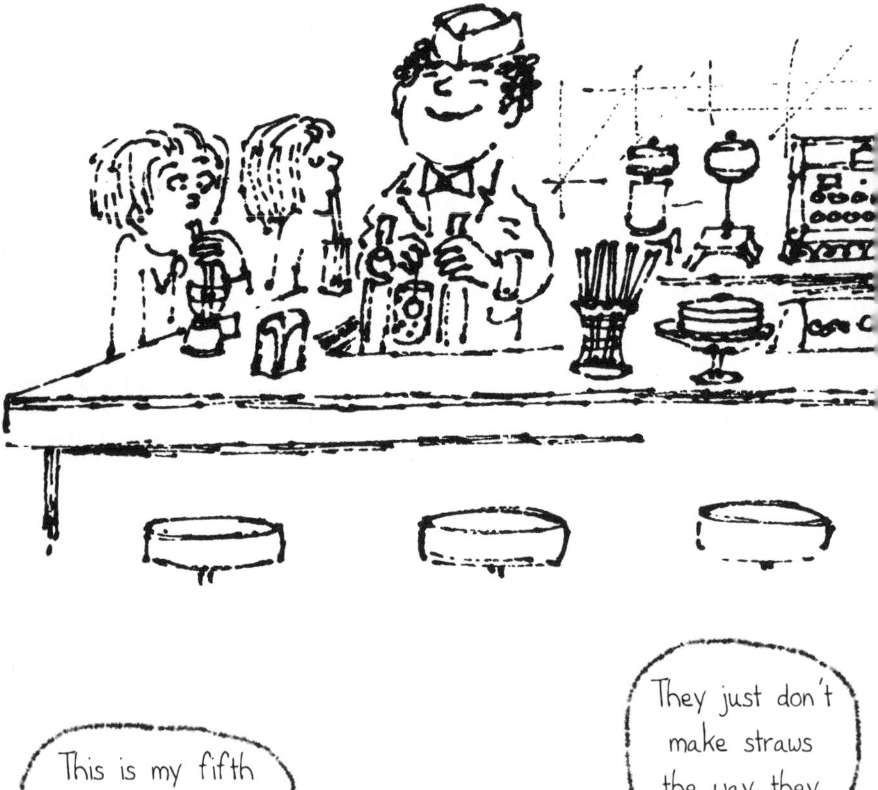

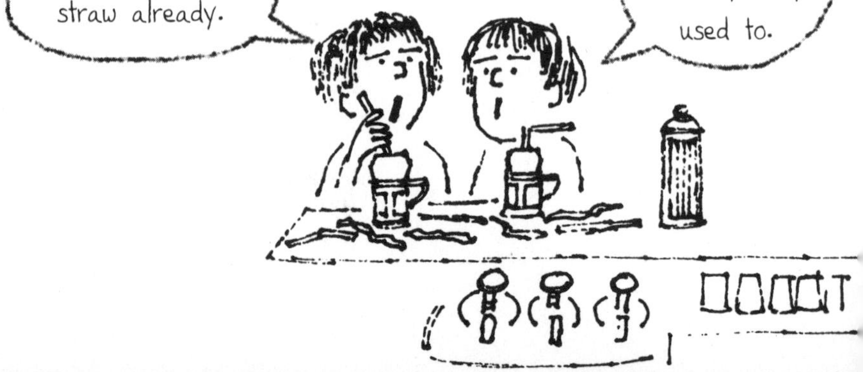
This is my fifth straw already.
They just don't make straws the way they used to.

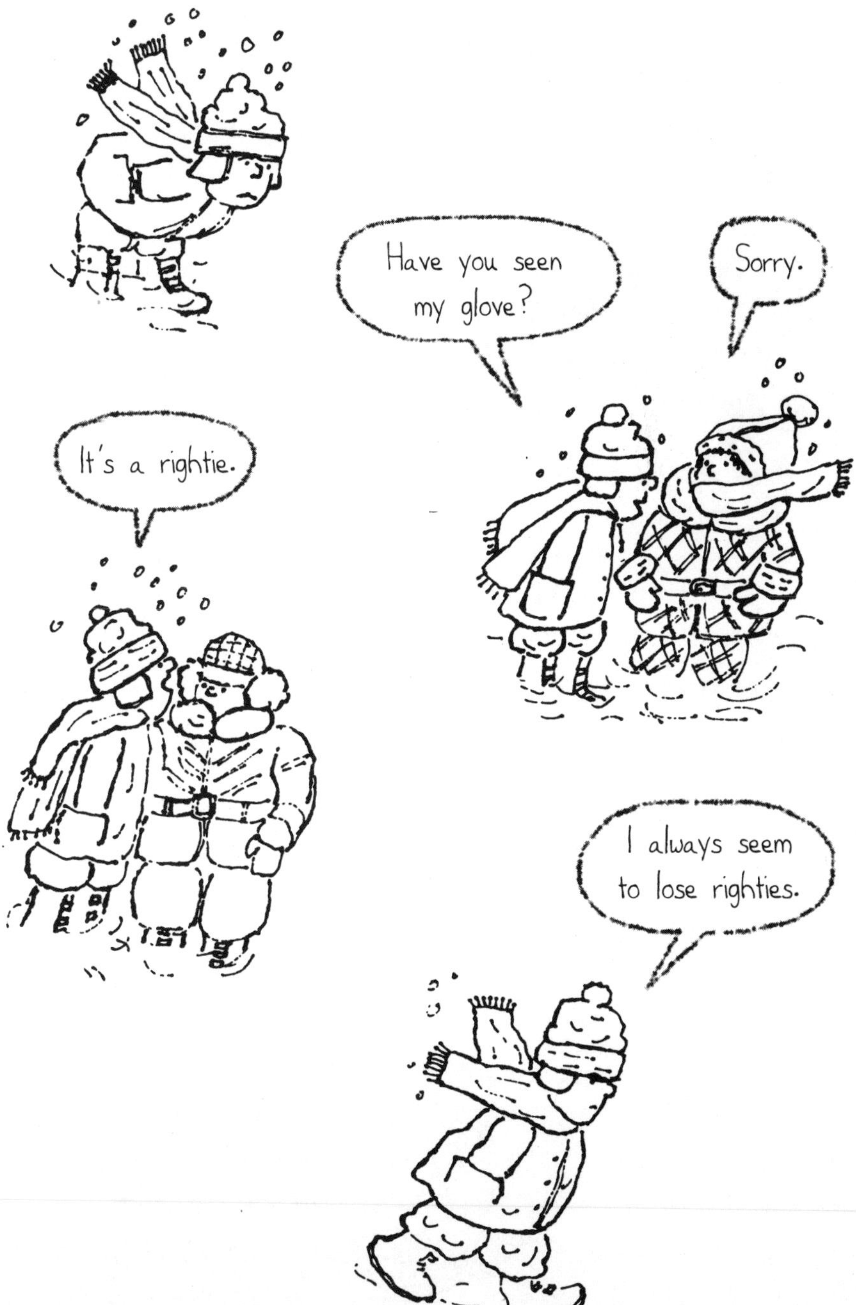
Have you seen my glove?
Sorry.
It's a rightie.
I always seem to lose righties.

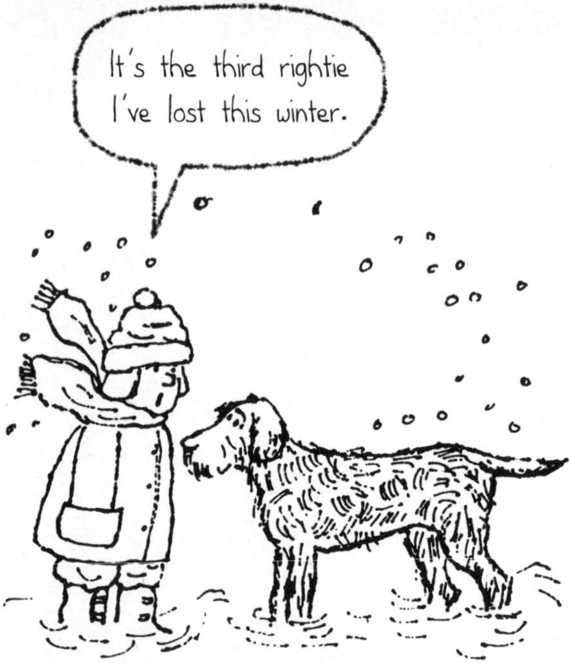
It's the third rightie I've lost this winter.

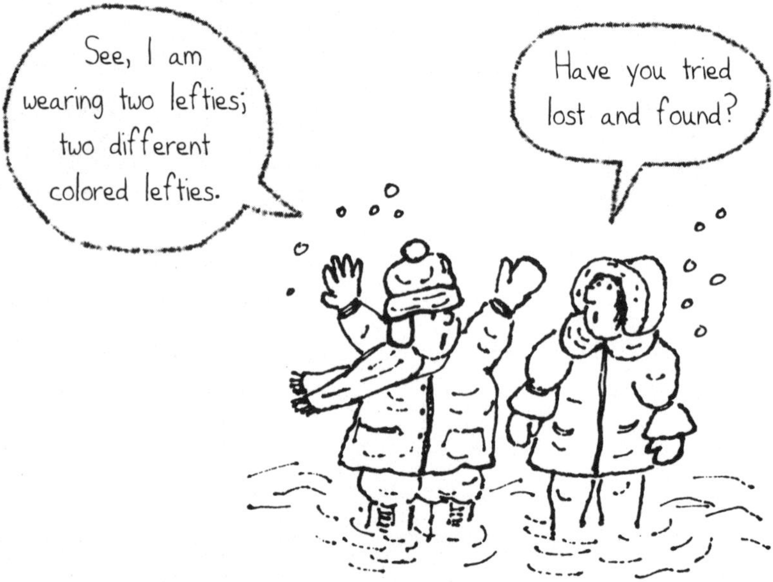
See, I am wearing two lefties; two different colored lefties.
Have you tried lost and found?

"PETER PERFECT SLEEPS WITHOUT A NIGHTLIGHT." —HIS GRANDFATHER

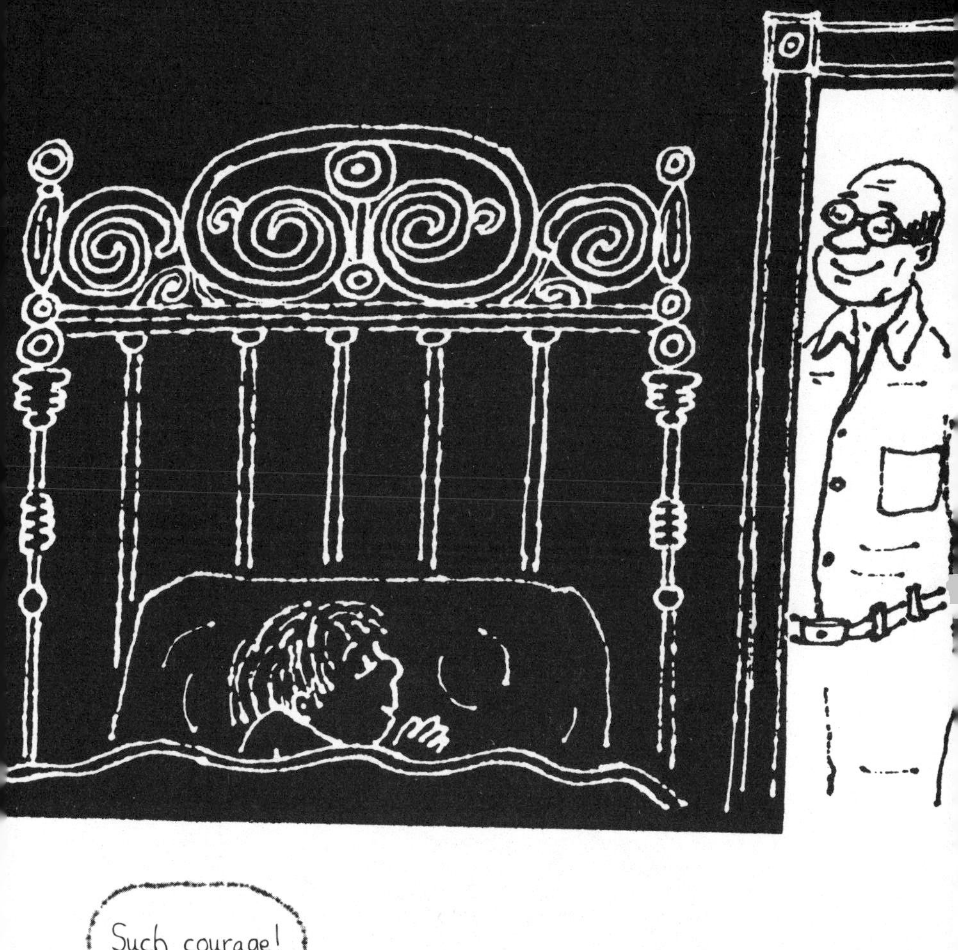

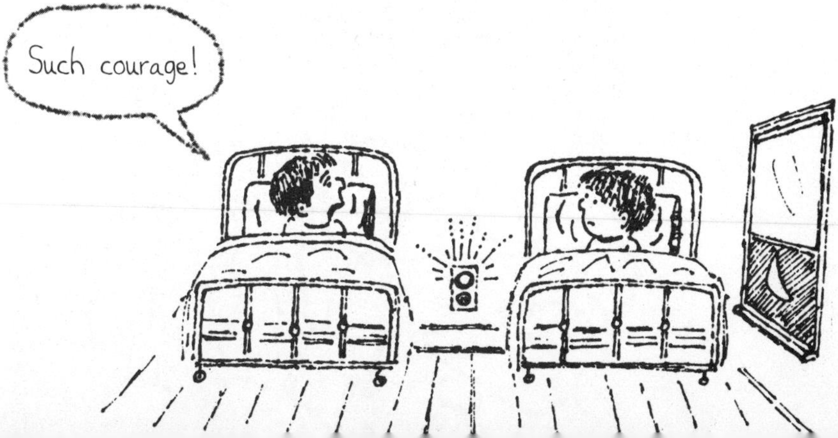
Such courage!

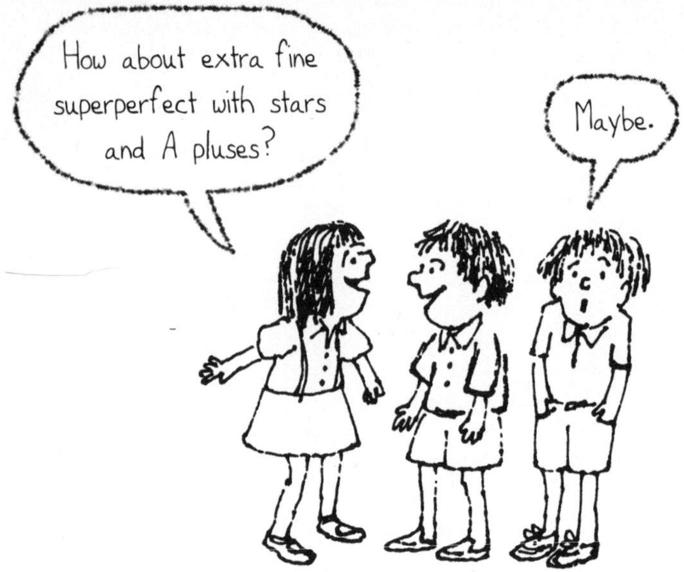
How about extra fine superperfect with stars and A pluses?
Maybe.

"PETER PERFECT IS PERFECT BECAUSE I RAISED HIM PERFECTLY."
—HIS FATHER

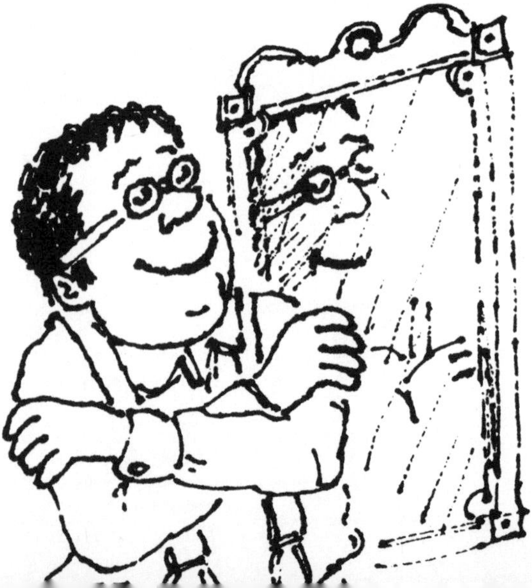

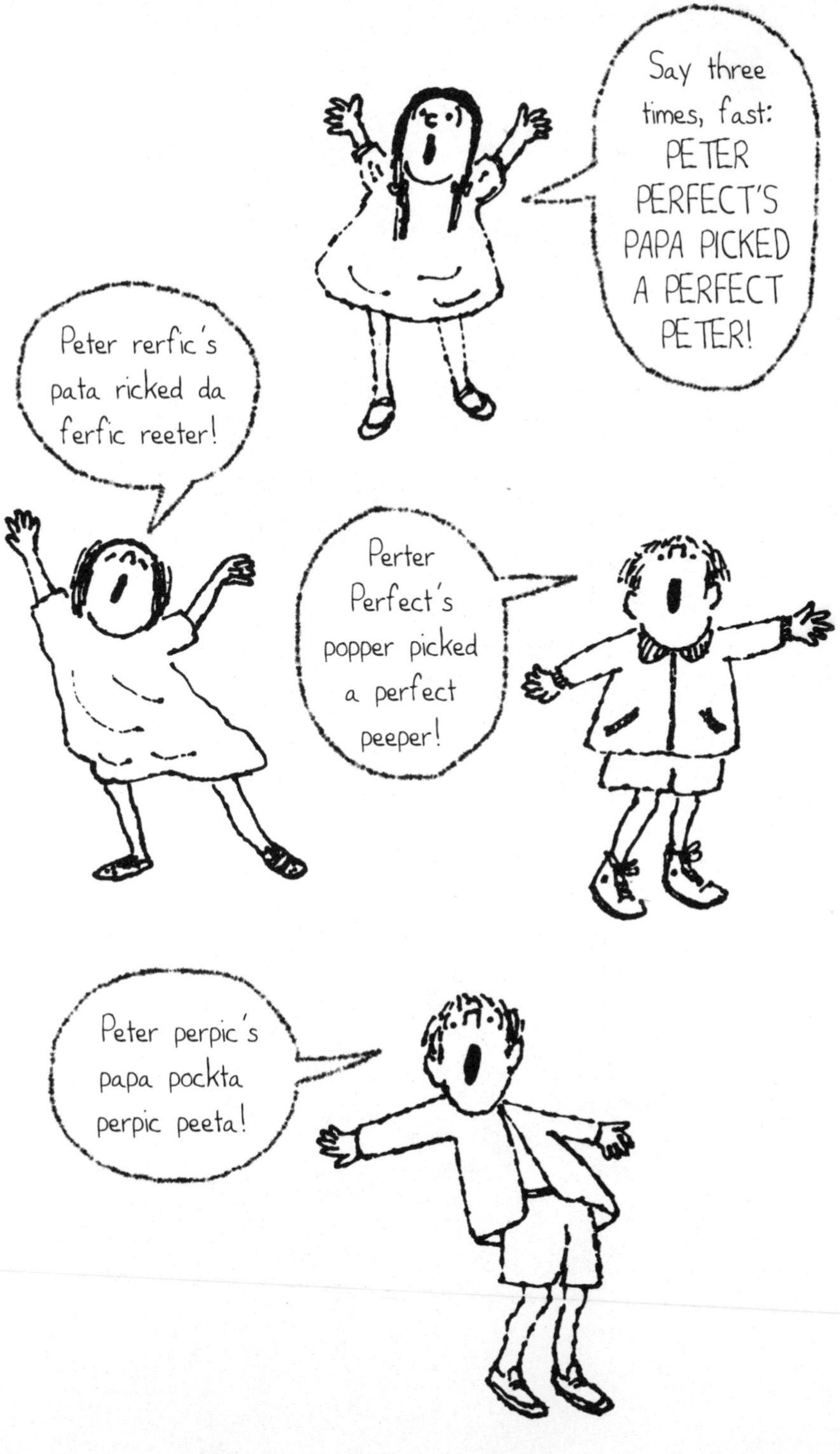
Say three times, fast: PETER PERFECT'S PAPA PICKED A PERFECT PETER!
Peter rerfic's pata ricked da ferfic reeter!
Perter Perfect's popper picked a perfect peeper!
Peter perpic's papa pockta perpic peeta!

IF ONLY YOU WERE
REAL, PETER PERFECT!

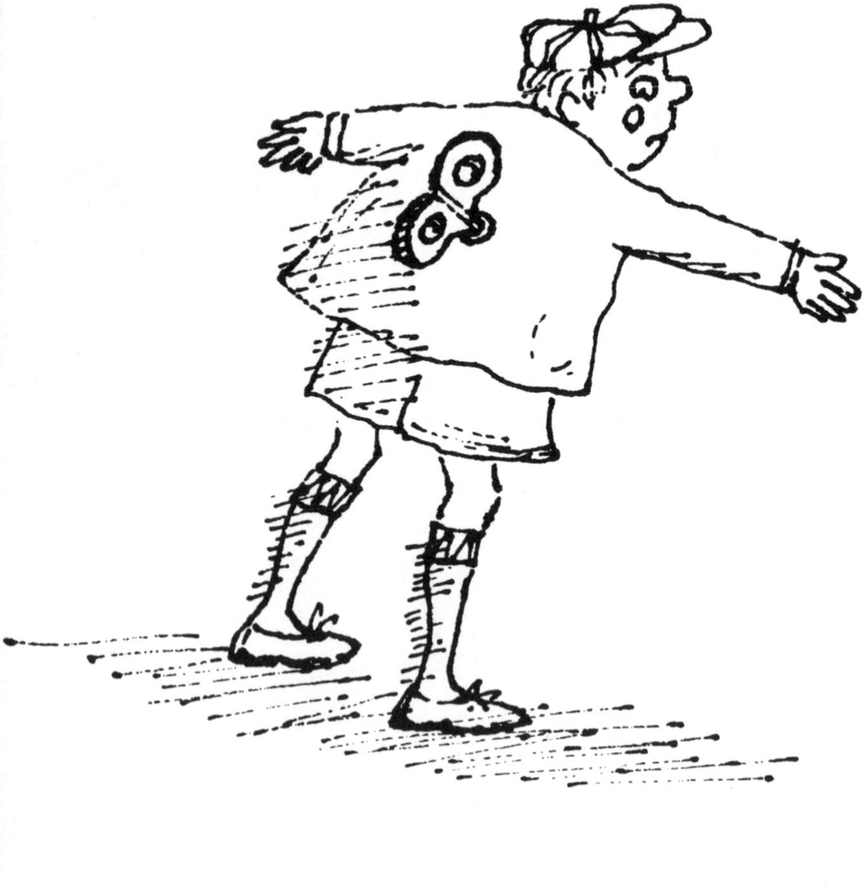

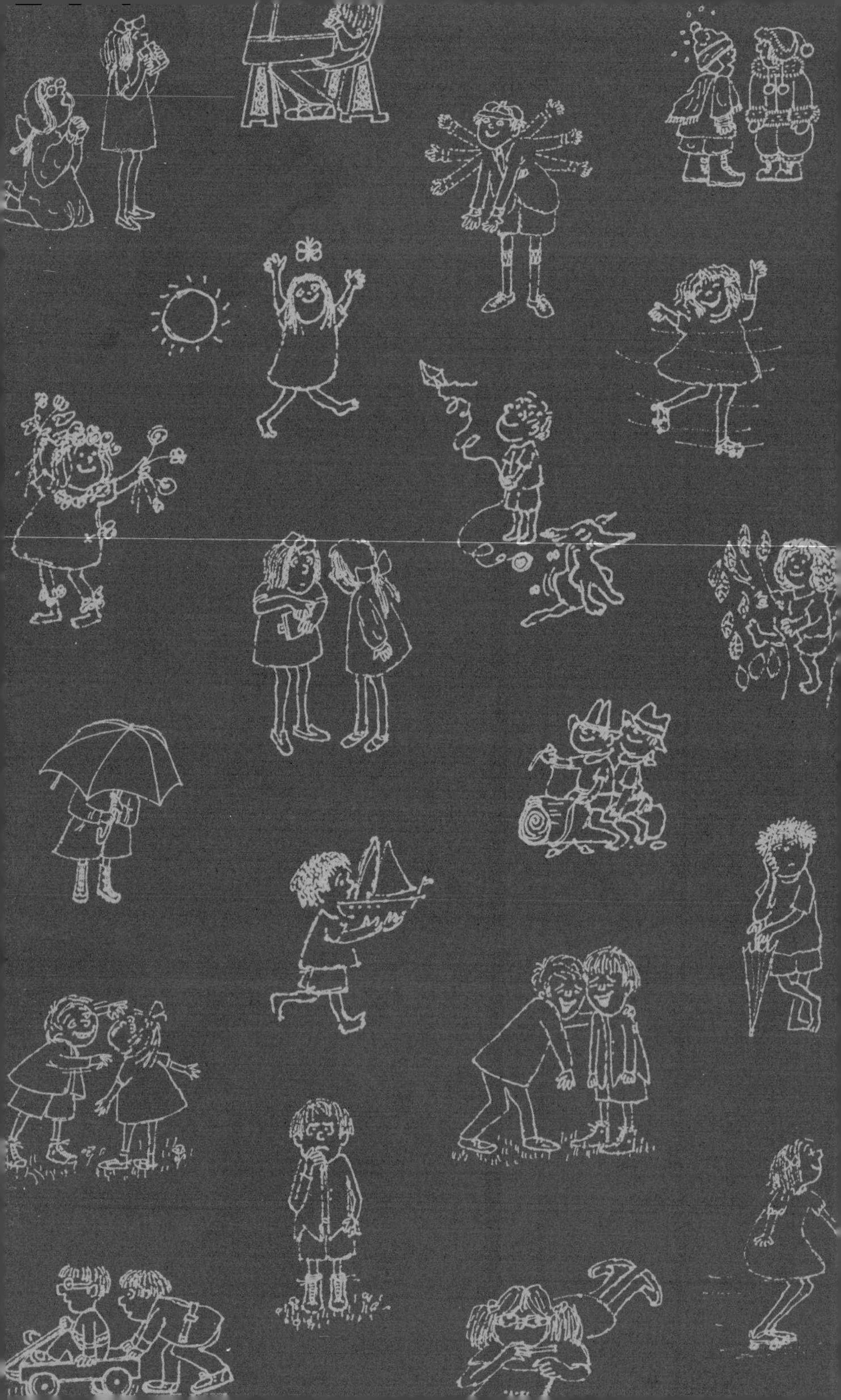